Instant Daddy, Just add Rum

MARY OLDHAM

Print: ISBN: 979-8-9907139-9-4
Kindle: ISBN: 979-8-9907139-6-3
Ebook: ISBN: 979-8-9907139-7-0

Any references to historical events, real people, or real places are used fictitiously. Names, characters, and places are products of the author's imagination. **No parts of this book were created using AI.**

Story and Grammatical Editor: Arleigh Rodgers
Cover Design: Lynn Andreozzi
Interior Book Design: Teri Barnett/Indie Book Designer
Author Photo: Tanith Yates

Printed in United States of America
By-Creek-Ity Publishing
Portland, Oregon
www.maryoldham.com

For my BETA readers. I could not do this without your help.
Hugs, M

CONTENTS

"Holy crap," Jack Brewster muttered to himself when he got a good look at a barely-there patch of red fabric covering what he could tell was a very lush female body.

A parade of well-oiled beauties had walked along the white, sugar-fine sand of Saline Beach on the French Caribbean Island of Saint Barts and not drawn his notice. But this woman, this woman in the red bikini, was different. Sort of like how a firecracker is slightly different than a candle.

At first, the brief hint of color moving against a bright, pastel landscape had drawn his lazy notice, causing him to sit up straighter and knock over his beer. It was a jolt of well-needed energy to his sexually dehydrated system. The woman strolling along the edge of the surf, as if she didn't have a care in the world, was wearing a bright red bikini. It was as if she were daring someone to ask her to remove it on the predominantly nude beach. She was in good company. Jack, who wore a set of baggy navy swim trunks, observed the action from afar, not wanting to display his assets freely either. But for her, he might make an exception.

Miss Red Bikini's long blonde hair whipped around her body in gentle billows as her feet made a trail in the pristine, sugar-like sand. It was then that he noticed her fingernails and toenails were painted the same red as the bikini. It was a small thing, but he liked the attention to detail and wondered what it would feel like to kiss each one of those red tips. It had been a long time since someone had knocked him off his perfectly balanced axis.

There were other women on the beach who looked at Jack in open invitation as they suggestively rubbed coconut oil on their bare, tan breasts, paying particular attention to their erect nipples, daring him to approach. Not in the mood for the kind of woman who touched herself in public, Jack's full attention fell on the woman who covered herself with a simple red bikini. If he could spend time or have a conversation with anyone on this beach, or this island for that matter, he'd choose her. But he didn't just want to talk to her. He wanted to touch her. Find out how it felt to run his fingers through that flaxen hair and touch that smooth, tan skin that offered a hint of peaches and cream.

As lustful thoughts about that little red bikini coursed through his brain, she glanced over her shoulder, her eyes falling on him.

At that moment, their eyes met.

He felt guilty. She'd caught him looking. He had no other choice but to smile at her. Offer her the best he had to give. There was a hint of a smile on her face in return. She offered it to him, then turned her back and looked in the direction of the numerous sailboats, which lingered in the translucent aquamarine water, their white sails bright against the azure sky. He wondered if she belonged to one of the boats or was just a tourist like himself. Nothing would surprise him at this moment. He could tell she was special.

And in that moment, he felt a curl of jealousy. Was she with someone? Some rich sugar daddy? Or his worst fear: What if she was on her honeymoon? Was her sated groom back in their hotel room sleeping off a night of passion? Lucky bastard. Sometimes, life was very unfair. Why couldn't he have someone like her in his life? This situation is what his mother always calls his "future tripping."

His mother had no room for dreams or whimsy. No, she was a hard-nosed businesswoman. Heck, he had heard how his parents met, and it did not warm his heart. His grandparents had practically arranged their marriage. His mother's family came from one of the largest printer companies in the Pacific Northwest. No wonder they got a permanent deal on all the labels for their beer.

Thankfully, his parents had fallen in love, or their version of love. Well, that kind of "arrangement" wasn't for him. Not that his mother hadn't tried for years to play matchmaker for the right kind of girl. Heck, if the Pretzel King had a daughter, his mother would find her and demand that Jack marry her. He could almost hear his mother say, "Do something good for the family, Jackson. What goes with beer? Pretzels, of course." No. Thank. You.

Jack continued to create Miss Red Bikini's backstory as if he knew her. Maybe she was a model, taking a break from her latest photoshoot. Or maybe she was one of those antique dealers who scoured the world looking for treasure for rich clients. Fair or not, he was already spinning the tale. If she were his, if she graced him with her smile, her attention, he'd never let her out of his sight. At that moment, she paused, leaned forward, and picked up a shell from the sand. At the sight of her lush ass pulling tightly against the red fabric, Jack's heart skipped a beat, and he was glad for the nearby towel that he could drape over his suddenly attentive "assets."

What was wrong with him? He wasn't some randy teenager with his first hard-on. He was in his mid-thirties, for fuck's sake. He'd had his pick of beautiful women from his family name alone, which hadn't interested him. Well, he'd grown tired of the shallow connections. Yet, truth be told, he had to admit, they didn't make anyone that looked like her back home in Portland, Oregon.

A relationship with her wouldn't be shallow. No. Not her. He could see the intelligence, the curiosity, the humor bubbling just behind her large sunglasses and that carefree smile.

After a long moment, when he thought of his mother's scowl, his grandmother's love of mothballs, and, finally, his parents kissing, he lost the wind in his sail. It was the "ew" factor he needed to regain control of himself. Bye-bye, unfortunately timed erection. Jack unfolded from his sitting position on the blanket and stood, brushing sand away from his legs. He'd made a decision. It was time to see how close he could get to that little red bikini. She was something special. And if he let her go without talking to her, he would never forgive himself.

She had a good lead on him, and it would take some effort on his part to catch up, but she was worthy of the attempt.

As if she knew she was being pursued, the woman stepped around a large outcropping of rocks and disappeared. By the time Jack hastily picked up his towel and overturned beer, making it to the outcropping of rocks she had disappeared behind, he caught a glimpse of the red bikini. She was riding away on a bicycle. Her hair blew out behind her in the wind.

He'd waited too long. He'd played it too safe. He'd lost her in that moment.

"Nicely played, Red," he said aloud to no one.

Jack had a few more days on the island before he needed to leave and go back home to resume his life. There would be some new changes, so nothing would be the same, which was a big improvement over his dull existence. He had escaped from the monotony six months earlier when he decided to take his new idea involving the family business in a new direction: *Rum*. Three generations of the family, except for that time during prohibition when they'd made root beer, had predominantly been fermenters of very popular, world-famous beer. The family had been talking about distilling hard alcohol since Jack was a kid. It had always sounded like something that was unattainable. A pipe dream to be discussed during holidays while sipping a *Brewster Reserve*. But his ancestors had been too chicken shit to take a chance and make it happen. Jack Brewster wasn't scared of anything or anyone, well, except his mother.

His older brother and heir to the family business, Charles, was back home and could keep the home fires burning with all the beer they brewed, while Jack had other ideas. It meant he had to go to where rum was made and learn everything he could.

His family hadn't exactly been excited when he had presented the idea to them, but then Jack had formed his own LLC, used a portion of his inheritance from his grandmother, and the question of what the second son, the spare son, in the family would do was all but answered. Everyone, especially his parents, could breathe a sigh of relief. He would branch out on his own, with a bit of help from the Brewster name and the reputation it carried.

He remembered his mother wrinkling up her nose and saying, "You want to do what?"

"I want to make rum," he'd said.

"Oh joy. Every frat boy's first foray into hard liquor. Alcoholic sugar water," she said, wrinkling her nose.

"Would you prefer I arm wrestle Charles for control of the business?"

"Oh, for god's sake, run off to the Caribbean and figure out how to make your sugar water. And when you come back, make some damn money."

He had done the first part. Part two was next. He already had money, but as his mother liked to say, "You can never have too much." Thankfully, he didn't really agree with this statement.

He was fine. And the things he wanted now, money could not buy.

The local family he had spent time with on St. Thomas, just a couple of islands over, hadn't easily let go of their secrets, but a small donation of that Brewster family money had gone a long way to make introductions. And they were nice people. After the initial strangeness, they had come to respect and like each other.

The last six months had been educational. Jack felt like a monk learning to make champagne. Now, he had a much-needed vacation to remember who Jack Brewster was before he was relegated to the role of a second son back home. He needed to shed his Jacques Brewster apprentice skin and re-assimilate into the docile son his parents expected.

Incidentally, this little transition period also meant that he had some time to find Miss Red Bikini.

His cell phone chimed. He glanced at the screen and swore before answering it. Miss Red Bikini, on her pink-and-yellow bicycle with the big tires, became just a tiny speck in the distance.

"Jack?" It was Charles, his older, stick-up-his-ass brother.

"Hey," Jack said and waited. It wasn't easy being the younger sibling. It *was* easy to be his older brother's punching bag. He had hated it when he was ten but despised it now that he was in his thirties. The only difference was that Charles wore a suit every day and had gone soft, and Jack was pretty sure he would win a physical altercation.

"When are you back?"

"I have another week," Jack said. "Why do you care?"

"I'm climbing Mount Hood later today. I'm meeting up with Derek and Seth on the mountain later tonight. We are shooting for a sunrise summit. Mom's guilting me about it because you're out of town. She wants me to wait until you're back. Same Mom guilt bullshit."

It did make Jack happy to know he wasn't the only one who

dealt with their mother's guilt. Even if you hadn't done anything wrong, she had a way of making you feel like you had. It was pure talent.

"You should wait, you selfish bastard. My itinerary hasn't changed. But let me guess. You didn't look."

"This might come as a surprise, but some of us have been working hard to keep the home fires burning. I'm not globetrotting half a world away on a tropical beach. I'm working. This window for climbing opened up, so we took it. It isn't like you just climb Mount Hood when you want to. It takes planning."

Yet he was only telling Jack about it now. Charles had probably known for several weeks. Heck, he'd probably been going to the gym and jogging to work on his endurance.

There was a lot of stupidity and ego that went into such an endeavor, both of which Charles had in the exponential range.

"I don't really care, but isn't it too early to be on Mount Hood? I mean, it is still technically winter. And the last time I looked, you weren't in your top shape for a mountain climb despite your desire for daredevil activity."

"I go to the gym four or five times a week," Charles replied. "And I've been amping up the cardio with jogging in the last few weeks."

Of course. Because this had been a plan for a few weeks.

Jack smiled to himself. Mount Hood didn't serve cucumber water and fresh towels that Charles had become accustomed to at his swank gym.

"Good for you," Jack said as he shook his head.

"We are going early to avoid the tourists that descend. They aren't professional climbers like we are. We could climb this mountain in our sleep. It isn't like we haven't done it before. We will be fine. And I don't need second-guessing when it comes to our decision. I'm not asking your permission."

Always defensive.

Always with the chip on his shoulder.

Always a bully.

When was the last time Charles had climbed anything? Oh yeah, right after college—fifteen years earlier. The pompous asshole.

"Good, because I'm not giving you my blessing, but I will say, please be careful."

"Save the concern for someone who needs it. By the way, it would be nice if you stopped with the vacation and got back to work. We could use an extra body. We are a tad busy running an international company," Charles complained. "Brewster International Brewing can get you on a flight tomorrow. Knowing her baby is on his way back will help distract Mom. So, what do you say? Can I tell Mom you'll be home tomorrow?"

Jack thought of Miss Red Bikini and said, "Not a chance."

"Thanks for being a team player, you dick," Charles said. "Hey, you want to bet on my summit time?"

Jack had not missed this part of his relationship with his brother while he'd been in the Caribbean. Always a bet or wager. It had to be competitive. Never friends, never brothers. Jack was so over it. "I do not. Be safe."

"Yeah, well, fuck you, too."

Instead of responding, Jack did what he knew Charles would do. He hung up on his brother.

He needed to enjoy this time while he could. When his mother got a look at how long his hair was and when his antiquated father scrutinized his tan, they wouldn't be listening to a word he said. He didn't want to think about going home to cold, rainy Portland. He didn't want to think about the haircut and severe business suits in the wild colors of light to dark gray that awaited him back in his grandmother's house, which he'd inherited when she died, and his brother didn't want.

Everything, from the suits to the house, would all need to be dry cleaned or aired out to remove the smell of mothballs. He'd think of it later as in…well…seven days. He had other things on his mind now.

Thanks to the markings on Miss Red Bikini's getaway vehicle, which happened to be yellow and pink, he knew where to start looking for those long, tan legs that belonged to her. The Beachcomber Saint Barts Hotel was known for its yellow and pink theme.

Chapter One

Ella Martin sat on a bar stool and watched the ocean break gently against the rocks as the sun began to set towards the west. She was wearing her favorite black dress, a halter that was too sexy for work, so she rarely had occasion to wear it. She paired it with some strappy sandals her friend Cindy had snared for her when they'd come into her resale shop.

"They are Stuart Weizman's, and they are brand new. They don't have a scratch on them!"

Ella had four days left of her vacation before she returned home to Portland and settled in for the last cold and damp vestiges of winter. Her skin was starting to get a caramel glow, and, happily, she had tan lines. She wouldn't have them if she wasn't such a prude, but just because the beaches were nude didn't mean she had to be. Besides, when she was back home, the tan lines would remind her that she had actually been on vacation.

Working usually seven days a week led to deep burnout, which could only be soothed by the tropical sun in the middle of winter. She lived for these seven days and saved all year for this one indulgent treat. She was determined to enjoy every moment to the fullest and was already sad about how quickly the vacation was going by. For the last three days, she'd laid on the beach, read a pile of romance novels, and drank exotic fruit juices mixed with large quantities of rum that came with colorful paper umbrellas and pineapple wedges; all the while, she was in paradise. This was vacation at its finest. The fact she was alone again this year…well, she didn't need to dwell on it.

When she'd left her apartment four days earlier for the airport, her neighbor Padma had to scrape ice off her car windshield before giving Ella a ride. Portland and all Ella's responsibilities were almost four thousand miles away. She had only called once, yesterday, to make sure her pride and joy—her shop, *Marcella's*—was running smoothly. Cricket, her assistant, was handling everything in Ella's absence. Ella remembered their conversation and smiled to herself.

"This isn't a great way for you to spend your spring break," she had said to Cricket. "I'm sorry."

"Are you kidding? I get to read a bunch of smutty books and meet hot doctors from the hospital. I'm averaging two date requests a day. Okay, I should admit, some of these dudes are older and, I suspect, married, but they could still show me a good time. You shouldn't be interrupting your vacation to check in. Everything is fine. We are even making money."

"I trust you, Cricket. You are the best. Please be careful of the good-looking doctors, especially of the cute ones. Avoid the married ones at all costs. Look at their—"

"I know. Look for the indention on their left hand for the wedding ring they might have conveniently removed."

"Exactly," Ella warned. It had happened to her.

"And hey, I get to try different baked goods on them. The 'cockies' sold out in two hours."

"Cockies?" Ella asked.

"You know, naughty cookies, shaped like anatomy," Cricket explained. "You should see what I can do with some melted chocolate and a piping bag. People *love* them!"

"Please, please don't let the children see them."

"Relax, it is cool."

Oh good, *it is cool.*

The cobalt blue-haired Cricket had a quick, crooked smile and a personality to match her name. She was overtly flirtatious. Men assumed that because she was so out-there with her hair, dress, and outlandish repartee, that she was an easy and potentially good lay. She probably was, but Ella didn't judge her friend. Cricket was just twenty-one, a junior at Portland State University, and happy for the week of earnings she was going to get from handling seven days at *Marcella's* during her vacation. Ella was actually a bit jealous of her outlandishness. She wished she could be that free. Why couldn't she say cockies with a straight face?

"I bought you a bottle of rum today. I also got you a beautiful coral bracelet and a t-shirt," Ella said.

"Stop buying me stuff. I don't need to be bribed. I'm having fun. You go enjoy yourself, make some bad choices."

"Well…"

"Seriously, Ella, you are always wound so tight. Enjoy your time. Get drunk, screw a local, and get naked on the beach!"

Ella laughed. She knew that Cricket was kidding, but there was some truth in it. She should enjoy this and savor the small amount of time that she had before returning to her reality.

Once Cricket graduated from PSU, Ella wasn't sure what she would do. She maybe had one more year of having Cricket available to help her, then what? Close the store for a week when she needed to take her vacation? That wasn't going to happen. She couldn't afford to do that. The bigger problem was that Cricket didn't just work this one day a week. She worked at *Marcella's* on Saturdays, and each semester, she and Ella worked on her schedule to give her hours at *Marcella's*. Ella worked around her. It was something that worked well for both of them. Besides, Ella needed the occasional help and the ability to go to a dentist appointment or to get a pedicure.

She only hoped that Cricket would keep making the baked

goods for her small coffee bar. It had been a serious money maker, and Cricket knew her way around a scone.

Ella shouldn't borrow trouble. She knew that. Her work was her life, and even being gone for a week could take a serious dent out of her profits, but Cricket was good at upselling and had shown a moxie well beyond her twenty-one years. Ella didn't know what she'd do without Cricket.

But the truth of it was, when Ella was away from her shop, profits dipped because people came to *Marcella's* because Ella could almost predict what they needed. She was fantastic at matching people to the right book, piece of jewelry, gift, or knick-knack that they could not live without. Cricket had a lot of talent, but that inherent, unspoken talent for reading the needs of people when they crossed her threshold wasn't one of them.

As she contemplated her second Mojito, Ella ordered an appetizer of shrimp and tropical salsa off the bar menu. She could admit that it had been harder this year to relax. There were rumors that the hospital near her shop was going to expand and wanted to take the land under her shop for a new wing. This would also impact where she lived, which was over her shop, not to mention her kind neighbors on either side, who were her family by choice.

The rumor mill said the hospital expansion was several years away, but Ella didn't think that was true. She didn't know what to do about it except to stress and wonder how *Marcella's* would survive. She had to face it when she got home and started planning for the worst possible outcome. Part of her thought she should fill out an application for a sales position at *Nordstrom* and be done with it. Heck, maybe she should apply at *Home Depot*. She might meet eligible men there.

The usual sun and surf of Saint Barts hadn't quite curbed the edgy unease she felt this year, which was unlike her. She supposed it was a kind of torture to come to a place like Saint

Barts as a single woman, but she had worked hard and looked forward to this trip for a year. Just because she didn't have a guy in her life didn't mean she couldn't come to a beautiful tropical island for a vacation. Life was to be lived. And at the end of her life, she didn't want to have any regrets. Sure, she'd like to make this trip with a boyfriend, someone she really, really loved or at least liked a lot. But how was she supposed to get one of those? How long had it been since she'd been on a date? A year and a half?

Yes, it had really been that long since a man had held her in his arms and made love to her. *Michael. Her ex.* They had dated for eight months. He had disappointed her in the end when he showed signs of very controlling behavior. And then he'd accused her of not needing him. Well, she didn't. She was a self-made businesswoman. She didn't need a man to support her. Aside from sex and the occasional large object that needed to be moved, she was fine on her own. And if she wanted to eat tuna fish out of the can while standing over the sink, no one could stop her. Michael couldn't figure out why she didn't want to be saved. Somewhere along the way, he'd decided he would save her anyway. It hadn't been a pretty ending when he'd started to advise her on her business and pouted when she didn't take his stupid advice.

Not thinking the breakup would last, he still called and dropped by *Marcella's*. Despite any of his unwanted attention, she was clear that they were through. It had been a long time since she'd been attracted to anyone. She was starting to feel that darkening edge of gloom that equated to being a spinster or a nun.

She hadn't given up on the idea of romance, although she was contemplating getting a hairless cat which she would name Slick. This year, she had done something quite out of character, although she knew it was more of a message to the universe than actual reality: She had packed condoms and a *Lover's Kit* from her very own shop in her luggage.... Just in case. She was ready to love again.

In case of what? In case of mind-blowing, earth-shattering sex, of course! That wasn't going to happen because, despite the racy kit and condoms, she didn't get that close to anyone that fast. Besides, maybe to have such detritus in her luggage sent the wrong message. And Ella wasn't that kind of girl. Of course, she wished she was, but she kept getting in the way of herself. Wearing a bikini on a nude beach for starters...

There *was* that guy. That very good-looking man who had stared at her while she'd walked on the beach. She still felt the flutter of butterflies in her stomach when she thought of him. She should have done something, but what could she do? Maybe she'd go back tomorrow and see if he was there again. And then what? Talk to him? She needed possibly a third Mojito.

Well, she was already picturing the moment that she'd return the little kit she'd stolen back to the shelf next to all the other love enhancements and potions. How ironic! Someone would buy it, never knowing the *Lover's Kit* had been out of the country and not put to use. How pathetic, yet *so* Ella.

She bit her lip to keep from laughing. Sure, there was a part of her that longed to be seduced and treated like a drunk virgin on prom night, but her bark was bigger than her bite when it came to sexual prowess. She was a bit shy, kind of aloof, and nothing could or would ever change that. Ella—according to her friends, family, and neighbors—quite frankly *needed* a man, and fast, before Slick the cat became a reality. Well, when she got back home, she'd better start investing in cat toys. Because it was highly likely she would be a single cat lady.

She just wasn't the kind of woman who would have sex just for the satisfaction of the action. She was old-fashioned. She needed that all-too-elusive brain, body, and spirit connection. Basically, she was a pent-up prude. For as much as everyone around her thought she needed a man, the moment she got one, there would be cautionary tales of all the horrible things that could happen if she actually entered into a relationship.

Don't move too fast.

Keep your options open.

Get to know him.

Date several men at the same time.

Don't get too physical too fast.

Men don't buy the cow if they are getting the milk for free.

The right man will wait until the time is right, the commitment is there, and he loves you.

Whatever! Why did she feel there was one set of rules for her and a slightly different set of rules for everyone else? Well, in the last few months of deep thought and deliberation she had come to a conclusion. She was enough. A man coming into her life would be for entertainment, not with the promise of forever.

What if she wanted to be swept away? Caught up in the moment? What if she wanted to fall into a relationship? Or a relationship of the moment? The answer was simple; she would.

She was so tired of hearing how everyone else could, but when Ella did it, there were consequences not to be taken lightly because she felt too much and cared too deeply. She would get hurt. What was her protective mother always saying? She vacillated between warning Ella that she would be an old maid someday and cautioning her not to jump into things too quickly. The point and counterpoint were only one thing: consistently annoying. She was tired of it. And wasn't she old enough to make her own decisions?

Remembering her current nun-like status, she decided to change the subject, or at least give her brain a break from an argument that was always circling in her mind. She placed her linen napkin in her lap and reached for a fork. At least she could satisfy her appetite for the spicy food that called to her. The elegantly arranged shrimp on the plate that had been placed before her was so fresh, she could still taste the saltwater on its perfectly firm flesh. A drop of pineapple juice sated with lime and salt and a splash of habanero lingered on her lower lip after the first bite. Her tongue caught it before it could slip away. Ah, it was sweet, hot, and delicious... The burn was intoxicating.

No restaurant back home had ever satisfied her so completely. And how could it? She was in paradise, where the ocean provided background music, and the setting sun provided the subtle light. It was romantic, even though she was alone. She felt sexy, despite the knowledge that the only one enjoying her cleavage was the person looking down at it (herself!), and she hoped she wouldn't drop a shrimp tail because no doubt it would end up in her cleavage.

She speared another morsel and savored it, shutting her eyes in deep contentment. At that exact moment, she knew she was being watched. Before she could turn and glance at the stranger who had taken the barstool next to her, she heard his voice, perfectly accented French, speaking to the bartender. She chanced a quick glance. He was, she realized, no stranger at all. It was the man from that morning at Saline Beach. He'd stood out to her because, aside from her red bikini, he was the only other non-nude on the beach. He wore rather conservative navy swim trunks. She wondered at the time what he'd thought if she'd strolled up to him and pointed out the obvious fact that neither one of them was naked. But she wouldn't do that kind of thing. Okay, she had thought about doing something like that tomorrow morning, but she'd never been good at talking to handsome men, let alone strangers. Besides, he was too tan. His hair was too long. He had to be a local. He *was* a player. And she bet she wasn't his type. It would have no doubt annoyed him and embarrassed her in the end.

But he was here again, right next to her. She could be polite. Okay, so take romance off the table. She wasn't his type. She knew that. He looked like he came with a warning label. Couldn't she just have a nice conversation with someone?

Slowly, with only a hint of her head-turning, she looked at him again, but still quickly, and registered the spicy trouble less than two feet away. She thought she'd blown it that afternoon when, instead of starting something that would only surely disappoint them both, she'd lost her nerve and escaped on her hotel bicycle like a scared animal. Was fate giving her a second chance? Was it a second chance at the gorgeous man? Or a second chance to make a fool out of herself? Maybe she was just drunk. Why couldn't it just be simple? Why did everything have to be so complicated? Just have a damn conversation. *Duh.*

"Bonjour. Ça va?" he asked, turning and smiling at her with recognition. Close up, he looked even more formidable, and Ella liked what she saw. Long lashes framed green eyes deeper than the ocean that lay only a few feet beyond them. Earlier today, those beautiful eyes were covered with sunglasses. His blue-black hair was pulled back into a short ponytail contrasting with a gauzy white linen shirt, unbuttoned to mid-chest and displaying a nice smattering of chest hair. The translucent fabric caught in the warm breeze and moved like waves over his tanned skin. There was a beachy, exotic scent coming off him, which had to be an expensive cologne, but she had never smelled anything like it before. If it was called *Ocean Seduction,* she wouldn't have been surprised.

He was the human equivalent of dynamite. Glad she wasn't his type.

Be cool. Try to be *cool.*

Touching her napkin to her lips, as she sat up straighter, she replied. "Bien, et vous?" With that statement, she had reached her full and unimpressive mastery of the French language. She was good, better than she'd been all day because of who was sharing this space with her.

"Jacques," he said, extending his hand. "Like the explorer Jacque Cristaux only spelled with an 's' at the end."

Taking it on her own, Ella felt that touch as it raced through every nerve ending in her body. His skin felt like someone who worked with his hands. Not too rough, not too soft. Possibly, just right.

Okay, there was no way she was his type, but she could still dream a little. As her fantasies took hold, and she met those emerald eyes head-on, packing the condoms and the sex kit no longer seemed like a foolish idea. Her stomach and points south were already tingling, which was ridiculous, but she was glad to know she could sense attraction when it sat next to her.

"Ella," she said and added, "Je ne parle pas français. Parle-tu anglaise?" She'd learned that being able to tell people you couldn't speak French also came in handy in a predominantly French-speaking country.

"I speak fluent English," he said, the smile breaking across his face. It made the hard lines soften as his lashes gracefully dropped in a manner so sensual, so delicate that Ella found herself mesmerized. Men should not be blessed with such beautiful lashes.

Damn, he was gorgeous.

"I saw you this morning on Saline Beach," he said enthusiastically and winked. "You wore a very petite rouge bikini."

"Yes, I was in my red bikini." Had he remembered *her*? Was he making fun of her? Did she trip or look stupid? Was the bathing suit unflattering? Was she too big for a two piece? Maybe she should revisit the bikini.

"Tu avais l'air sexy."

What?

Ella laughed as the heat kissed her cheeks, blushing as scarlet as her bikini. She didn't need a translator to know he'd just complimented her. Score one for the bikini. Why was he talking to her?

Smiling lasciviously, he pointed to her drink. "Do you like your drink?"

"It's a Mojito," she replied. "It's good, bien."

"Is it made with Bacardi cent cinquante et un liquor?"

"I don't know," she said, shaking her head, to which he pointed to a bottle of Bacardi 151. Understanding, she said, "Bacardi 151? I don't know what's in my drink. Maybe just rum, some mint, and lime. It is good. I'm trying to decide if I should have another."

Jacques pointed to himself and said, "Fabricant de boissons alcoolisées pour Bacardi. I work for a company like Bacardi. Allow me to get something I know you'll like."

"No, I didn't mean—"

"No, I want you to try something that I know you will like," he said.

Just then, the bartender arrived, and Jacques ordered each of them a Mojito made with some kind of exotic rum. There was a long string of French words Ella couldn't understand, but as she watched the bartender smile appreciatively and then make their drinks, he did so with rum that came from an ornate crystal bottle on the top shelf of the bar with a label she didn't recognize.

She wondered how much the specialty liquor would cost. Thankfully, there was a high limit on the card she had with her. But when the bartender said something to her new friend, he produced a credit card and handed it to the bartender. She began to protest, and he said, "Please, this is on me. Start a tab, please." To her ear, he used such perfect English. It was as if he was American, not French, and not accented, but she convinced herself that it was her imagination.

For the rest of the evening, her glass never went past half full before it was replaced by another fresh Mojito made with the ornate bottled rum, fresh mint, and lime. Then, other ingredients were added. At first sip, she'd been able to tell the difference. It was almost a completely different drink. It is much smoother and, she feared, much stronger. The other additives, the fruit, things she'd never tasted before, seemed to explode in her mouth. Lots of pineapple and her favorite, passionfruit. Were Mojitos supposed to have pineapple and passionfruit? She didn't think so. How long had it been since mint was added to her drink? A few drinks ago. Somewhere in the evening, they'd started drinking something altogether different.

Platters of shrimp arrived with other delicacies like conch salad and lobster.

They talked of Saint Barts, beaches, travel, and food. They talked about a lot of things. She told him she owned a small jewelry store. And she did, but it didn't just carry jewelry. He didn't need to know that. She felt more sophisticated with this one tiny lie.

He was in the rum business. She wasn't sure what he did exactly because he'd told her in a mix of French and English and used words like overseer, distiller, and fermenter. She let it go because there were more important issues to discuss. They managed to convey that they were both single and had never married. Ella considered his relationship status to be the most important information she needed to know. She also thought it was interesting they both wanted to get that point across. She hadn't taken him for the kind of man who was looking for one woman.

He surprised her. She didn't know how she felt about that.

"Why did you come to Saint Barts? Business?"

"No," she said, shaking her head. "Pleasure. Some warmth in the middle of winter."

"By yourself?" he asked.

She shrugged her shoulders as if to say, "What was I going to do?"

"You are by yourself," she pointed out. He shook his head. "I'm with you."

Such rapt attention, smooth dialogue, and the liquor led to two very interesting consequences for Ella. First, she could never be exactly sure how many drinks she'd consumed. For a woman who was always in control, this was something new. Second, her grasp of the French language seemed to improve with the more she drank. She'd taken two years of French in high school and thought she'd forgotten much of it, but the liquor seemed to unlock the darker recesses of her mind.

Jacques asked her where she was from, and she said, "United States."

"États-Unis? J'adore Americans," he replied lustfully, and they laughed harder. "I love America and Americans. Especially pretty blonde ladies who wear red bikinis."

She shook her head. Could she really believe him?

The sun, which had been uncomfortably bright in the sky and warm when Jacques had originally sat next to her, had quietly faded to a deep blush of magenta as Ella and Jacques chatted in a mix of English and French. Fueled by high-proof rum, everything they said to each other was incredibly funny. Ella's cheeks hurt from laughing so often. Ella had no objections when Jacques's arm encircled the back of her chair and then landed lightly on her bare, suntanned knee. And when, some-time later, he leaned toward her and whispered in her ear, she leaned into him, enjoying his crisp, fresh scent and the way his lips tickled her as he spoke.

When the bar closed, neither one of them wanted the evening to end, and they hesitated over the final call. Jacques signed the tab and must have tipped well. The bartender glanced at the bill, then looked shocked and thanked Jacques profusely.

At last, it was time to leave, and Jacques held her hand as they walked through the empty restaurant and through the deserted, open-air lobby of her hotel. They continued to a path that would take them either together toward her room or apart to unknown destinations.

Ella felt stressed. Either destination had consequences.

Making his decision clear, Jacques pulled her into the shadows of the tall tropical plants and kissed her. His lips were soft and warm on hers, the teasing brush of a cool petal against bare skin. Leaning into the kiss, her need to touch and be touched pushed away any lingering shyness. His arms tightened around her. His hands were warm and sure, heating her through the thin chiffon wrap that fell loosely on her shoulders.

They faced each other in the shadows, her eyes searching his for something that would confirm the truth. She saw no warnings. No smooth seduction. Only a kind of honesty that surprised her.

"Am I really your type?" she asked and then wanted to kick herself.

"I think you might be more perfect for me than anyone I've ever met," he said smoothly.

He kissed her again, and his lips became more demanding, opening so that his tongue could taste her. Returning the favor, she leaned into him, her body aligning with his as she tasted his sweet mouth and ran her hands over the rough linen that covered his chest.

It had been a long time since she'd been held and kissed. And much longer since she'd been kissed this thoroughly. The liquor made any warnings or inhibitions become a subtle white noise she no longer heard. All she wanted was another kiss. She didn't realize that she'd been this thirsty and that he was the only elixir to quench her thirst.

"Where is your room?" he asked in almost perfect English. Was it her imagination, or did he sound like an American again? She'd find out later. First, she needed to have the experience of him. How far would this go? The red flags needed to stand down. Tomorrow would come…tomorrow.

"This way," she said, taking his hand in hers and leading him through the tangle of lush, dense jungle toward a long row of rooms that faced the ocean. This man—this solid, beautiful specimen that sent tiny spikes of electricity along her skin with merely a look—trailed willingly behind her. The next day and for many days after she would wonder if she knew what she was doing or if the exotic alcohol had taken control of her senses. Later, she'd blame everything that happened that spectacular night on the alcohol. It was the easiest solution to digest.

Pausing to find her key, she looked up and found Jacques smiling down at her. Her smile faltered as the reality sunk in. Then he leaned in and kissed her again, and she couldn't wait to get inside and see what might happen next.

If they crossed the threshold, there would be no turning back. She would be getting swept up in exactly the way she had dreamed of, and the thought of it made her scared to death and completely excited.

She wanted this like nothing she had ever wanted. Chocolate sundae? Nope. Designer gown? Nope. Wealth beyond her wildest dreams? Nope, not now. She just wanted Jacques.

She pushed the door open to her obscenely expensive guest room, which was completely decorated in white. The floors, furniture, walls, shutters, lazy ceiling fan, tongue and groove vaulted ceiling, and last, but not least, the linen on the whitewashed four-poster bed, which dominated the space in monochromatic elegance. The only color was from a bouquet of red and pink ginger blossoms that she'd purchased earlier in the day.

Once the door was closed, Jacques pulled her to him, dipping his head to kiss her again. Then he lifted her in his arms. She went willingly, sliding along his body, devouring every inch she could feel.

Yes, this was serious. Playtime was over.

After a moment, Ella had a thought, tried to dismiss it, but then said, "Wait just a second, I promise, just a second...I want this to be perfect."

"It is perfect," he said. Then he looked more than a little perplexed as he reluctantly released her, her feet gently touching the floor. She smiled and held up a finger to signal she just needed a moment.

Eyes on him, she tossed off her thin black chiffon wrap, ran to the dresser, picked up a box of matches, and began lighting candles throughout the room that she'd bought on her first day of vacation. Ironically, she'd chided herself for the frivolous purchase, but now she was glad for the foresight.

The exercise of lighting the candles was part delay and part tease. She felt Jacques's eyes on her as he watched hungrily from the sidelines, his green eyes iridescent in the candlelight, a slight smile on his lips. She paused to open the doors to the private balcony, allowing the sound of the ocean and the tropical breeze to enter the bedroom. Tossing off her shoes, she turned her back to him and took off her watch and large silver bracelets, placing them on top of the dresser as she casually opened one of the white wicker dresser drawers to make sure the box of wishful condoms was still there, waiting for any bad deed she chose to do. She snatched the box discreetly, turned, and watched Jacques, who met her gaze with an eager smile. Her bare feet padded lightly on the wood floor as she made her way back to Jacques, who opened his arms in invitation.

The candlelight made dreamy shadows on the walls, while splashes of color from the bouquet of ginger blossoms swayed in the warm wind perfuming the heady air.

Jacques didn't speak. He didn't ask for permission. He simply took her in his arms, lifted her off her feet, and carried her to the bed. Then he set her on the fine linen. She fell back against the soft pillows and watched as he stood next to her and unbuttoned the last few buttons on his linen shirt.

Despite the fact he'd been almost as modest as she was at the beach, in his navy bathing trunks, he didn't seem to have the same issue when he tossed off his shorts and then his silk boxers. Ella bit her lip as she took in every detail of his well-muscled body. Each tanned inch of Jacques was beautiful. Her eyes lingered on the impressive erection that gently swayed with each motion he made, closing the distance to her. At the very sight of it, she took a deep inhale of breath. Yes, he wanted her as much as she wanted him. And soon, they would be making love. It wasn't a question any longer.

Her heart beat so fast she thought her chest might explode as a blush once again crept along her skin. When he joined her on the bed, she smiled and tried not to think of how wonderful it would feel to have him inside of her. All the warnings that had been well ingrained in her since she was a teenager simply fell away. Ella was getting swept up in the fantasy.

* * *

Jack looked down at the beautiful woman sprawled on the bed in front of him, so lush, so sexy...

He'd made the initial mistake of assuming she was French. By the time he discovered his mistake, it was too late. The idea that she thought *he* was French suddenly seemed like a very interesting element of her seduction. He should come clean. Tell her he was an American, but he didn't want to do one thing that might change the mood or what they were about to do. He could apologize later.

Her breath came in shallow bursts, her chest heaving a little. He recognized the signs of her arousal and wanted to prolong them for as long as possible. Slowly, he ran his hands along her body, feeling firm breasts through the thin fabric of her dress. He kissed the peaches-and-cream skin between her breasts while his fingers danced teasingly along the edge of her dress's bodice.

Leaning into her, his weight dipping the mattress, Jack encircled Ella with his arms. Jack was nothing if not playful when it came to seduction. He traced the fabric of the halter dress that still covered her breasts to the fastener behind her neck. He wanted to linger there for a while, but flashes of the red bikini had his adept fingers dispensing with the knot that held the fabric together in record time. He peeled away the top of the dress, their eyes meeting as her breasts lay exposed to him. They were perfect teardrop shapes, their rosy nipples the color of the center of soft pink plumeria blossoms, erect and inviting. His mouth watered at the thought of tasting them. He wanted to feast on them, but he had other, more pressing places to explore first. Smoothly, he divested her from the rest of her dress, the glossy lining rippling along her skin as he exposed more silk and lace. The scraps of lingerie that covered her intimately did not disappoint. Giving into his more primal instincts, Jack kissed her through the red silk panties, the lace tickling his cheek. She did look lovely in red.

"Rouge, bien," he murmured as he blew air on her hot skin.

"I like red," she said, her voice soft and slurred as her lips curved into a small smile as she murmured, "At home, I wear a lot of black and red."

Jack smiled, and she smiled as he snagged the edge of her panties with his teeth and slowly peeled them down and off her legs. His fantasies that morning at the beach weren't half this good.

Jack started at her ankle and placed a trail of kisses and gentle caresses, which led to Ella's knee and along her inner thigh to the juncture of her femininity. When he finished with one leg, he started at the ankle of the other. She liked this. He could see it in her expression, but it wasn't enough for her.

It wasn't enough for him either. He needed more but wasn't ready to take her yet and feared losing control of himself too soon. The anticipation was amazing.

"Jacques, please...." Ella begged, her voice carrying an edge of desperation that grabbed hold of him and wouldn't let go.

"Se détendre...relax, darling," he managed as he spied the box of condoms at her side and paused to quickly open the box, free a condom and sheath himself. Then he spread her legs wide, took up position between them, and gently slipped inside her. She was ready for the intimate invasion. He saw her exhale in relief when he was inside her. Their eyes met as she said, "You feel so good."

He leaned forward and kissed her, their hands joining as he moved with her.

Her eyes glazed over as she seemed to look through him. He lost himself in the passion and heat of her body as she moaned beneath him, a climax building within her.

He liked the feel of her, the taste of her, the way she looked as she got ready to unravel. He felt himself losing control too quickly. He could hear the ocean and the sound of the bed hitting the wall in perfect rhythm to his thrusts, but most of all, he could hear her keening the first time she screamed out in release. Other animal sounds joined in, rising and blocking out all other sounds. It was only then that he realized the sounds had come from not only his lips but hers as well.

Chapter Two

The warm, tropical sun fell across Ella's cheek as she slowly awakened the next morning. Jacques lay next to her, his arm wrapped around her middle, his head turned toward her. She didn't dare move for fear of waking him. Her body was stiff and sore in places where it had not been sore for a very long time, and for good reason. There was no delicate way to explain what her body had been through the night before. And it had been well worth it.

Turning onto her side, she looked at Jacques. He looked peaceful as he dozed, which was quite a contrast from the passion he'd delivered with such ferocity several times the night before. Reaching out, she touched a lock of his blue-black hair, feeling the softness between her fingertips. He was one of the best-looking men she'd ever seen, let alone made love with.

The arm wrapped around her middle began to move, searching for and finding her breast. He opened his eyes and displayed a sly smile. By way of greeting, he leaned over and sucked on the raised nipple as his arms encircled her and pulled her close.

"Good morning," she said, her hand traveling to his hair as he continued to lavish attention to her breast.

"Bonjour mademoiselle," he murmured.

It didn't take long before they were making love again.

She sat astride him, his hands on her hips, guiding her as she rode him for all it was worth. Happily, she'd remembered the condoms, but she had an odd feeling that she hadn't remembered it every time they'd made love the night before. She would worry about that later.

Spent once again, they snuggled together under the crisp white cotton sheets and eventually dozed, only to be awakened when the maid knocked and asked to clean the room. By mutual agreement, they decided it might be a good idea to get out of bed and have something to sustain them before they made love again.

Jacques indicated his watch and held up three fingers as he said, "The lobby *à trois?"*

"The lobby, this hotel, at three today," she replied.

"Oui," he said as he kissed his way from her breast to her lips. "Unless you'd like to come with me now."

"I really want a shower and to redo my makeup."

He shrugged and said, "You look beautiful. Three seems a long way away."

It was just after one. A couple of hours would give Ella much needed time to get her bearings before another night of passion. She desperately wanted a shower and to freshen up her hair and makeup.

"I know. Don't be late," she said and kissed him back.

"I won't, my darling." Later, she would remember his last words to her and swear that there wasn't a hint of his previous French accent.

* * *

Jack was staying at a hotel five miles from Ella's. Having found Ella by recognizing the bike she'd been riding as belonging to one of the more popular hotels, he'd taken up residence on a wicker settee with a book in the hotel's lobby. After waiting for several hours, he decided to go to the hotel restaurant and cliffside bar for a drink. When he walked up to the bar and saw Miss Red Bikini, now dressed in a black halter dress and matching chiffon wrap, he remembered his family business motto: *It was better to be lucky than good any day*. And just how had he gotten so lucky?

Ella was spectacular. Could he have fallen in love with her after one night? It was a cliché, but so much how he felt.

Now back in the suite of his hotel, he immediately heard the telltale buzz of voicemail from his cell phone. Back to reality. The phone was where he'd left it on the dresser in his bedroom. In his haste to find Ella, he'd forgotten it the day before, which was out of the meticulous, responsible nature of Jack Brewster, businessman. It was very much his new laid-back Jacques self, the maker of rum. The light on his desk phone blinked with several unheard messages. He felt his stomach lurch. Something was wrong.

Twelve missed calls indicated that something was very wrong. Stepping out onto the balcony, he ignored the white sugar sand beach beyond, placed the phone to his ear, and listened to his messages. After the first voicemail, he swore and dropped into a waiting deck chair before falling. There had been a terrible accident on Mount Hood involving his older brother, Charles. The asshole had always considered himself to be a daredevil, believing himself invincible, as demonstrated by hiking Mount Hood in the middle of winter.

Hitting the speed dial on his phone, he waited.

"Jack?" his mother asked, her voice somewhat frantic as she answered. This was bad.

"Yeah, is everything okay?" he replied, selfishly trying not to think of Ella and the night ahead.

"Where have you been?"

"I lost my cell phone and just got it back today. What is going on?"

"We will discuss your forgetfulness later. What a time to be characteristically irresponsible. Charles has been in an accident on Mount Hood." At the last part, her voice broke.

"Didn't he just start on the mountain today? What? Did he trip in the parking lot at Timberline Lodge?" It was the wrong thing to say to her, and he realized it the moment it was out of his mouth.

"Leave it to you to joke at a time like this," his mother said and then inhaled into a sob.

"I'm sorry. That was wrong of me. Is he okay?" Jack asked.

"He fell in a crevasse on his way to summiting Mount Hood. He was airlifted to Good Faith. He has several broken bones and a head injury. He was talking when he was riding in the chopper, so he isn't mentally impaired, thank God. But it is serious. And where are you? Just playing on the beach on some island while your brother fights for his life. Why am I not surprised?"

"Mom, I'm sorry. I'm sorry about the phone. I was only able to get it this morning."

"That doesn't account for the fact I called your hotel repeatedly. You weren't there last night. I tried you early this morning, but you weren't in your room. You were probably passed out on some beach after drinking too much, or you were sowing your oats and having some one-night stand with a floozy."

Ella was neither a one-night stand nor a floozy. At the very thought, he bristled.

"Thanks for thinking the best of me, Mother."

"I'm not wrong, am I?" she said with a certain knowing that made Jack bite back a harsh retort.

"I'll come home right now. Once I get off the phone with you, I'll call the airlines."

"No need. The family plane is waiting at the airport in Saint Barts. We sent it for you because we knew you'd want to stop screwing around and be by your brother's bedside."

"Thank you. I'm packing as we speak."

"It is horrible. Two of his friends died. That Derek, who I never liked, and that Seth, who I always thought was trouble. They got all tangled in each other's ropes and went into a crevasse that opened up due to the warm winter. They shouldn't have even been climbing at this time of year."

Jack paused and shut his eyes.

Derek and Seth were two of Charles's best friends. They had all grown up together, were also from privileged backgrounds. Seth just had a child with his wife last year. Jack felt sick. Their families would never recover. That poor child would grow up without a father. But his mother kept talking.

"What if something happens to Charles? What if he has a brain bleed or something they haven't found? What will I do if my baby doesn't survive?"

"Mother, it is going to be okay. He's getting wonderful medical care at Good Faith. Trust them. I'm on my way."

"You don't know that. They could miss something. If I lose my sweet Charlie, what will I do? He is everything to me."

"Don't think that way. You're not going to lose him. I'm packing now, and I'll see you soon."

Jack didn't think. He just reacted. Grabbing his luggage from the dressing room, he threw his clothes haphazardly inside. After he reassured his mother for a third time that Charles would be okay, he hung up and immediately made another call to the airplane he knew was waiting for him at the airport. Then he called the concierge and reserved a seat on the airport transport, leaving in ten minutes.

Once packed, he paused, thoughts racing back to the woman with whom he'd spent the most wonderful night of his life. He didn't have time to go back to Ella's hotel and explain the situation. Hell, he'd been so confident he'd see her again he hadn't paid attention to the little details like her room number. He couldn't remember her last name. He wasn't even sure she'd told him her last name. He didn't even know where she lived in the United States. It hadn't mattered because he had the means to visit her and, often, wherever her home turned out to be. But he hadn't asked. He was a fucking overconfident idiot.

He could admit there had been other things on his mind, like how it would feel to hold her, how it felt to seduce her. Maybe he was a scoundrel. Hadn't that been what his mother used to call him? Maybe she was right. He was ashamed that the details of a respectable initial conversation when you first met someone had all but flown away. He remembered that she said she had a jewelry store. Despite his acumen with liquor, he was a cheap drunk.

He'd planned to come clean when they met again and let her know he wasn't French. As it was, he'd created a mess that he didn't have time to fix. It had been fun at the moment, but it now had horrible consequences. She would think he was an asshole.

Pulling out a piece of hotel stationery and an envelope from the suite's desk, he also retrieved a business card from his wallet. Then he wrote a note to Ella, which explained not only his quick departure but also his sincere apology for not being able to keep their date. He told her he wanted to see her again. Hell, he had to see her again. As he sealed the envelope, he realized he meant it. He really wanted to see her again. He only hoped that after she read his note, she wouldn't hate him for lying.

Grabbing his luggage and the note, he ran for the lobby of his hotel. Pausing at the concierge's desk, he quickly explained the situation about his brother and tossed the man several hundred Euros along with the letter for Ella after giving him a small map to her room in the other hotel. If there was anything his upbringing had taught him, it was that if you had enough money, you could get people to do anything you wanted. The concierge smiled and assured Jack he would deliver the message to her door. But once Jack was out of sight, the concierge pocketed the cash and tossed the envelope into the nearest garbage can.

37

Chapter Three
Twenty Months Later

"I've texted Ivan," his mother said. "The car will be in front of the hospital in three minutes."

Jack shook his head, "I'm going to walk. I need to have a look at the proposed space."

His mother scrunched up her face, her wrinkles defying the monthly Botox injections. "Why? Jack, it is cold out there."

"I have this very nice Burberry coat from *Mario's*. Remember? You gave it to me for Christmas last year."

"Of course I remember," his mother snapped. "I'm not that old."

"And this is something I have to do, thanks to your assurances to the board. I'll see you back at the office."

"Well, if you get sick, don't expect me to drop everything and wait on you. I've got a lot to prepare for the holidays—"

He walked out of the room. Sometimes, like now, she was too much. Besides, he had a housekeeper who had proven to take better care of him than his mother ever had.

Jack took an elevator to the hospital lobby and then walked east along the tree-lined Lovejoy Street in Northwest Portland. Now that they were fully into autumn, the trees were beautiful in colors of golden rod and red.

He'd just come from a two-hour board meeting at Good Faith Hospital, the oldest hospital in the city and one of the largest in Oregon. He'd spent a considerable amount of time inside that main building, first as his brother recovered from the devastating accident on Mount Hood and then when he took his brother's position as a member of the hospital's board. Not that he wanted to, but circumstances had intervened, and his parents had insisted. He despised setting foot in the place. He didn't care about the strong relationship between his family and the hospital. He thought it was all a bit morbid. This was his mother's passion, not his. Even the sterile smell of the place bothered him.

Generations of the Brewster Family held a mostly honorary position on the hospital board for over one hundred and fifty years. As he gazed skyward at the intersection of NW Lovejoy and 21st Avenue, he could already see the shadow of *The Brewster Family Center for Orthopedics* extending in front of him, as the architect had envisioned, where now there existed three small businesses his mother liked to refer to as "*...those damn dilapidated shacks.*" He doubted she had ever set foot in any of the cute little shops, and he was angry that the role of intermediary dream-killer had now fallen to him. Even though she hadn't wanted him to go today, she had assured the board that he would have some magical power to do so.

"Jack will smooth it over with the shop owners. Surely, they will see his...our position, how this hospital expansion will benefit the community much more than their shabby shops...Who wouldn't go all in with something so wonderful for the entire community?"

But Jack knew that the three shop owners who had established clientele were living their own dreams.

Jack thought the three independent businesses, three livelihoods they were destroying, wouldn't quite understand the benefit to the community. The hospital board and his mother were seriously out of touch on this issue.

The idea of funding and naming a hospital wing had been in process for over two years. But in light of Charles's accident, it had gone from being a cancer or obstetrics wing to an orthopedics wing, whether the hospital needed more orthopedics space or not.

It had been almost two years since his brother's accident, which had forever changed the course of Jack's life. Charles had never quite recovered from the fall down Mount Hood, which had claimed the lives of several people, including Charles's two friends, in one of the worst accidents ever on Mount Hood. Charles had recovered from his physical wounds, but he was no longer the son whom the family trusted to lead the international family business into the next generation. He might be physically all right, but something had scrambled his brain, and he now had a conscience. He was much less of a jerk. Jack no longer recognized him. Jack thought Charles had found his humanity. Maybe the guilt of losing his friends had changed him. Some mellow, nice guy now occupied Charles's body. It was completely unnerving.

"Bro," Charles had said in one of their last conversations before he strapped on his beat-up backpack and left in search of his salvation. "We are just small, incidental cells on this beautiful big blue marble. We owe it to ourselves and the planet to experience life and to respect all the beautiful creatures. I want to help the less fortunate. That is my purpose, bro. I know it."

"You really want to walk away from all of this?" Jack asked, knowing the truth.

"It isn't about money, bro. It is about experience. Life. The more you experience, the wealthier you are. Do you think Mom would mind if I sold Grandma's engagement ring to fund new wells in this village in Tanzania I discovered?"

"I think she would kill you and end your journey on this beautiful big blue marble," Jack said with certainty.

"Bummer. She is so uptight. Even the Dalai Lama understands. As his holiness says, *"Love and compassion are necessities, not luxuries…"*

"Please don't say that to Mother unless I'm around. I want to see her reaction," Jack said.

Jack sometimes missed the old Charles. He respected the new Charles much more, but it would cost Jack dearly. His future trajectory had been derailed.

His business-oriented parents no longer trusted Charles to lead the company into the next generation. Someone so enlightened couldn't be trusted to sell legal, addictive intoxicants. Jack and Charles had switched places of importance in a matter of seconds. The responsibilities of The Brewster International Brewing Company now fell to the "runner-up" son. The slightly ignored child. Jack had been called into service like the runner-up at a beauty pageant after the first-place winner had been forced to resign due to some sort of scandal involving sex, videos, or politicians, maybe all three.

Charles's once-driven personality—a seriously conceited one of self-importance, which had always pushed him toward success—had somehow flipped in the exact opposite direction. Charles no longer had the drive which had forced him to climb every mountain in the Pacific Northwest. Plans to travel to Katmandu and conquer Everest while eating gourmet food and drinking Brewster alcohol on the highest point on the planet had simply vaporized. He'd still made it to Nepal, but now as a United Peace volunteer on a humanitarian mission to make sure children had food, water, and schools. Six months later, he'd headed for Africa to do the same thing. Which country, the family wasn't sure, but he had the sense to employ armed security guards, which eased his troubled mother's heart and hit her bank account.

The new Charles took some getting used to and his appearance and new attitude came with the notion of filling his own dreams and shattering his younger brother's.

As he'd explained in his last cryptic letter home, *"Wherever there is suffering, I will be there to ease the pain..."* He did not consider his family or the family business, however, to be worthy of his attention any longer, except to pay for his security detail and provide "funds" for his special projects. On some level, Jack admired Charles, but he still wanted to punch him for stepping away like a righteous, abdicating monarch, the jerk.

Jack hoped Charles would come to his senses and return, but he didn't think it likely. Not only to lead the company but also to dedicate the hospital wing that had been funded in his honor by his family and his family's powerful friends. When Jack finally found Charles with a satellite phone a week earlier in some yurt on the other side of the world, he'd merely laughed at the idea that there was a wing being named in their family's honor. And then he'd shared with Jack the irony of how the money raised for that hospital wing could go so much further in a third-world country to help the countless masses, feed the hungry, provide clean water—heck, even build schools.

On some level, Jack not only believed him but was proud of his brother's new humanity.

Their mother had taken to crying, a lot. It was quite disturbing to see her act human. On the way to the board meeting that afternoon, she confided that she had spoken to Charles the day before. "Do you know what he asked me?"

"No, I'm assuming it had to do with money," Jack had guessed.

"He thinks we should sell the business and give away the proceeds. He says we don't need the houses we have, that I don't need my jewelry. He wants your father to sell his Mercedes, Maybach."

"Not the Maybach," Jack answered in mock horror.

"Here I am, trying to have a serious conversation, and you are making light of it. Have I raised two idiot sons?"

Jack couldn't disagree, as he'd always been good at seeing both sides of an argument. But with Charles out of the picture, the responsibility of not only the company but also to propel the hospital project to completion had fallen squarely on Jack's shoulders. And with that new power coursing through his veins, Jack made one concession. Instead of being called the *Charles Brewster IV Center for Orthopedics*, the wing would now be called *The Brewster Family Center for Orthopedics*. That way, Charles didn't need to make it back for the dedication, where he might feel the need to share his thoughts on the third world or the Maybach to a large audience, including the press, thus embarrassing the family.

Now, after Jack walked and wool-gathered along Lovejoy, he thought more intently of the glass and steel structure that would one day occupy the space where the shops currently resided. They were cute, the quaint shops, and they had what appeared to be apartments above them with small decks. He wondered how life might have been different if he had lived in one of those apartments after college instead of his parents' house. Maybe he'd have more compassion. Maybe he'd have met someone lovely, like Ella from the Caribbean.

It hurt to think of her. She had reached a mystical, dream-like status in his memories. There were times he wondered if he'd ever met her. She had never called, and he had spent a lot of time wondering why. He couldn't change the reality of what happened now, so he changed the subject to the present.

He tried to feel good about knowing that his family had chosen this wing to be their personal family memorial for this and future generations. Strangely, he didn't. He wished he could go to Africa and build schools like his brother, but as the second and final son, that wasn't an option for him. His time for freedom had come and gone.

Each generation of Brewsters had dedicated a memorial to their generation. It was tradition. Thanks to Great-Grandfather Charles Brewster there was The Brewster Fountain in downtown Portland, which was a popular place for the homeless to bathe and wash their clothes.

Grandfather Charles Brewster II had dedicated The Brewster Park to honor fallen firemen, which was a popular place for men to find dates with brightly dressed women who charged by the hour. Now, Jack's father and mother, Mr. and Mrs. Charles Brewster III, would be responsible for a hospital wing, which unfortunately would not be dedicated to their oldest son, Charles Brewster IV, businessman, mountaineer, accident survivor turned globe-trotting do-gooder.

Jack had better things to do on this crisp but sunny fall afternoon than further irritate a group of angry shop owners. He'd rather have a root canal. Considering his mother's feelings about the shops on the street, he wished she'd been the bearer of this personal appeal. It might have humbled her, but his mother didn't like to get her hands dirty. Rumor was that one of the proprietors, Ms. Marcella Martin, owner of *Marcella's*, a gift shop, was about to become the spokesperson for her neighbors. He had yet to see what he was dealing with, so he needed to meet Ms. Martin and try to see what kind of adversary she'd be. He hoped she'd be a reasonable, bohemian grandmotherly woman who had a favorite grandson about his age. That was the best-case scenario.

Most of all, Jack wanted to get back to his company, his office, his label design, and the excitement he felt of doing something that didn't involve his parents. He was a few short weeks away from bottling his first batch of *Brewster's Redrum* if the lawyers could get him the name. When Charles had his accident, everything changed, and the idea of *Brewster's Redrum* was put on the back burner. Considered by his family to be a hobby, Jack's rum was now treated like the illegitimate cousin no one wanted to talk about.

Jack walked along Lovejoy Street until he stood in front of the three shops that were on the chopping block in the name of progress. *Cindy's Cedar Chest*, a resale shop, offered a collection of hideously outdated clothing in the window. Looking at a display of sherbet colored polyester dresses, he had to wonder: Who bought this crap? Some rebellious teenagers, he was sure.

He'd be doing the world a favor by closing this ugly shop.

Next to *Cindy's* was *Marcella's* boutique, owned by their potentially biggest and most outspoken opponent, Marcella Martin. Next to her was the *Curry Leaf*, an Indian restaurant that had once made him sick for a week and he thought should be shut down by the health department. Not sure his stomach could handle even the scents coming from the *Curry Leaf*, he decided to start with the middle shop and face the enemy head-on.

Entwined hearts and a neon pink sign proclaimed he was about to enter *Marcella's*. Damn, he did not want to do this. He wanted to be back at his office with his dog, looking over different marketing concepts. Instead, hat in hand, he had to befriend some bohemian shop keeps and bribe them, if it came down to that.

He'd heard from the board that the owner, Marcella Martin, was very passionate about her livelihood. Not that he could blame her, but she wasn't going to win this fight. She'd found a bleeding-heart liberal lawyer who'd taken the case pro bono and was going to battle the hospital's right to eminent domain. *Good luck, little lady.*

Jack was trying to do the right thing. He would introduce himself so she would know the face of her enemy. Maybe, just maybe, he could get her to see reason. He certainly didn't need a handful of Portland's finest citizens protesting in front of his distillery the day he released *Redrum*. Not that he could really blame her. If someone were trying to take away his distillery, he'd fight like a wolverine. But then he knew that would never happen. He would always have enough money to win any battle —well, any battle that didn't involve his parents.

Pausing by one of the bay windows that framed the old-fashioned Dutch door below the sign, Jack noticed an artfully arranged selection of coffee table books including *Champagne, Chanel, Plantations*—nice, tasteful books—and then, further back, there was an *Eroticism in Rome, Love Voodoo for The Soul, and Recipes for Love.*

What kind of shop was this exactly? He'd been told it was a high-end gift shop with a bend toward the romantic, mystical even. He heard there was a barista bar and a few baked goods. Well, he wasn't sure he believed this shop was that innocent after reading some of the book titles. He had a feeling Marcella Martin wasn't the grandmother type after all.

Maybe it was a high-end sex shop with equally expensive edible underwear and high-tech vibrators just behind the facade.

Moving to the other bay window, he noticed heart-shaped silver jewelry, heart-shaped boxes of high-end chocolates in elaborate red boxes, and other odd totems he wasn't sure he understood or wanted to understand, for that matter. It wasn't close to Valentine's Day. What was with the hearts? Then he saw the tiny sign in the corner, elegantly written, *"Love is Every Day."* Okay, she was one of those optimistic people. Too bad Charles wasn't here; he and Marcella would probably like each other.

He continued to scrutinize the display with a jaded eye. He jolted when he saw one object, which brought with it the bittersweet memory that took him back nearly two years to his time in Saint Barts. He'd only seen the box once, but he knew what it was. Knowing what was inside that simple brown wrapping brought back sweet memories of one of the best nights of his life, if not *the* best night of his life.

The label on the box read: *Lover's Kit.* Indeed. How many places carried this? Well, probably every high-end sex shop in the western world. He remembered glancing at the ingredients label during the night with Ella and reading that it was manufactured in Canada. It appeared the Canadians knew how to have fun.

He thought of Ella again and felt that familiar pain. Why hadn't he asked her where she lived? Why hadn't he gotten her last name? He should have gone back to her hotel that day. He should have talked to her in person. His mother be damned. Charles be damned. He had blown it on such a large scale. There wasn't a day that went by that he didn't think of Ella. Where was she?

Chapter Four

Ella checked on baby Xander, where he lay napping in the back room of her shop, which had been set up as a safe nursery area for her precious child. She had a video baby monitor, but she just didn't trust it one hundred percent. She also never wanted to let him be completely alone. She was very protective. He was a sweet-natured baby, whom she still didn't know what she'd done to deserve. But one thing was for sure: he was the best thing that she'd ever done. He was the spitting image of his father. And although they had only spent one night together, the memory of Jacques's face was as real to her as if she'd seen it for a thousand nights.

She no longer tortured herself with ideas of how to get in touch with Jacques to tell him about his son. He'd lost that chance when he ran out on her after their one unforgettable night. It was still difficult to understand why he'd chosen to leave after all they'd shared. It might not have started out as anything but a one-night stand, but it had evolved into something more, at least for her. Over time, she had no alternative but to accept that Jacques hadn't felt the same way. It was his loss, but it still hurt.

Someday, she would have to explain it all to Xander. She only hoped that when the time came, she would figure out how to tell him that his father hadn't wanted to be a part of her life and hadn't known Xander even existed. Maybe Xander would choose to do a DNA test and find his father that way. She heard stories like that all the time. Maybe Xander would do it and get lucky.

More than once the thought crossed Ella's mind to swab the inside of Xander's cheek and send it to Ancestry or one of the other record keeping sites, but that took the decision away from Xander and something told her not to do it.

Ella still remembered the thrill and the fear that came with the discovery of her pregnancy. She always knew that she would have children one day. She just hadn't expected it to come as a surprise, nor had she thought that she would be doing it as a single parent.

As she'd broken the news to her mother, there had been swift reproach and a series of lectures that were hard to hear. Thankfully, her other family—the shopkeepers, her neighbors, and friends, on either side of her shop—had rallied around her and welcomed Xander with open arms and provided her a shoulder to cry on when Ella was overwhelmed.

Walking around her eclectic shop, she tidied various displays. *Marcella's*, a wonderful escape, was in its seventh year of operation and, thankfully, profitable. Marginally, but still, profit was profit.

At *Marcella's*, you could lose yourself in an afternoon. She had almost named the shop *Saturday Afternoon* because, as a young woman, she had loved to window shop and explore. She had her favorite haunts. One was a small, local bookstore where she could get lost among all the wonderful titles. Then, there was a coffee shop that made something called Chocolate Mocha Muds. Her favorite beverage of all time, where she'd also indulge in a sugar cookie. Lastly, she loved the artisan jewelry store *Wire*, where she would buy funky jewelry that was afford-able to a teenager.

As she got older and lived on her own, she used to go to the local farmers' markets and buy fresh ingredients that she would make into a special Saturday night dinner that usually involved pasta and cheese, unless she had a date, then she might be looking for something special to add to her date routine, a new mascara or perfume. Maybe a new blouse or skirt. But that was before the baby. Now, she cruised baby shops and discount stores online. Aside from a couple of new work outfits in black or red each year, she didn't buy things for herself.

Her shop was meant to remind her of all those lost Saturday afternoons. Cricket had played right into Ella's emotions sharing that she liked to bake, so Ella had given her a chance. Ella opened a bakery space, making only one request: sugar cookies. It had been a good idea and had turned out to be very popular with Ella's clientele.

With any luck, the bakery part of Ella's business might expand when Cricket had more time to dedicate to it. If that was the direction Cricket wanted to go.

"You'd really do that for me?" Cricket had asked when Ella suggested the idea.

"We could put in another case over there," Ella said, pointing at a space, "You know, for cakes and whatever else you can come up with."

Cricket hugged Ella.

"You are my dream boss, you know that?"

Ella smiled. "Only because you are my dream employee. Now if we could only find a way to make a bunch of money!"

Ella liked to think of herself as the eternal optimist.

One wall of the eclectic space was filled with books on travel and distant locations, from Athens to Zanzibar. She sold out of her books on *Erotica in Rome* within a couple of weeks of each reorder. She was quickly becoming a favorite among the local romance novelists, as she loved carrying books from local authors. She had started monthly author signings on Saturday afternoons, and they were making Saturdays her biggest sales day.

Her shop, being in such close proximity to the hospital,

brought in a steady stream of customers who needed everything from a small stuffed animal to give to a loved one to hold for comfort or a book to read while waiting for news of their loved ones. Then, there were the nurses and doctors who had a bad day and needed an escape. *Marcella's* offered that oasis.

Her shop was upscale but perceived by the narrow-minded as a modern-day sex shop who latched onto the dozen or so "questionable" products she offered among the sweet detritus. They could think what they wanted, but Ella didn't sell whips and plastic penis windup toys. Nothing vulgar ever crossed her threshold because, despite all outward appearances, Ella was a bit old-fashioned. But she did sell heart-shaped boxes of chocolates all year round because love didn't just exist on Valentine's Day; love is every day.

She liked to think of herself as a pharmacist who filled prescriptions for love.

There was also an irony with being so close to the largest hospital in Portland. Many of her clients were medical staff, including doctors and nurses, who liked to wander around her shop during their occasional breaks. More often than not, they confided to her about a difficult day or a tragic case as if she were their best friend or therapist. She'd recommend they sit at one of the café tables that were arranged eclectically around the space, have a cup of tea or espresso, a cookie, and look through a book on beaches in Africa or Houses by Frank Lloyd Wright. The distraction, even for a few minutes, helped.

That was the thing about *Marcella's*: there was always a pot of tea waiting to be shared or a sweet sugar cookie to enjoy. She was partial to flowers and puppy-shaped cookies, although Cricket's giraffes were very popular with children. The giraffes had once been her infamous cockies, but they sent the wrong message, so Cricket had transformed them into giraffes. Most importantly, they all had a thick layer of buttercream frosting.

More than one medical professional had thanked her for a

suggestion of a *Lover's Kit*. Maybe they'd had a bad day and didn't want to take that energy home to a partner. *A Lover's Kit* could change someone's mood like nothing she'd ever seen.

If there was one thing Ella wanted to achieve with her shop it was the idea that love manifested itself in many ways. Still single and pining for the father of her child who she'd known for fewer than 24 hours, she didn't have to wonder why she found love in the photo of a book or a customer's smile. She was the epitome of the hopeless romantic. Somedays she could barely stand herself or her optimism, but she was glad she had it.

On this particular day in late October, there was a new chill in the air that bothered her more than it should. It wasn't just that the hospital wanted to take her shop away to build another ostentatious wing to their healing monstrosity. It was that they hadn't asked her nicely. She didn't intend to go quietly, nor did she intend to allow them to claim eminent domain. If they wanted to take her livelihood and home away from her, it was going to cost them. Considering all the money The Brewster Family had raised for their steel and glass egomaniac-eyesore, which had a slight bend toward the phallic, she thought they could be more than a little generous with her and her two neighbors.

This was politically charged Portland, with two prominent law schools in close proximity. You couldn't swing a Columbia River salmon without hitting a hungry lawyer. Cliff Potter was just the lawyer for this job, or so he'd told Ella the day he'd volunteered to take their case. Ella was pretty sure they were going to lose because, on some level, Cliff was an idiot, and they didn't have a leg to stand on. This knowledge did not deter Ella, far from it. She knew if she wanted this job done right, she was going to have to step in at some point and do it herself. As for Cliff, it was his job to keep her from getting arrested or sued. In just a week, she was going to take her message to the streets.

It wouldn't be easy. The edgy products Ella sold made her store an easy target. For as many people who loved her shop, there were those few flies in the ointment who only wanted to see her fail. Failure wasn't an option for a single mother. Ella wasn't sure what she would do if *Marcella's* had to close. Having a sunny yet determined personality, she was fixated on the idea that good things came to those who worked hard and were kind to others. She pitied the overconfident fool who underestimated her.

However, if the hospital expansion went forward, she wouldn't just be losing her shop. She would be losing her home. She and Xander lived in a tiny two-bedroom apartment over the shop. It wasn't huge, but it was nice and safe. Besides, the rent was affordable. And she liked her neighbors, as the two other shops that shared her block were her neighbors by day and night.

The thought of relocating her shop kept her up at night to the point she had dark circles under her eyes. If she had to relocate and redesign her shop, it would decimate her meager savings, not to mention the medical bills that hadn't been covered by her crappy insurance when she had given birth to Xander. Most importantly, she had to think of Xander's well-being and security, plan for his future, and give him all the love and support she could. She might be raising him alone, but he didn't need to suffer from her mistakes. It was time to think of a way out of this mess.

Chapter Five

After Jack had thoroughly examined everything displayed in the bay windows, he begrudgingly entered *Marcella's,* which assaulted his eyes as well as his senses. The place was part Harry Potter's workshop, part Guinevere's castle, and reminiscent of an adult shop down by the train station known as Madam X's. However, there weren't any dildos or inflatable sex dolls in sight, which was a small consolation.

The quantity of stuff reminded him of all the tourist shops he'd seen in the Caribbean. He had to admit, this place appeared to be much more upscale, almost European. On closer examination, each item in the shop was of pretty high quality to his critical eye. The price tags weren't for the faint of heart. It was as if someone's great aunt had opened her steamer trunk and decided to display her treasures from her world travels, controversial or not. The place was literally packed with artistically displayed items. It was colorful yet pleasant. He was almost dizzy with the assault to his senses.

Customers milled around like star-struck zombies throughout the store, looking at all the wares offered.

A flash of red caught Jack's eye. There was something about the woman across the room with her back to him. She wore a long red dress. Her blonde hair cascaded down her back, straight and lush, held neatly in a tortoiseshell barrette. It reminded him of another woman he'd known who looked good in red. She spoke quietly to the customer in front of a display of books. He got a look at her profile and felt the air leaving his lungs. She picked up one of the titles and handed it to the customer, who looked as if she'd been given a treasure. They looked through the book together. Then, both women walked toward the register, and Jack was able to get a better look at Marcella Martin's face, but he already knew it.

"Holy shit," he muttered as an invisible wave of emotion threatened to knock him off his feet, his eyes straining wide in recognition. Almost tripping over an unseen object, Jack gained his composure quickly. No one had noticed his reaction—not yet.

Thankfully, Ella focused completely on the customer she was helping, allowing Jack to scrutinize her as his brain tried to make sense of what he was seeing. It had been almost two years since he'd gone to Saint Barts, since his brother almost died falling off a rocky cliff and into a deep crevasse on Mount Hood. Twenty months since he'd made love to the beautiful woman with the red bikini and the peaches-and-cream skin. The woman now helping a customer at the register.

A child's cry from somewhere close by had Jack nearly jumping out of his skin.

"I hope your nephew loves the book. Please let me know how he likes it. Thanks for stopping in today," Ella said before she hurriedly ran from the room toward the sound of the crying child.

The ringing in Jack's ears drowned out the sound of her high heels on the hardwoods and of the crying baby. The woman he'd been with in Saint Barts did not have children. The ringing grew louder as he thought of possibilities. He reasoned that just because she had a child didn't mean it was his. Hell, she could be married for all he knew. But, deep down, another truth was whispering in his ear.

A moment later, Ella emerged from the room carrying a small boy in her arms. Jack grabbed the nearest item he could find, opened it, and held it in front of his face. He carefully looked at Ella over the top of the pages as she comforted the child in her arms and walked in slow circles.

"Well, hello there, Xander. Look how big you've gotten," a woman who was seated at a café table said. "Ella, you are so lucky, he is a beautiful child."

"Oh, thank you," Ella said sincerely. "I think he's special, but I'm a bit biased. I love my Xander." She happily bounced him and then kissed him, which made him snuggle tightly against her.

"He's going to be a heartbreaker someday," the woman said with a knowing nod.

Ella smiled and comforted the child as she added a bit of sarcasm to her voice and said, "I can't wait."

Then, turning back to the little boy, she said, "Xander, it's all right. You were just having a bad dream."

So much for coincidence or the idea that she was married to the father of the child in her arms. Jack knew better. He would've recognized that face anywhere. Xander was Jack's mirror image at the same age. Xander had to be his son.

His mind flashed with a dozen images: the red bikini, the lovely blonde woman sitting on a barstool with the ocean just beyond her, the curve of her smile, her aquamarine eyes, her soft laugh, the curve of her breast just under the thin cloth of her black halter dress, her red silk lingerie, the warmth of her body as he slid inside her and claimed her as his own.

Oh, hell…

And in that Mojito-infused memory, there was just one thing he couldn't remember. Had he worn a condom every time they made love? If he were a betting man, he would've bet against himself on that third time, just before dawn, when they were both still half asleep.

With the images and this new information flooding his senses, Jack did the only sensible thing he could do at the moment. He set down the book, turned on his heel, and left *Marcella's*.

As he hurried down the sidewalk, telling himself not to run, breathing didn't come easily due to the tightening in his chest. Pausing, he looked over his shoulder back at *Marcella's*. Ella stood in front of her shop, holding her baby and looking back at him. At the sight of her, he stumbled, caught himself, and then picked up the pace.

By the time he was halfway back to his office, he was hyperventilating. Once inside the sleek Brewster International Brewing building, he grabbed a paper shopping bag out of a garbage can, emptied the contents, and held the empty bag to his face. For the next five minutes, he sat on a step in one of the fire escape stairwells and willed his lungs to relax as he breathed into a paper bag. *He had found Ella. He had a son.*

Ella stepped out onto the sidewalk with Xander in her arms and looked in both directions to see which way the man had gone. She didn't like it when customers left before she could greet them. It was bad business, and a shop full of customers was no excuse. There was something about him…something that tapped into a feeling she hadn't had in almost two years.

As she glanced down Lovejoy Street, she caught sight of him. His stride indicated he was in a hurry to get somewhere fast. Ella was about to go back inside when the man paused and looked over his shoulder back at her. Jerking in surprise, he lost stride. It was at that moment that Ella recognized her son's father. His black hair was short and professional. He was wearing a dark gray business suit under a black wool coat, but the man was Jacques. If she hadn't had Xander in her arms, she would've chased after him.

"Jacques?" she managed, but there was no way he could hear her. She'd have to scream.

He not only looked familiar to her because he was Jacques. She'd seen him looking like this before. Where? When? Who was he?

By the time she thought to yell, he'd turned a corner and disappeared. Reluctantly, Ella returned to her shop, bouncing a smiling Xander as she went and wondering if her mind was playing tricks on her.

Her emotions around Jacques had never been logical, made worse when she discovered she was pregnant. She'd made attempts to find him, embarrassing as it had been. She'd called most of the hotels in Saint Barts and made up an incredible story about a man named Jacques, whom she'd wanted to thank. The hotel bar where they'd met, and he'd paid for their evening with a credit card, was reluctant to give out any personal information about their guests. In the end, after a terse back and forth, they'd given her nothing. Every rum distillery in the Caribbean had refused to discuss any information about their employees, especially a Frenchman named Jacques. One of the distilleries had threatened her with legal action if she didn't stop harassing them.

Explaining to her friends and further about the absence of the father had come at a high personal cost to Ella. Her widowed mother basically disowned her after she'd explained the circumstances of her pregnancy, the result of an encounter with a stranger.

When Xander was born there was a slow defrost for his benefit. Ever the doting new grandmother, Beverly Martin, had eventually taken to Xander, but her relationship with her daughter had yet to find its warmth.

"Maybe you should just give him up for adoption," her mother had suggested while Ella held Xander in the hospital.

"You can't be serious," Ella had replied, looking at Xander's perfect face.

"You are single and barely making it. Now, you have a baby. It is a mess if I've ever seen one. I don't know what you can do to get yourself out of this. Really, Ella. How disappointing."

Thank goodness for the generosity of her other family, her neighbors. Not only had they rallied around her, but they had also helped her prepare for Xander's arrival by setting up her crib and nursery. Cindy almost single handedly provided baby clothes that were from her shop. They all visited often with food and offered regular babysitting so she could take a moment for a much-needed nap or moment for herself.

The day she saw the man who resembled Jacques, Ella closed *Marcella's* at six-thirty and took Xander upstairs to their apartment. She fed him and gave him a bath, then put him down for the night. He was a good baby, and, more likely than not, would sleep through the night. For an eleven-month-old, he'd had a big day, spending more time standing and making motions that indicated he wanted to start walking; the sooner, the better.

She didn't know what she'd do when he was more mobile. Up until now, she took him to a daycare just a few blocks away, Tuesday through Friday. On Saturdays and Sundays, she worked a half day, Xander with her, usually playing in his huge playpen behind the counter where she could keep an eye on him.

Once Xander started walking, he'd be able to pull things off shelves in the shop, which was not child friendly. She hadn't figured out what she would do on the weekends short of hiring a babysitter.

Her assistant, Cricket, who had become a good friend, was a great help with Xander, but then she was only there twenty hours a week, with several of those hours dedicated to baking. Thankfully, Cricket had decided to get her doctorate in psychology. Ella knew she'd have to pay more if she was going to keep Cricket, but with funds tight, she might have to start opening on Mondays and consider adding another part-time person. Summers were great because they were her busy season, and Cricket worked more hours each week.

Ella thought of everything she was facing and tried not to fixate on the fear. It was overwhelming, her mind going from one dire scenario to another. Something had to change before she fell into the abyss. If she found a new location for *Marcella's* and found a new place to live, then she'd just have to figure out childcare and Cricket's schedule. Piece of cake!

As she cleaned up the dinner dishes, her thoughts lingered on the man she'd seen earlier. It was ridiculous to think he could be Jacques. Jacques was probably still in the Caribbean seducing more women just like her! Yet every time she thought of how the man had looked back over his shoulder at her, she thought she'd seen recognition in his face. She remembered the time they'd spent together and how it felt when he disappeared. She still felt the pain of his disappearance anew and had to wipe away an errant tear.

Never in her life had she had such a connection with a man.

Never in her life had the man just disappeared.

It might have been twenty months, but it still hurt.

There was only so much pain and suffering one person was worth.

Chapter Six

J ack sat behind his desk and looked at samples of rum labels the designers had presented to him earlier. It had been hard to maintain his cool during the presentation, and that was before he stopped by *Marcella's.*

Really? How hard could the label design be? *Redrum*, a twisty play on the horror film *The Shining*, was supposed to look scary. But there was also a version he was favoring that had a silhouette of his dog, Moonshine, who was a sensitive and smart Hungarian Vizsla. Going off of the dog and calling it *Red's Rum* would avoid any copyright infringement and was the direction his lawyers advised.

A cartoonish pirate holding a rose in a hook, bleeding red petal drops, was supposed to be the epitome of *Redrum*. He shook his head. How could the designers have misunderstood the idea of elegance? Red bottle, scary label with the slogan: *It is always better to be lucky than good.* He would have even conceded to one small rose to be symbolic of Portland, the City of Roses, if the rose had been done right, stylized, sexy…

He was considering that the label needed to have Moonshine holding a red rose in his teeth with the label: *Red's Rum.*

He had a headache. It appeared that even the simplest of decisions were beyond him this afternoon.

This should be one of his proudest moments. Two years of work coming to fruition…

Ella. His mind replayed every moment of his time at her shop earlier in the day.

She lived in Portland and had a son who looked exactly like him. He didn't believe in coincidences.

Pushing aside the labels, he picked up his phone and called his personal lawyer and best friend, someone who was good at getting the kind of information not readily available to the general public.

Flint Dixson picked up on the first ring. "Hey man, when can I come by for my free sample?"

Jack smiled tightly and then winced.

They'd met in college, where Jack had always been popular for his proximity to beer swag from the family business.

"I'm looking at labels for my first bottling. And they are going back to the drawing board. Everything looks comical, not elegant. The whole *Shining Redrum* thing is missing. I've decided I don't want to be sued for that anyway."

"That's why you have all those corporate lawyers. You'll figure it out, and it better be in time for the launch party."

Jack glanced at the calendar and said, "Seven weeks from today."

"My calendar is clear...is it my imagination, or is something wrong?"

"Yes, very wrong, I think. What gave me away?" Jack asked.

"You sound strange, like your dog died."

"Moonshine is alive and well. Don't jinx him," Jack said, thinking of his beloved year-old Vizsla puppy. "I need you to do some quiet digging for me. It's regarding the new hospital wing my family is dedicating. Find out about the shop owners that we might be putting out of business. I'm most concerned with the owner of *Marcella's.*"

"I'm most concerned about the *Curry Leaf.* I can't believe you are taking away my favorite place in the neighborhood for Indian food."

"I can't believe you'd go back there after what happened to me," Jack complained.

"Hey, I can't help it if you can't handle a little heat."

Jack shook his head. "Just look into the shops, especially *Marcella's*."

"Interesting, I've heard about her. There is a blog about the new hospital wing, and she has been very vocal about her disdain for everyone Brewster."

"Great. That is just great."

"Will I need to take out a restraining order to protect you after you take away some hot chick's livelihood?"

Jack thought about this for a long moment, thinking about the woman he'd seen earlier in the day. "I hope not. Why are you calling her hot? How do you know her?"

"Because she's hot. I've seen her in her shop. Sexy hot," Flint said. "Maybe I should do some in-person recon. I'd like to help her through this difficult time."

Jack didn't like the idea of his best friend lusting after Ella.

"Mine," Jack said, and his tone had the other man chuckling.

"Okay, okay, jeez, calm down. I'm on it, but I don't think even you are handsome enough to get a date with her after you take away her business. Give me a couple of days to check her out."

Jack hesitated and then said, "There is something else."

"Of course there is. What?"

"Flint, for my own peace of mind, tell me: Who pays your retainer?"

"What the hell, Jack? You do. I'm your personal attorney."

"That means that we have secrecy between us. Anything I tell you stays with you, correct? My family would never be privy to our communication, correct?"

"Yes, of course. Mama Brewster could and would torture me, but I can't tell her a thing. Okay, you're scaring me. Invoking thoughts of your mother makes my scrotum retract into my groin. It's a self-preservation thing."

"Good, then you understand that this is something big and needs to be kept private. There is something else, but I need you to be discreet about this."

"What the hell...okay.... What is it?"

"Ella...Marcella Martin has a baby. I guess he looks like he is around a year old. I actually think he's about eleven months old. The thing is, I think I met her when I was in Saint Barts about, oh, twenty months ago."

"Wait a minute, doing the math, bro. Holy shit. Dog, did you and the pretty Marcella Martin do the horizontal Mambo? Are you the father?"

Ignoring Flint, he said, "I don't know if it is her. Just a feeling. That is when Charles fell off the mountain. I left her, but I should have stayed. Biggest mistake of my life."

"Kid a boy or girl?"

"Boy. I heard her call him 'Xander.' And, well, he looks like me."

Flint demanded the pertinent facts about Jack's time in Saint Barts and then warned him: "Stay the hell away from Marcella Martin! Jeez, talk about a honey trap. You should talk to a friend of mine. He can tell you about visitation, custody, etc. I'll call him and set it up."

"I think it is too soon. I don't know what I'm going to do. This just happened a couple of hours ago."

"If what you told me is true, it is never too soon to start cleaning up this mess, and make no mistake; this is a mess, my friend..."

After Jack ended the call, he put his head in his hands and wondered why she hadn't contacted him. Had lying about the French accent really been that big of a deal? She hadn't mentioned she was from Portland. In truth, he hadn't asked because there had been other things on his mind, like seducing her.

His office door opened, intruding on his thoughts. No knock, no surprise. It was like she wanted to catch him doing something bad, like when he'd been fourteen and stolen his brother's *Playboy*.

His mother, Dolores Brewster, marched into his office, her hands on her hips. She was resplendent in a black Chanel suit, which contrasted nicely with her snow-white coiffed hair. A striking beauty in her early sixties, she'd obviously just returned from an important meeting, something no doubt he should have been at, that she didn't tell him about so she could yell at him… Like now. Long ago, he'd come to realize she liked yelling.

Jack wondered where his father was currently hiding, as they usually came as a matched set attached at the hip.

"Hello, Mother," he said without looking up. "Thanks for knocking."

"Do you know what I received in the mail this afternoon after I returned from the board meeting at the hospital?" she asked.

"Publishers Clearinghouse notification? Did you win a million dollars?" he asked, tongue in cheek, which he knew would annoy her.

"No," she said, waving her hand in front of him as if he were an annoying gnat. "Those people are threatening us with litigation. They want more money for their little shacks."

"Those people? What people?" he asked, but he knew.

"Those horrible shop people. The ones the board wanted you to speak with. Did you do that? If you did, you obviously didn't do a good job."

"I've been busy," Jack said as he held up one of the sheets containing label samples. "You know, getting ready for the launch of my distilled rum? You know, the project I've been working on for over two years? I scoped out the shops today. I'll go back soon."

"I know you're busy, but do I have to negotiate with these money-hungry shopkeepers myself?"

Jack thought of his mother running into the woman who may or may not be the mother of his child. "Look," he said. "I'll take care of it. You don't need to bother yourself with it. Besides, it will give me an excuse to meet potential constituents. You know, in case you ever convince me to run for mayor?"

"Our wish for you to consider a career in politics is not a joke, Jackson. Our family has a responsibility for this community, and it would be nice if you started to take that responsibility seriously. Having money isn't where responsibility ends."

"Wrong son, Mother. Remember? Charles is your politician."

"I wish your brother were here. He was always so good at talking to people. They just seem to gravitate toward him. He has a natural charm and charisma."

Jack felt the jab. "We both wish Charles were here. Because if Charles were here, I could focus on my real job, running my arm of the family business and integrating new products like *Red's Rum*. But since he decided to save people in every other place in the world but here, I guess you're slumming. I'm all you've got."

"That's not what I meant, and you know it. You were always my sensitive child. It's just that Charles was destined for great things. Your father and I were so proud to think that he might run for mayor," she said, her hand automatically going to her pearls to make sure they were still there. "It was tragic what happened to him and his friends on top of that mountain, but it didn't mean he needed to change his life so drastically. If he wanted to help the poor, we could have found poor people in Portland for him to help. There are many fabulous worthy charities right here in his own hometown."

"Well, that's not what he decided to do. He went global."

"You know Jackson, you really would make an excellent mayor with a bit more training and polish. I just wish you were married. I think it is time for you to settle down. You should add that task to your focus."

"Mother?"

"Yes, dear?"

"Get the hell out of my office."

Nonplussed, she turned her back and started to leave but stopped short of the door just like she had no doubt planned. "One last thing. I was seated next to Lindsey Pritchard's mother, Evelyn, at lunch yesterday at the country club. She said you never called Lindsey for a second date. I told her you'd been busy. Lindsey is expecting a call."

Jack groaned internally. Lindsey Pritchard was awful. A perfect little snob with an inflated opinion of herself and about the most boring dinner companion he'd ever shared a meal with. He'd lied about being tired after a busy day and dropped her back home within fifteen minutes after their check had arrived. He hadn't kissed her goodnight, nor had he mentioned ever seeing her again.

"If she's waiting for another date, she'll be waiting a long time. I'm not calling her."

"Really, Jackson, she is the perfect girl for you. She's pretty, smart, and educated, and she has made quite a name for herself as a fashion buyer at Nordstrom. Standing next to you at a podium, she'd look wonderful. You'd make pretty children. What else do you need? Stop being so stubborn."

"If she is the perfect girl for me, I'll never get married. Stop with the matchmaking," he said in a harsher tone than he'd meant, but he needed to accentuate the point. In light of the current Ella and Xander situation, the last thing he needed was his mother chumming him out as fresh bait for sharks like Lindsey Pritchard. There was a good chance he already had a good-looking child with an unwed mother, who he'd never gotten off his mind.

Dolores made a face that brought no reaction from her son.

"This isn't a battle you're going to win," he said. "So, I'd suggest you do something nice for Lindsey Pritchard and set her up with some other son of one of your many crony friends."

"Jackson!" she exclaimed, her voice sounding shrill. Thankfully for Jack, that tone had stopped working between high school and college. Moonshine, who'd been quietly slumbering in his dog bed, raised his elegant head and let out a concerned woof.

"I see you brought in the dog."

"He was invited. You weren't."

"I'm so offended—"

No longer in the mood for polite conversation, Jack stood, walked past his mother, and opened his office door. "Mother, please."

"You are more like your father than I give you credit for."

"I'm sure he is hiding in his office, so why don't you harass him for a while? He seems to like it."

Dolores stalked past her son with one parting remark. "I hope you will be in a more cordial mood on Sunday. Please leave that dog at home." Sunday was their once-a-week mandatorydinner.

Jack bit back a snide reply about Moonshine and kissed his mother on the cheek. "Looking forward to it."

Chapter Seven

J ack walked from his office on NW Everett and 10th Avenue to *Marcella's* on 21st Avenue and NW Lovejoy. It was almost two miles, but he enjoyed the feel of the crisp fall morning. To be honest, he needed the walk to calm himself down. He hadn't slept at all. And he didn't know what he would face the moment he darkened her door. More to the point, he had no idea what he would say.

After he'd been home from Saint Barts for about two days and his brother's condition stabilized, it dawned on Jack that Ella hadn't called. When he racked his brain and figured out that he had no way to get in contact with her, he called her hotel and asked for her but was told there wasn't a guest by her first name. No amount of bribery could get him her contact information. Shamefully, he'd tried with ever-increasing sums of money until they had sternly told him to go away.

Walking along the sidewalk littered with leaves crunching under his feet, Jack couldn't admire all the beautiful fall shades of red, orange, and yellow. He didn't smell the woodsy, crisp scent of fall in the air. Instead, his terror increased with each step he made. As he rounded the final corner that would put him on NW Lovejoy Street, he had the briefest hesitation. He'd always thought he'd have children, but the thought of committing to one woman and being a family man had never been high on his list of priorities. What had he gotten himself into?

It was just after ten in the morning, and *Marcella's* had only been open for a few minutes. This time, he didn't linger outside looking at display windows; he stepped through the door intent on facing this problem head on. He couldn't remember a time when he'd been more terrified.

As soon as the woman inside heard the bell, she stopped arranging the display at her fingertips and looked up. There was instant recognition in Ella's twinkling aquamarine eyes.

Ella was strikingly beautiful, her blond hair and perfect red lipstick accentuating a glamorous face reminiscent of a silver-screen Hollywood actress on the level of Veronica Lake or Carole Lombard. From the neck down, it was all about elegant lust. Dressed in a black wrap dress and knee-high, stiletto-heeled black patent boots, she was more of an edgy rock star than the sweet lover he'd seduced. His heart felt the same rush. At that moment, he didn't have the words to say how he felt. Sensual need clouded his analytical mind just as it had that day she'd worn the red bikini on Saint Barts. He wanted her; he'd never stopped wanting her.

"You were here yesterday, and then you ran away," she said as she took a couple of steps toward him, her tone somewhat threatening yet chiding at the same time. Challenge accepted. This wasn't going to be easy.

"I didn't run away. I just couldn't believe it was you. I was shocked and didn't handle it well. As soon as I had a moment to catch my breath, I came back," he said. She took a step back, and he immediately knew why. He didn't have a French accent anymore, and she didn't know what he wanted or why he had suddenly appeared.

"Why are you here? Visiting from France? Oh wait, did you lose your accent?" she asked, confirming his assessment, her face contorting unpleasantly as if she were looking at an archenemy.

"I live in Portland," he said, taking a step closer to her.

"But of course you do. You don't have a French accent.

You're an American, probably always were," she said, shaking her head. "Wow, I really was an idiot in Saint Barts. That must have seemed very funny to you. Especially after all those alcohol-saturated Mojitos, or whatever they were. You must still be laughing at my stupidity. It must have been a big joke when you got home."

"I should have told you. I was going to tell you when we met up at the hotel that afternoon," he said, taking a step toward her. The discussion wasn't going as he'd planned. "I figured when you got my note as to why I had to leave so suddenly and saw my business card, you'd understand my reasons and not judge me too harshly. Frankly, I was surprised I didn't hear from you. I wanted to see you again. Hell, I mentioned it at least five times in the note. I wouldn't have left the note if I wanted to get away from you."

"What are you talking about? You left. I didn't get a note, a card, or anything. I thought something had happened to you. I was worried. Like an idiot, I called the hospital and the police. Then, I realized I'd been dumped. It was all quite humiliating, *Jacques*. I'm sure everyone I talked to had a big laugh at my expense."

Jack felt the color drain from his face. The note had never made it to her. She must hate him. He'd have hated her if the scenario was reversed.

"No, no, I didn't dump you. My brother was in a terrible accident on Mount Hood. I found out as soon as I got back to my hotel that morning. I'd left my cell phone in the room the night before. My family, well, my mother, had been calling it almost every hour on the hour. I had twelve messages from her at the front desk. I had to fly home immediately. I left a note with money for the concierge at my hotel to deliver it to you. I gave him several hundred Euros."

"Sure," she said, giving him a look that showed she didn't believe him in the least.

"You really didn't get it?" He felt sick.

"Hmm...yeah, I think I would have remembered that," she said sarcastically.

"I'm so sorry, really, Ella. I don't know what to say," he said, feeling like he'd had a gut punch. He'd hurt her so badly, but he hadn't meant to. Far from it.

"So you have a brother? Is he okay?" she asked.

He wiped his face, feeling dizzy. She hated him. He couldn't blame her.

"Yes, he's recovered. It just took a while and his personality kind of changed, but he is okay. His two friends died, which was incredibly tragic. Five other people died that day on Mount Hood. You can look up the news story. It was the day we woke up together in your room."

"I'm sorry for the tragedy. That is awful."

"Look, could we maybe sit down and talk somewhere?" His knees were about to buckle.

"About what?" she asked incredulously.

"Everything. I really wanted to see you again. I've thought about you every day...My name is Jack. Really. That is the truth."

"Your actions don't indicate that I should believe anything you tell me. If the tables were turned, I would not have just left you a note. I would have gone to your hotel and explained. You acted like a complete jerk. You hurt me. You left me after all that we shared, *Jack*. How could you?"

"I made a mistake. The biggest mistake of my life. I'm sorry, Ella. Please. I'd like to make it up to you, at least talk it out," Jack said, his thoughts going to the little boy and his need for answers.

Ella folded her arms and shook her head as if the very idea was too horrible for words.

"I saw you with your son," Jack said and then asked the question which had haunted him through a sleepless night. "Is he mine?"

She opened her mouth to answer, and the bell over the door chimed as a customer stepped inside the shop.

Ella motioned for Jack to step closer, and then she whispered, "I can't talk about this right now. I'm working."

"We need to talk. I need to see you. I need to know," he said, leaning toward her, so close he could smell her perfume, sweet freesia—much like the ginger and plumeria in Saint Barts.

Then he whispered, "Please."

She'd been here the whole time. Ella. His Ella. He'd be damned if he'd let her go again.

* * *

Ella saw the hurt and anger in his eyes, the eyes that had haunted her dreams for twenty months. She'd thought of him each day, especially at night, as she lay in bed and tried to fall asleep. The day she'd found out she was carrying his child, and even when she'd given birth, she'd pictured him. She'd speculated countless times as to where he was and if he had a wife or family of his own. She'd wondered if he'd ever thought of her.

Keeping her voice low, she said, "Fine, whatever, I suppose we probably should…talk. Now is not a good time."

"When? Today? Later today?" he asked desperately, not waiting for her to answer, his polished veneer cracking ever so slightly. "I'll meet you anywhere, anytime…please…"

"It's hard with my son. He's at daycare right now, and I must pick him up by six-thirty after I close here. Then I have to get him fed, bathed, and ready for bed. I'm not available until eight-thirty or nine. By then, I'm tired and have things to do like laundry and cleaning up after a baby."

"I'll make it work. Just tell me when and where. I'll move anything in my schedule to talk to you."

"Maybe I could get a friend to watch him one night this week. I could give you a call."

Jack shook his head. "No, I can't spend another night like last night. I have to talk to you. What time tonight? I need to talk to you sometime today. I haven't slept all night. I can think of nothing else but you since I saw you. Since I saw him."

Something about the way he said it let Ella know that there would be no escaping this man. It would not only be futile to put him off, but also it would be torture for her as well. But if she had a few days she could think about what she wanted to tell him.

"Well, that is too bad because tonight won't work. I'm sorry. I could possibly make tomorrow night work. I'll close at six, six-fifteen if there are customers. But, like I told you, I'm not available to talk until eight-thirty, maybe nine, and by then, I'm tired." She wanted to punish him. She wanted to make him suffer a little.

He pulled his cell phone from his pocket, his voice unsteady, as he said, "Where do you live?"

Looking up at him, her lip trembled, and she bit down hard on it. Her own nerves were getting in the way, and her entire body shook as if she were cold. Taking a minute to find her voice, she pointed toward the ceiling as she said, "I live above the shop in an apartment. The steps are off the alley just off Marshall. I have the middle apartment, 203."

Clumsily, Jack reached into his pocket and pulled out a business card. She noticed that his hand was shaking as he extended the card to her. Ella glanced down at it, reading his name as the air left her lungs.

"What the hell? Is this some sort of joke?"

"No, I came by to talk to all the shop owners. That is why I was in your shop yesterday. I'm so sorry. I had no idea."

"You're Jack Brewster. Oh, shit. I cannot believe I didn't

recognize you. Without the long hair and tan, you look so different." Arch enemy, evictor, dream killer…liar…baby daddy.

"And you're Marcella Martin."

She nodded, too stunned to speak. Thankfully, she didn't have to. Another customer entered her shop and made a beeline for where they stood.

"Ella, oh, thank goodness you're here! I need your help. I need to get some books for my daughter, the sixteen-year-old. She broke up with her boyfriend and is quite beside herself… She isn't eating. She isn't sleeping. I don't know what to do."

Ella spoke softly to the other woman, who stepped to the side. Then she faced Jack again.

"I'll see you tonight, at nine?" he asked, ignoring the woman who could probably hear their conversation.

"Tomorrow night," Ella corrected him. "If you come tonight, I will not be home."

"But you will be home tomorrow night?" he asked, the desperation clear in his voice.

"Do I have a choice?" she whispered, her heart hammering in her chest as her anger bubbled to the surface.

"No," he said, shaking his head, then he whispered, "If I have to sit on your doorstep all night, I will."

She wanted to hit him, knock him down, and hurt him as much as he'd hurt her. Despite her dark thoughts, she was in her place of business and needed to project a sense of civility.

"That won't be necessary. Tomorrow night. I'll make it work. Don't ring the bell. It will wake the baby. Just a soft knock, okay?"

"Xander," he said as Ella assured her client that she would be with her in a moment.

Turning her attention back to Jack, she clarified, "Yes, his name is Xander. I need to know. Were you living in Portland two years ago?"

"Yes, I grew up here and never left," he said and asked, "You?"

"My entire life," she said, closing the distance between them and adding in a whisper, "Let's get something straight."

"Okay," he said, his green eyes narrowing.

"I don't like the way you just disappeared. I'm sorry for the tragedy, for your brother, for his friends, but you should have come to tell me in person," she whispered, her voice low and menacing. "And nothing you can say, no excuse, is ever going to change that."

"I never wanted it to be like that. If I could go back, I'd never have let you go. I'm just asking for a chance to talk."

"Aren't I lucky?" she said, narrowing her eyes.

Chapter Eight

Waiting for that elusive 9 pm visit to Ella the next day was hell. Jack got nothing done and had a second night of no sleep. He stared at the ceiling above his desk in his plush office for hours as his world imploded. His dog repeatedly put his head or paw on Jack's knee, knowing he should add comfort to his master but not knowing how.

Moonshine whined and then nuzzled Jack's hand.

"It's okay, boy," Jack said as he absently petted the coppery velvet fur of his best friend, finally pulling Moonshine into his lap for a much needed snuggle.

His brother Charles the IV's empty office was next door. His father, Charles the III, had the corner office where he had a fondness for naps and cigars when he wasn't at his wife's side.

Of all the offices, Jack's was the smallest. Today, it felt incredibly claustrophobic, the walls tightening with each hour.

Ella, the woman he couldn't get out of his mind, had been here the whole time. The. Whole. Fucking. Time.

Jack visited the distillery building with Moonshine in tow, who sported a red collar and matching leash. He checked on his new rum production, which didn't soothe his frayed nerves in the least. All day, a cloud of impending doom hung darkly over him. Ella hated him. He reasoned that a person wouldn't have such feelings for someone who'd simply disappeared unless there had been consequences. He'd have bet his entire trust fund on the consequences equating to a little boy named Xander.

For almost two years, a woman living less than two miles from his office had carried his child and given birth without Jack knowing a thing. His son went to daycare somewhere close by. Ella probably shopped at the same market he did. She probably went to the same dry cleaner and ate at the same restaurants— well, except he'd never darkened the door of the Indian restaurant, the *Curry Leaf,* again.

Heck, the day before yesterday, he had never set foot in *Marcella's.* Sure, he'd seen it and even wondered what kind of shop it was. But it wasn't his kind of place. It wasn't the kind of place he would go seeking out. And it sure as hell wasn't the kind of place where a Brewster should be raised. He wasn't the kind of man who would take a child from his mother. But when he thought of Ella's visible hostility toward him, he thought again about Flint's family attorney. He'd talked to the man, but he didn't want this to get ugly. He would be a part of his son's life if Xander was his son. Who was he kidding? He knew it in his heart: Xander was his child.

By eight that evening, he'd gone to his house on Vista Avenue in the Portland Heights neighborhood to shower and change into more casual attire. He made sure Moonshine was settled in and fed. He killed time back at his office. The last hour was the worst. If Ella were any other woman whom he was meeting at nine o'clock at night, he'd have taken flowers or at least a bottle of wine. Waiting for nine o'clock to arrive felt like waiting for a dentist's appointment to get a particularly painful procedure. Heck, he might have preferred the dental appointment.

* * *

Ella never thought of her career as very stressful. She made people happy. It was what she liked to do. She loved her job, but today, there wasn't any happiness to give. A man she longed to see every day for the last year and a half had reentered her life the day before. And instead of profusely apologizing for standing her up and leaving her after one of the most sensual nights of her life, he'd had the audacity to act surprised and slightly shocked!

Okay, so he apologized. It didn't mean anything. He wasn't the one who had carried a baby for almost ten months, fed and cared for the child. He was a clueless playboy. She'd be damned if he was going to get close to Xander. Not at this age, maybe ever, the jerk.

She should have met him last night, but she was angry and wanted to punish him. Unfortunately, she had only punished herself.

All that pent-up longing that she'd always thought would transform into happiness at the sight of him had morphed into anger in a matter of seconds. She had a lot to say to him, and none of it was good. So much for the warm embrace and platitudes of happily ever after. The only thing she felt now was the strong desire to punch him in his perfect jaw! But she couldn't do that either because of Xander. And at the thought of her sweet child who looked so much like his handsome father, she had to blink back tears...*again!*

And, to add insult to injury, she *knew* this man. She didn't know Jack personally—well intimately, yes—but she knew his family. How had she not noticed it before? There had been photos of the Brewsters in the news for years. Mainly, it had been Jack's parents and his older brother, Charles.

And damn it, she remembered returning from Saint Barts and hearing about the accident on Mount Hood. Heck, it was all anyone could talk about for weeks. There had been a question of whether Charles Brewster would make it. She'd been seeing her doctor at the hospital to confirm her pregnancy the same day Charles was released from the same hospital in the middle of a media frenzy. And Jack, he'd been so close on that day. If only she'd known. Would things have been different if they'd run into each other in the hall, maybe the elevator? So different.

Things would be different now. Her simple, happy life was about to slide off its axis. And to think, the day before Jack Brewster entered her store, she had problems? She had yet to understand the depth of the problems she was facing. The Brewster Family were a bunch of pretentious, political, self-serving Portland socialite snobs whose lineage dated back to the birth of the city. From all the articles she'd read and everything she'd heard, they still believed they were entitled to run Portland. She thought of the recent news about the family going into the rum business. It was no coincidence that Jack had made sure she always had a rum drink in Saint Barts. The jerk! No doubt his research was the reason he was in Saint Barts to begin with. He'd said he'd worked for a company that made rum, but he'd been vague. Heck, he'd spoken French.

As the day wore on, after a near sleepless night, Ella fought back tears for a variety of reasons. When it was finally closing time, Ella picked up a tired Xander from daycare and made her way up the stairs behind the shop to her apartment. Walking inside, she turned on the lights and then sat and played with Xander for a few minutes. She put on a Sesame Street movie for him to watch as she made his dinner. Tonight, he was getting one of his favorite things, smushed up macaroni and cheese. She felt like a horrible mother for the junk food she was about to give her child, but tonight, she needed his utmost cooperation. As an afterthought, she added green beans, his new favorite vegetable, which she smashed to oblivion, picturing Jack's face as she did it.

Like clockwork, Xander was ready for his bath thirty minutes after he'd started on his dinner. And in their house, bath time was playtime. Xander played with his favorite water toys: a foam shark, an otter with a pontoon tail, and a small blue and white boat that was regularly submerged by the shark and otter working in tandem.

By the time Xander was in his pajamas and had a bedtime story, his eyes were heavily lidded, and he was ready for sleep. Ella was exhausted and damp from the splashed bathwater. After Xander was down for the night, she had exactly fifteen minutes to make herself presentable for the man who'd given her Xander. The best she'd been able to manage was a quick change of clothes, a washed face, and fresh lipstick. Several minutes were spent tidying the apartment to reassure anyone who should enter that it was a suitable place to raise a child.

Looking older than she had in Saint Barts, she felt on the old side of twenty-nine as she glanced in the bathroom mirror. Her mother had told her more than once that she finally had to grow up when she had a baby, and stop "playing with your little store." Her mother hadn't thought she was an adult until she'd had a baby even though she thought Ella should give Xander away. Now, her mother's idea of helping her was to suggest anti-aging cream and internet dating. It was possibly best to accept that she would never make her mother happy.

How old was Jack? Older, obviously. Thirty-five? Forty? Either way, dressed as a corporate lawyer, he looked older too. No one would have mistaken the man in her store today for a carefree beach bum pirate he'd been the day she met him. Goodbye Colin Farrell, hello dignified Colin Firth. Was he dating? Did he have a girlfriend? Was he married?

She shouldn't have agreed to this. She should have closed the shop and made an appointment with a lawyer to understand her rights. Xander's birth certificate didn't list a father since she hadn't known "Jacques's" last name. What would Jack do? Demand a paternity test? Visitation? Did he have other children? What if he wanted to be a part of Xander's life? What if he didn't?

The soft knock stopped her mind from making one more stressful leap into the "what ifs." Show time.

Chapter Nine

Hesitantly knocking on the yellow paint chipped door of apartment 203, Jack tried to calm his breathing. His child, his son lived here. He was just behind the closed door.

"Jack," Ella said as she greeted him with a tight, unsure smile and stepped back so that he could enter.

She had changed from the black wrap dress, heavy eye makeup, jewelry, and black boots that she'd worn to work. Now, her face was almost devoid of makeup. She wore blue jeans and a red cashmere sweater to ward off the fall chill. She had pearls at her ears and wore no other jewelry. All he could think of was how beautiful she looked.

"Ella," he said and stepped inside the doorway to the small apartment. It smelled good and homey, like dinner had been something comforting. He was, for a moment, jealous of this time she'd spent without him. He wanted to be there and share this time with her. Why hadn't he suggested that he bring dinner? Because he was stupid.

His body's response was an unwanted distraction. He remembered how she'd looked in the red bikini. Was it somewhere in the apartment now? For months after their night together, he couldn't get that damn bikini out of his mind. He'd fantasized about slipping his hand under the edge of that tight red fabric to stroke a breast…Since she'd given birth, her nipples were probably larger now, rosier…

Shoving his hands in his pockets to keep from touching her, he stepped forward and entered the cozy space. The furniture was an eclectic mix that he would describe as sophisticated bohemian meets an old-world mansion. It was clean despite the fact that she had a young child. At the thought of Xander, lustful thoughts vanished with a solemn, silent reprimand.

"Where's Xander?"

"Asleep, so let's keep it down. Would you like to sit?"

Jack took the end of an oversized couch patterned in red and gold fabric in a heavy jacquard. It held a lot of coordinating silk pillows in deep jewel tones with tassels. Ella sat opposite in an oversized hunter-green velvet chair that complimented many of the pillows on the couch pulling the look together. Between them sat a leather ottoman, which featured three stuffed animals who seemed to be watching him.

"I'm sorry about the way I came into your shop yesterday morning," he said, "I hope I didn't disturb your business."

"It was a shock to see you," she said nervously. "Especially since I never thought I'd see you again. I pictured you differently. A bit more like the last time I saw you."

"I should explain. I was in Saint Barts after working with one of the small-batch local rum factories and researching rum production in the Caribbean. I was soaking up the culture and taking a last-minute vacation before heading home. I knew once I got to Portland, there would be no fun and games. My family, heck, *I* expected myself to hit the ground running. The French persona, in retrospect, was a bit dishonest."

"A bit," she said, her eyes glowing with unspoken anger.

"Okay, it was a lot dishonest. I didn't even realize it at the time. You see, I'd spoken more French in those six months than I had English. It seemed natural to continue doing so. Everyone called me Jacques," he said, knowing that he was talking too much and not talking about the important reason why he was there. He had a hard time not kicking himself, seriously thinking he should have brought flowers or wine.

"I feel like a real jerk," he said.

She nodded in agreement. "I can't disagree with that."

"I'm sorry. I'm really sorry."

His eyes slowly scanned the space, taking in the details. She'd done a lot with not much. The lath and plaster had seen better days, but she'd painted the ceiling and trim a soft cream color. The walls were a light sage green that accentuated the colors of the couch and chair very well. IKEA bookshelves held an interesting assortment of books, music, and movie DVDs, including a large selection of Disney movies for Xander, arranged in alphabetical order. It surprised him as he thought only he was that meticulous.

Ella had a view of the West Hills. If he took the time to look, he bet he could see part of his house. The idea was more than unsettling, considering all that had transpired.

"Interesting that you could lie so easily," she said. His explanation did little to melt her anger.

"It wasn't that I'd done the French accent on purpose just with you…"

"Oh, so you did it with all the women you met," she said, finishing his statement, but not to his liking.

"No, I was learning about rum. I wasn't there to meet or seduce beautiful women. It was a working vacation. And you were a wonderful surprise. Why were you there?"

"Vacation," she said vaguely and leaned forward in her seat. "I always gave myself a week off in the winter. Not now, obviously. Not with Xander. So you're in the family business?"

"Trust me, if it hadn't been for Charles's accident, I'd have happily been doing my own thing and not involved in the business or the hospital at all. I'd planned to start my own company and not be involved with my family." Damn Charles.

"What do you mean?"

"He is the favorite son. Charles was slated to run the business. He's been competitive with me since we were kids. He's always wanted what I've had, even though he had everything. In this case, he was hurt pretty severely when he fell into a crevasse on Mount Hood, but then he healed and had an epiphany. I think it was because he lived. He probably made some detailed bargains with God. Anyway, once he was better, he decided he wanted to control his own destiny, so he dumped the leadership of Brewster International Brewing on me and decided to become this other person, someone no one in the family recognizes. In a way, I should thank him. If he hadn't decided that life was more than running an international company, you'd be dealing with him, and I might never have found you again."

"And I could have gone on wondering what happened to Jacques—the man, the myth, the dream—that turned into... well, I have Xander, so I can't say nightmare."

"More likely, Charles would have hit on you. He's the playboy of our family."

"Should we cut to the chase? I'm very tired, and I have a long day tomorrow, so I have a limited amount of time tonight. What exactly do you want?" She was tougher than she looked, not that it came as a surprise. She was tired of the small talk.

"Is Xander mine?" Jack asked, tightness in his throat threatening to cut off his words. Did he have a son? Was he looking at the mother of his child?

Ella looked away, first to the window that looked to the West Hills and then down at her clenched hands, her fingers unclenching just long enough to reach up and bat away a wayward tear.

"Xander is your biological son, but that doesn't mean anything. I don't want anything from you. Xander might want to meet you someday, but that will be a choice for both of you to make. For now, we're just fine. So you can leave here tonight with a clear conscience," she said, her sparkling aquamarine eyes threatening more tears. "I'm not going to come after you for financial support. I'm not going to call a reporter. You have no responsibility. Xander is mine."

"I have a son," he said, more of a statement than a question, as a smile he couldn't contain broke free.

"No, I have a son," Ella corrected. "He doesn't know you."

Nodding, losing the smile, he said, "I need some time to get used to the idea. And I know we have a lot to discuss and work out."

"No, we don't," she said. "Something happened due to alcohol and a tropical setting, but that doesn't mean that we must be in each other's lives forever. In fact, now that you are here, just what exactly were your plans for the afternoon in Saint Barts if you hadn't been called home? Were you really going to show up or were you going to stand me up?"

"Hell yes! I was going to show up! Damn it, Ella, I was enchanted with you. I couldn't get you out of my mind. Heck, I don't think there has been a day since that I haven't thought of you. And, as I remember it, we discussed having a sunset picnic at Colombier Beach. It is supposed to be the best place on the island to watch the sunset and I wanted to share it with you. I was going to talk to the concierge at my hotel about a picnic, instead I gave him a letter for you, which he obviously didn't deliver."

"Then what?" she asked.

"Huh?"

Ella shook her head. "What would you have done at the picnic?"

"I'm sorry. I'm tired, I haven't slept for two days, and it is taking me longer to think. I was going to come clean about who I was on the beach, hopefully knowing you couldn't run too far away from me. I've been told it is a small beach."

"So, you knew enough to know you had deceived me and I might have a reaction?"

"Yes," he answered, not quite able to meet her eyes. "I only hoped you wouldn't hate me."

Ella let out a long breath as if to answer that yes, she did indeed, hate him, and asked, "Then what, *Jacques?*"

"I'd have offered my hotel room for hopefully another night together. Or your room if you'd have been more comfortable. I'm sorry, Ella, I didn't mean for any of this to happen."

She shook her head and shut her eyes. "Look, when Xander is old enough…"

Jack leaned forward on the couch, closing in the space that existed between them. "I

want to be in his life now. Not just when he's eighteen. He needs a father, and I want to be there for him and you."

Ella gave a cynical smile and shook her head.

"Are you worried I'd try to take him from you? Is that it? I wouldn't do that to you," he said.

"I wouldn't let you."

"Then what is it?"

She leaned forward, "I don't like you and I'm not scared of you, Jack, but I don't understand why you are taking me at my word on Xander's patronage. Don't you want a paternity test to prove he's yours? Most men would be denying that he was theirs."

"I'm not most men. He looks just like me at the same age. Unless you slept with a bunch of men around the same time, which I seriously doubt, that kid is mine," he said, feeling suddenly possessive of someone he didn't even know.

"Why do you think I didn't have any other male companionship on my vacation?" she asked, raising her chin in defiance. "Did you sleep with only me on your vacation, Mr. Mayor?"

She'd obviously researched him since he arrived that morning. The article about his possible run for mayor in the next election had only been published a week earlier. His mother had planted the story, and he was still mad about it.

"As a matter of fact, you were the only person I had sex with while in the Caribbean," he said, leaning forward and making sure he was maintaining eye contact. "Yes. I wanted you the moment I saw you on the beach in that skimpy red bikini. I would have stripped that suit off you right there and made love to you in front of everyone who wanted to watch. I don't think you were with anyone else because you had a new box of condoms and a *Lover's Kit,* which I recognized in the window of your shop yesterday.

"I haven't been able to get the memory of how you looked at me when I was deep inside of you out of my mind. Or the way you moved underneath me when you were moaning with pleasure that I was bringing to you. It still haunts me. I want you right now, as much as I did then, if not more. Ella, I wanted to see you again. You must believe me, if Charles hadn't gotten injured on Mount Hood, I'd have been there in your hotel lobby at three. I shouldn't have let him intrude on our happiness. I should have told my mother to deal with it. Hell, I don't know if I could ever let you go. I'll do whatever you want, but I'm not going to walk away. And I'm certainly not going to trust my future to some thief masquerading as a concierge. Trusting him was the biggest mistake of my life."

* * *

Each of his words had the effect of soft tickles in places that shouldn't be aroused during such a serious discussion, especially by a man purposely trying to get under her skin. Ella felt the heat lap along her skin as memories of their night together played through her brain. She remembered the *Lover's Kit* with its tiny bottles of oil. He'd poured the vanilla oil all over her body and then licked it off. When he'd finished, she'd returned the favor, only with a bottle of almond oil. The two mingling scents went together well.

Her breathing wasn't steady, and she couldn't find her words. Swallowing hard, she looked at him and saw the determined look in his green eyes, the same look a hungry lion gets when it spots a limping gazelle at the edge of a clearing.

"So, just to be clear, you're not going to demand a paternity test?" she asked, breaking the spell between them.

He smiled the pirate smile she hadn't seen in a year and a half and said, "He's mine, and so are you. We just need to get past what happened. I need you to know how sorry I am."

Ella rejected his choice of words for their possessive nature. Xander was *hers*, not his. How dare he make such assumptions about Xander and about her? They had been on vacation. This was real, and they were on opposite sides of it. There were too many obstacles. Too many hurdles. They couldn't recapture the magic of that one night.

She asked, "How does it feel to know you're going to take the only home your son has ever known away from him and his mother for a steel and glass monstrosity in the name of your family?"

"Nice," Jack said, leaning close. "One, any place would probably be an improvement over this neighborhood, which is too dangerous for children and their mothers. I don't like thinking of you here. Two, didn't you hire some lawyer to make all of us bad, progressive people with a vision for the hospital go away? Let him do his job. Heck, I'm curious what he has to say and what tactic he will take. You will be okay. I'll make sure you and Xander are always okay."

"At least my son has a mother who loves him and has been with him since day one. As for this neighborhood, it's culturally diverse and interesting. Cindy, who owns the resale shop, is from Croatia and has traveled the world. Padma and Hiram, who own the Indian restaurant, live next door. We all watch out for each other. I couldn't ask for better honorary aunts and uncle to look out for my child. They are a second family to me."

"Oh yes, I forgot about the resale shop and the Indian restaurant. Here's a piece of advice, don't buy any of those ugly clothes. And don't, for your own health, eat at that restaurant. Just the smell of it, which I can smell now in your apartment, is nauseating. This is Portland, not New York. You can have a house with a lawn, fresh air, and a wonderful neighborhood. This downtown experience has got to be old by now. Xander needs a yard."

"Well then, there is another reason for you not to meet Xander," Ella said, leaning forward in her chair, the stuffed animals keeping each party at a safe distance. "I ate Indian food every day that I was pregnant. Butter chicken, Naan, and Raita were the only things I could get down for months. Xander loves Indian food. Maybe he really isn't your child after all."

"I was the only man you'd been with, so you can cut the crap. He looks exactly like me at the same age."

"Your word against mine."

"I'd bet every dollar I have that you don't sleep around. When can I see him?" he demanded.

What could she do? Argue that she was some sort of slut? She wasn't, and they both knew it.

"I told you, he's sleeping, and he is scared of strangers. It would be best to meet him during the daytime in a very casual setting, like a park."

"Fine. Tomorrow? When? Where?" he asked impatiently.

"You're not going to stop, are you?"

"He's my son," he said, holding his hands up in surprise.

"You were the sperm donor."

"Ella, please have a heart," he said, his voice carrying an edge of desperation that surprised her. "When can I see him? I've got to see my son."

"Maybe tomorrow," she said. "You can call me, and I'll see if he is in the right mood to meet you."

"You know that I'll keep coming here until I get to meet him."

"I think I liked you better when you were the jerk who stood me up after a one-night stand."

Ella had perhaps taken the war of words too far. Jack, in his blue button-down shirt and khaki trousers, with his matching crocodile belt and loafers, no longer resembled the calm and controlled businessman he had been since he'd stepped over her threshold.

"It was not a one-night stand, and you know it," he corrected, his words short and definitive.

"You could have fooled me," she said, licking her lip seductively and smiling.

"What will it take for you to believe me?"

"More than a quick mercy visit, Mr. Brewster."

Something snapped in Jack's reserve. Stuffed animals flew off the ottoman with a swipe of his hand, and a moment later, he had her in his arms. Ella didn't know how he'd managed it, but he pulled her from the chair, and now he was holding her to him, his fierce green eyes just inches from hers. His heart beat hard in his chest. She could feel it against her breast, matching the rhythm of her own racing heart.

"Enough of this bullshit. Do you have any idea how much sleep I lost over you?" he asked, and then, not waiting for an answer, he kissed her. A desperately thirsty man in need of drink.

She couldn't resist something her body needed so desperately. Sinking against him, she let him continue to control her as his lips pressed against hers, his arms like tight bands holding her close.

Enough of the bullshit, indeed. She kissed him for all the reasons she shouldn't. There had been too many sad nights of longing, wondering where he was, what he was doing. She hated him. She loved him. When he'd disappeared, she had never felt whole again, realizing in some sick way that he completed her. She hated him, hated him for leaving her and not being there for their child, but she could be mad later. Right now, she just wanted him. She wanted to touch him. She wanted to be held by him.

Tripping on something soft, she fell against him and heard him grunt as an ill-placed elbow hit a soft target as they landed on the couch. If she hurt him a little, well, all the better. He deserved it for hurting her so. Wrapping her arms around his neck, she felt him tighten his hold on her waist, one hand moving up to capture her breast in a squeeze. His tongue tasted her and explored her mouth as it had explored her body on that warm night in Saint Barts.

"This is not a good idea," she managed between kisses as his hand slipped under her sweater and pushed past her bra to capture her bare breast.

"It is the best thing I've done in the twenty months since we did it last," he said as his hand moved from her breast to the waistband of her jeans. "There hasn't been anyone else, only you."

She wanted to ignore his words, but she couldn't. She'd affected him as much as he'd affected her. Yet, she didn't know if she could believe him.

Slipping his hand inside the denim, he toyed with the lacy edge of her panties and then stretched lower to reach the junction of her thighs. Stroking her through the silk, he asked, "We need more room. Where is your bed?"

"Jack, I have to get up early…"

"Think of how good it will feel for me to touch you right here," he said as the hand inside her jeans pushed past the edge of her panties.

"Jack…."

"Shh…" he whispered. He kissed the hollow of her neck in an especially sensitive spot he'd remembered from their first encounter as his fingers tantalized her opening with teasing feather-light strokes.

"I want to taste you right here," he said and kissed her, his tongue auditioning with her mouth for more serious roles yet to be played out.

"You can't be here tomorrow morning," she managed between kisses as she ran her fingers through his soft hair. Of all the things that were new about him, the short hair was the hardest to accept.

Jack stood clumsily, grabbed her hands, and pulled her to her feet.

"We have to be quiet. If you wake the baby…"

"I can be quiet," he said, "but I'm not sure about you."

Chapter Ten

Once inside her tiny bedroom, Ella shut the blinds and turned on a small lamp that cast a dim light on a queen-sized bed. Thinking of all the ways he could make love to her on that bed, all the possibilities, Jack smiled as Ella pulled back the covers and began to pull her sweater over her head. Before it was off, he was there, helping her. He took his time, feeling like it was Christmas, and she was the present he'd envisioned unwrapping for a whole year. By the time he was finished, her hands were shaking as she fumbled with the buttons on his shirt.

"Do you have any condoms, preferably not the same defective box we used in Saint Barts?" he asked, his hands running patterns over her skin as he reacquainted himself with her body.

The pain in her eyes alerted him immediately to his false step. "I didn't mean that Xander is a mistake, just a surprise, and possibly it is too soon for another."

"I don't think it was a defective condom. I think we didn't use one that third time."

"Before dawn," he said, slowly running a finger along the slope of her breast.

She nodded, her fingertip tracing the contours of his chest as they faced each other. The mood had sobered and was possibly ruined. Jack wanted to kick himself for being such an idiot.

"Thank you for clarifying that," she said, her hand no longer touching him. When his hand reached for her, she grabbed it, stopped it mid-touch, and continued.

"We need to talk before this gets any more out of hand," she said in a soft whisper, "We've spent more time in bed than out. In case you hadn't noticed, I have a child we need to discuss at length, but not tonight. I don't know how I feel about you coming into our lives, but I will try to keep an open mind as long as you don't try to take him from me. My livelihood and home are currently in jeopardy, and it doesn't put me in the best of moods. I really hate what your family is trying to do to me and my friends. It was never business. It's always been personal. You're on the wrong side of what is going to be a very heated fight. If you think by being intimate with me, you'll change my opinion or sway me, you have another thing coming. I'm only a little less protective of my home and livelihood than I am of my child."

He began to speak, and she shook her head. "Not finished yet. I might be able to overlook a lot for the fact we've made love before and I can separate my body from my business mind because I need to have someone touch me, hold me, and bring pleasure to me. You're capable of that, so that is why I'm even considering letting you into my bed. But I really don't know you. You could have a wife, children, or a girlfriend. I will not tolerate any of that behavior from the man who joins me in bed."

This woman, who for a hundred reasons was wrong for him, surprised him again. She was beautiful, smart, and had, he understood, a very strategic mind. She was the kind of woman he could fall in love with, perhaps he already was in love with...

"You have an interesting and complex moral code," he said, the curves of her lush body distracting him from clear thinking. There was a stretch mark on her hip, interrupting all the lovely peaches-and-cream skin. No doubt, it was a lasting mark of her pregnancy when she held his child inside her. He longed to kiss that mark and trace it with his fingertip.

She had, however, basically likened him to a prostitute who was only to be used for her pleasure and resulting satisfaction. She talked a good game, but he didn't believe it. He liked the idea of breaking down all that firm resolve, inch by inch and getting her to care about him. It was, he realized, the direction his mind was going. He wasn't the sort of man who could walk away from a challenge.

"Am I right about the wife, or is it a girlfriend?" she asked, moving her body another step away in a subtle but effective posturing.

Smiling now, he brushed the back of his hand over her left nipple and watched her tremble and jerk away.

"I'm not married, nor do I have a steady girlfriend. Believe it or not, and despite my mother's constant attempts at match-making to a suitable girl with the 'right' background, I've been busy pursuing my own career dreams. I find the conditions for satisfying your passion quite acceptable for now. I realize, in time, your feelings could change for the better or for the worse. We'll take it day by day."

Leaning forward, he kissed her lightly on the lips, registering surprise on her face.

"What? No live-in girlfriend?" she asked, truly skeptical.

"There's a housekeeper who has an apartment over the garage."

"Really? Does she take good care of you?" Ella asked as she turned her back on him and climbed onto the bed. Lying back on a pile of oversized pillows, she casually stretched an arm over her head, her smile one of satisfaction. Jack's erection throbbed to attention.

"I think she might have once been a fisherman in Alaska. She has big, scary muscles," he said as he moved in for the kill, joining her on the bed, covering her body with his own. Screw the condom. If he got her pregnant again, it would be worth it, and she'd be even more attached to him. The thought was terrifying and oddly appealing. What the hell was wrong with him?

He kissed his way down her body, giving special attention to that little stretch mark on her hip. Her hips were, by chance, a tad wider, making her look curvier. He loved it, loved the lushness of her. Touching him back, softly at first, her hands ran through his hair, followed by her lips, exploring his body almost shyly. When she made a trail of wet kisses to where his erection strained in painful need, he took in a large breath and waited, hoping he wouldn't resort to begging.

"By the way," she whispered as she teased him, "I'm on the pill, but I'll need you to wear a condom because I don't trust you. Nor do I like you."

"I know you don't believe this, but I'm not going anywhere," he managed.

Ignoring his words and turning away from his body, Ella opened the nightstand drawer and pulled out a box of condoms. Detaching one from the rest of the chain, she ripped open the package and handed it to him. Sighing in defeat, he took it from her and sheathed himself, still thinking of how it would feel to make love with her without a condom. She'd told him about being on the pill just to irritate him. Fine. For now, he'd accept it.

Smoothly, he rolled her onto her back, pushed open her knees as his hands slipped under her butt and raised her hips. Then, in one long stroke, he sunk into her body.

Their eyes met and held. He'd wanted to be gentle with her, assumed it had been a long time for her. He hoped it was her first time since she'd given birth to his child, but the ready box of condoms hadn't eased his now troubled mind. He wanted to murder anyone who had shared her bed before him.

One of the last times they'd done this, they'd created a child.

"Please..." she whispered, "I don't want you to be gentle..."

He didn't wait for her to ask him twice.

After a few minutes of calming breaths after a fierce climax, Ella tapped his shoulder in a way he would not describe as gentle.

He tenderly kissed Ella's cheek and asked, "Are you alright?"

"Yep," she said unemotionally. Her hands no longer caressed his back but now patted the mattress in a pattern of boredom.

"I didn't mean to be rough," he apologized, feeling uncomfortable with her silence.

"That was just what I needed, thanks," she said in a flat, businesslike tone, adding, "Don't fall asleep. You need to get dressed and leave."

"But I..." Jack tried but couldn't finish. He'd hoped for round two. How could there not be a round two? He was just getting warmed up.

"And try not to be seen. I don't want to have to explain you to my neighbors," she said, wrinkling her face as if he were smelly garbage she would have to dispose of.

Odd, but he was finding it hard to remember why he felt so sorry for the mother of his child living in an apartment above her strange curio shop.

Then the successful businessman, who'd once been number twenty-three among the Top 100 Most Eligible Businessmen Bachelors in the United States, felt a new emotion.

Jack Brewster felt used as he walked to his car. A few minutes later, he pulled the Audi onto the brick driveway of his grandparents' house. The estate on Vista Avenue was supposed to go to Charles when their grandmother had died five years earlier, but Charles hated the place and gave the keys and deed to Jack as a thirtieth birthday present. Surprised and miffed at Charles's easy disregard for a part of their family heritage, Jack had grudgingly taken the house. It was too formal and too pristine to feel like a home, but his home it was. He parked in the first stall of the four-car garage, walked out to the sidewalk on

Vista Avenue, and looked down at the lights of northwest Portland.

The hospital was an easy landmark to find. Looking slightly to the north, he picked out Lovejoy Street and at the same moment, picked out the red lettering that read *"Marcella's,"* From this distance he couldn't quite make out the full sign, only the top part of the "M" and an "l" were visible.

He'd left Ella there less than ten minutes ago. That wasn't quite correct. She'd asked him to leave fifteen minutes ago, and as he'd dressed, he'd done his best to convince her that he could stay for just a little while longer. She was having none of it.

Could he make love to her again? Could he maybe just hold her for a bit and talk? Her answer to all of the cajoling had been a flat, unemotional, "No, I'm sorry, you have to go." But she wasn't sorry. She'd wanted him out and smiled as she shut the door in his face with an unconvincing promise to call him the next day and arrange a possible meeting with *her* son.

Jack stared at the neon sign less than a mile from his home on the hill.

Ella had made her point. He'd hurt her in Saint Barts, and she wasn't going to forgive him anytime soon, even though what had happened hadn't exactly been his fault, just his poor thought. And by belonging to the Brewster family, by default, he was the enemy.

Jack predicted that before it was all over, they'd both have to make some major concessions. Tonight, he'd taken one for his team. The sting of her rejection was still smarting.

Chapter Eleven

Ella lay awake long after Jack left. She was physically and emotionally exhausted, but every one of her nerve endings felt alive and on fire with energy she hadn't felt in a very long time. She'd awakened yesterday morning, never knowing if she would see Jack again. Heck, she thought his name was Jacques. Now, her bed was warm from the heat of their lovemaking. She'd made a huge mistake. In the moment, it hadn't felt like a mistake, but she'd slept with a stranger for the second time. Technically, this was the fifth time they'd made love, but she didn't know how she felt about the man.

She didn't know what Jack ate for breakfast, his likes and dislikes for food, or any dislike for that matter. She didn't know how old he was or what he liked to do for fun. She'd had a picture of this man in her mind, yet the reality was something not only different but mind-blowing. Not only wasn't he French, but he also lived in her hometown. What were the odds? How often had they crossed paths and been unaware of each other? Was it fate that had put them together in Saint Barts or a simple coincidence? Her mind struggled to make sense of every twist of fate that couldn't be explained logically.

At least she knew his real name. And could there be anyone worse for her at this moment in time than a Brewster?

After another hour with no sleep, Ella got out of bed and checked on Xander.

Being as quiet as possible, she pushed open his door and

looked in on him. Curled up on his side with his favorite stuffed animal, a rust-colored dog named BeauBeau, clutched in his arm, he slept soundly. He was the sweetest child she'd ever known, and her bias had little to do with the fact he was her child. He was inherently sweet natured to the point of being sensitive, and for that, she worried. The only reason Jack Brewster knew of Xander's existence was for the fact that Xander hadn't wanted to go to daycare the day before and wanted to stay with 'Mama.' He'd twisted her heartstrings into knots.

She decided on a shower to wash away that exotic scent of Jack that reminded her of Saint Barts. He smelled like the ocean and cedar and citrus, all mixed together in a lovely potpourri of scent that did strange things to her insides.

Would she have told Jack about Xander if he hadn't seen Xander?

Up until a couple of days ago, wondering, obsessing about "Jacques" and what he would do if he knew he had a son, had filled many lonely hours. She had wondered where in the world he was. Turns out, about two miles away. The mystery now solved, what did she do next?

Before she let Jack further into their lives she needed to know more about the man, his background, his plans, the way he lived his life and the people whom he surrounded himself with. She needed to know if he would be a good influence on Xander. She needed to know that he wouldn't disappear again. She needed to know he wouldn't try to take Xander away from her.

She had picked up on one very important thing tonight, Jack hadn't wanted to leave her apartment, but she hadn't been prepared for him to stay. There was deep satisfaction that had come with asking him to leave. Besides, she couldn't be seen with him. And he couldn't be seen leaving her apartment in the early hours of the morning.

And what if someone did find out? She wasn't even sure she

would tell her mother about this newest development. But then, Ella's mother had never been her confidant. Hadn't her mother told her not to expect her help? It really hadn't come as a surprise. Her mother should never have had children.

As her mother liked to tell Ella often, she'd raised her child and wasn't about to put her life on hold for anyone ever again, including a daughter. That included emotional support. Her mother was now free to do all the things she hadn't been able to do when she'd had to care for a family. And she was doing them. Her mother didn't want to be a grandmother any more than she wanted to be a mother. Even the memory of her mother's harsh words still had the power to sting.

And what would she tell Cindy, Padma, and Hiram? They had been united so completely in their fight against the hospital, which meant they were united in their dislike of the Brewster family. What now?

What if they found out she'd slept with Jack again? What if they knew who Jack really was? She couldn't believe she'd made love with him again. Her only excuse had been the one she'd told him. She needed sex like she occasionally needed a good massage or a chocolate cupcake with vanilla icing. She just *needed* it. And if she thought about it anymore this evening, it would make her feel bad for being so weak when it came to the man who'd set the bar for every other man in her life. It was ridiculous, really. She'd spent less than a day with him in real time. But the way he'd touched her, it felt so loving...

Glancing down at Xander, who made soft noises as he slept, she thought of another, more important reason why she'd done it. She didn't want Xander's father to have been only a one-night stand. She wanted him to be someone who'd been important in her life. Well, she succeeded. Next to Xander, he was the most important man in her life.

She hadn't made love with him to sway his opinion on the hospital expansion. If he had his own feelings about that, it was because he had a conscious about his child and the mother of his child, that was his own personal issue. Not only did her future rest in his hands, but he also had a direct say in where she would be living, working and his involvement in her future with every significant moment in her son's life.

Any smart woman would see the danger headed at her. Ella had never been that smart when it came to men. They were her mother's words, not her own, but still there was some merit there.

Jack wanted to meet Xander tomorrow. She wasn't sure how she felt about that. As she tucked the blanket around Xander, he seemed to relax against BeauBeau. Did she want it to happen because she wanted to show Xander off? Or did she just want to see Jack again? Both. And wasn't that just a fine mess?

It had to be slow. Everything involving Xander had to be slow. If Jack wanted to be a part of Xander's life, he had to earn it. She wasn't going to hand Xander off for visits and overnights, not without her supervision. That would be totally unaccept-able. She didn't even know where Jack lived. How much more did she want to risk by having Jack visit her again at her apart-ment? Maybe for their next meeting, she needed to see where he lived. If anything, it might stall things a bit.

How would his family, especially his mother, whose photo Ella had come across in her research of Jack, think about having a grandson from a woman not married to her son? Of all the scenarios in her head, this one almost scared her the most. The last thing she needed was a grandmother disapproving of the way she was raising her grandchild. She already had one of those. After seeing the woman's photo today, she realized she didn't fear Jack half as much as she feared his mother. She had a feeling she might be able to control Jack with sex, sad as that was. What was sadder was that he could control her in the same way.

If Jack had been telling the truth, dear old Mom would have

been trying to set him up with nice, appropriate ladies. It was highly unlikely Marcella Martin with a bachelor's degree in business management from Portland State University, for which she still had student loans that she was three years from paying off, would be suitable for Dolores Brewster's son.

She thought of her shop and some of the more colorful items she sold. The books on erotic art in Rome were the first items of concern. There was no way this was going to come together peacefully. By the time the Brewsters were finished with her, she'd be lucky to still own her beat-up old Volvo. Looking down at Xander, Ella felt really scared for the first time in her life. She needed a lawyer, not the guy who was handling pro bono work against the hospital. She needed a ball-buster who could tell her what her rights were regarding her child.

* * *

The next morning, Jack looked down at the summons on his desk. In three and a half weeks, there would be a hearing to determine if the Brewster family could have their own hospital wing. Two days ago, he would have felt excited for the opportunity to win and get past this hurdle. Today, he felt sick to his stomach. The best he could hope for would be a postponement, say, for ten or twenty years.

Glancing at his watch, he saw that it was just after ten on this Friday morning, only three days after he'd discovered that he had a son.

Jack reached into his pocket and pulled out a business card he had grabbed for *Marcella's*. He hadn't slept well the night before, thinking of what he would say to Ella this morning. His feelings ranged from wanting to show up on her doorstep and kissing her to wanting to run far away from all of his troubles. His thoughts drifted to Xander, his son.

He had a son. It was a mind-blowing concept that his mind had yet to wrap itself around.

He knew if he waited for Ella to call him, he'd be waiting a long time. Before the controlled businessman who ran a multi-million-dollar company could lose his cool, he picked up the phone and dialed the number for *Marcella's*.

"Good morning, *Marcella's*, this is Cricket," the young woman said.

"Hello...may I speak with Ella, please?" Jack asked.

"I'm sorry Marcella is out this morning. May I take a message?"

"Do you know when she'll be in?"

"I'm not sure, she didn't say."

Jack picked up on a bit of defensiveness from the woman who called herself Cricket. She didn't want to be giving out information about her boss. And she just about reached the end of her patience with Jack.

"All right, no problem. I'll just call back later for her. Thank you."

"Are you sure you don't want to leave a message?" she asked, irritated now.

"I'm sure."

Chapter Twelve

Ella sat across from Eric Johnson, the family lawyer specializing in custody issues. It was going to cost her $500 just to speak to the man for an hour, but she considered the expense well worth it, especially since he could see her on the same day she called.

The man took feverish notes as she described her situation. Midway through her story, the gray-haired man with a serious face held up his hand and asked her to stop speaking.

"Ms. Martin, I'm afraid I might have to stop you right there," he said, looking all the sudden lawyerly in a way that was no longer so friendly. There was a chill between them now that Ella did not understand.

"Okay," Ella said.

"I'm afraid that I'm already representing the other party in this matter," Mr. Johnson said.

"What?" she asked. "You're representing Jack Brewster in the custody issue of my child? He got a lawyer?"

"I'm really not at liberty to discuss this with you, Ms. Martin. The only thing I'm able to share is that I'm currently under retainer for Mr. Brewster, which means I'm not available to help you. Obviously, I won't be charging you for today's conversation."

"Wait just a minute," she said as understanding blossomed. "Did he talk to you specifically about my child, or is he someone who just has you on retainer?"

"I'm familiar with your case," he said, the words hitting her like rocks.

The color drained from her cheeks. Jack had already lied to her. He said he wasn't interested in taking Xander away from her, but why else would he have chosen to meet with an attorney before he even met his son? Ella was in over her head. And for the first time, she felt a real fear about losing Xander. Without another word, she stood and walked out of the attorney's office. She waited until she was in the elevator before she started crying. Her hand was shaking badly when she handed her money to the parking attendant to get the keys to her Volvo. He looked at her strangely as he passed over the keys, but she ignored him. As she pulled away, the tears started again. She was crying so hard that by the time she was a mile away from the parking garage, she had to pull over to an empty parking spot because she could no longer see to drive.

For the first time in her life, she contemplated running away from a problem. Taking Xander and everything they could fit into the Volvo and just driving away, destination unknown. It wasn't the solution. But now, it felt like the only option.

Ella parked in her designated parking space in the alley. After washing her face with cold water and reapplying makeup, she deemed herself presentable enough to go to her shop. Remembering to smile, she greeted Cricket and asked how the morning had been.

Cricket gave her a funny look and said, "A man called for you. He didn't want to leave his name, which I thought was strange."

"That is strange," Ellis said. She didn't want to act as if anything was wrong, but something was very wrong. "I'll get the phone the next time it rings."

Ella did not have long to wait. Jack called within the hour. She held the phone to her ear and tried to sound chipper.

"*Marcella's*, this is Marcella. How can I help you?" Ella said into the phone.

"Ella? It's Jack. How does today look for you?"

Ella waited a long time to answer. "I don't know Jack. It's going to be a busy day, and I'm just not sure if we can get together. It might be better if we waited until Monday. I have Monday off. How is that looking for you?"

"Ella, have a heart. I'm going crazy here. I need to meet Xander. I haven't slept at all. I need to see you. I need to see Xander."

Ella wasn't feeling especially generous when it came to Jack Brewster. Her feelings, which had softened after making love with him, had hardened to stone the moment the attorney had told her that he already had a client in this potential custody battle.

"Yes, I understand you are unsettled," she said coldly. "I got that opinion from Eric Johnson this morning."

"I don't understand. What are you talking about?"

Ella had taken the portable phone from the front counter and was now talking to Jack from the back room of her shop. "I'm talking about the family attorney you put on retainer yesterday."

"Wait a minute. Did he contact you?" Jack's words lost some of their smoothness. The pity she was hoping to evoke had suddenly turned on the defensive.

"Why? Was he supposed to contact me today?" she asked.

"No, never. I don't understand. But no, no. I can explain this."

"Oh, I'm sure you can. But the question is, do I want to know what you have to say, or should I just cut off all contact with you? To be honest, I'm kind of leaning in the direction of the latter. Maybe Xander and I should relocate to another city."

"No...please... Ella, please, I don't know why he contacted you, but there was no reason for him to. I will call him as soon as we are off this call and ask him for a full explanation. I only talked to him because I got scared. I told you before I would never take Xander away from you."

"Yes, but you thought about it." Ella was crying again. She hadn't realized tears were streaming down her cheeks until one landed on the table in front of her with an audible 'plop.'

"Ella, please, please do not worry about this. I want to meet Xander. I want to be a part of his life. I want to be a part of your life. Last night was—"

"I don't want to talk about last night." To her distress, a small sob escaped her lips.

"Sweetheart, are you crying?"

"Don't you dare call me that! Yes, I'm crying. You'd be crying if someone threatened to take the most important person in your life away from you."

"You have my word. I would never do that. I will never take Xander away from you."

"As if I trust you? The man who disappeared," she said, wiping her face with a tissue.

"I can be at your shop in ten minutes. Please let me come over, and we can talk."

"No," Ella said firmly. "I don't want to have to explain you to anyone."

"Could we please just get together again? I want to see you. Please? I've got to meet Xander."

"Not today," she said definitively.

Jack let out a frustrated breath of air. On some level, it made her happy to know that she'd gotten to him because he had certainly gotten to her.

"How about tomorrow? You name the time and place. I'll make it happen."

She sniffled, wiping her eyes and nose with a tissue, and he heard it.

"Are you okay?" he asked, his voice barely a whisper. "Are you still crying?"

"You would be, too, if you had the morning I had."

"Tell me what happened," he ordered softly. "Tell me everything."

"No," she replied.

"What did Eric say? Was he mean to you? He should never have contacted you. There was no reason for it. I didn't authorize anything."

"Does it matter?"

"Yes, he wasn't supposed to contact you. I was just talking to him hypothetically."

"Yeah? Well, so was I."

Ella waited for the light bulb to go on in Jack's head. It didn't take long.

"You went to see him this morning," he said. "You went to him. He didn't call you."

"Yes, until he told me he was representing you."

"There is nothing to represent. I was just getting an understanding of the situation."

Ella didn't reply, she'd basically done the same thing, only to know he'd done it somehow scared her.

"Look, let me come over tonight. We can sit down and talk."

"Somehow, I don't think that's what we'd end up doing," Ella said. "We don't seem to occupy the same space very well."

"I'm not sorry about what happened last night. I don't regret it. I only hope it happens again and soon. I like you. I never stopped liking you. I care. I care about you. I care about Xander. Now please when I can I see you and when can I see Xander?"

Ella's need to punish him was strong. She couldn't, wouldn't, give in to seeing him today.

"Meet me on Saturday at Jamison Park at 2 pm. It's on 11th between Johnson and Kearney. Xander likes it because it has a big fountain." And there was no chance they'd end up in her bed.

"I know the place well," he said. "It's only a few blocks from my office."

"I know it is because when you're brewing your beer, it really stinks up the air at that park."

"We won't be brewing at 2 pm tomorrow," he said.

"Good, because Xander really hates the smell," she said and smiled. It was a well-placed kick to the family business's corporate jewels and completely worth it.

"By the time Xander is twenty-one, he is going to be glad for the family business he was born into."

Ella didn't feel like continuing the banter any longer. She let him have the last dig. As a way of ending the call, she said, "Sure. I will see you tomorrow at two."

Jack seemed unwilling to let the call go. He asked, "Are you really okay?"

"No," she said. "I don't think I like any of this."

Ella turned off the phone and walked out of the back room to where Cricket waited, leaning against the counter, her arms crossed. The shop, she noted, was completely empty, which was a rarity. She wondered how much Cricket had heard and figured out. Cricket was smart, and it wasn't going to take a rocket scientist to figure out that Ella was in trouble. In a way, she was glad because she needed to confide in someone. And she didn't want that person to be her mother or her neighbors.

Before Ella could speak, Cricket held up her hand and said, "Let me guess. You found Xander's father."

"Actually, he found me." At the declaration, Ella began to cry in earnest.

Cricket grabbed a small sign that they only used in case of emergencies. It read: *Sorry! We'll be back in a half hour. Please come again. Thank you!*

Ella saw the sign in Cricket's hand. She nodded to the other woman and watched as Cricket put the sign into a bracket on the front door and then turned the lock. Together, they escaped to the back room, where Ella told Cricket about the last three days of her life.

Cricket, a pretty woman with beautiful mocha skin and now had bubblegum pink dreadlocks, said, "Holy fuck-shit. *Jack Brewster*! What the fuck are you going to do? He is like the prince of our city. You don't fuck with the Brewsters. Well, it appears you already did."

"Great. I haven't decided what to do yet, but I have to let him meet Xander. That is going to happen tomorrow afternoon in Jamison Park. I thought that would be a good time and place because I knew you were going to be in the shop. And it is neutral territory. Besides, I might need your moral support when I get back."

"You know what the press would do with this story if they figured it out?" Cricket asked. "You wouldn't have to worry about whether that wing would be built. You'd be the secret mistress of the Brewster heir. Think of the scandal. Think of the money. Advantage Marcella! Way to go."

"I don't want to think about it, but I'm not going to the press," Ella said, picturing the fallout. Then she wondered if Jack would try to buy Xander from her. She wouldn't put it past him or his family. "I don't want you to even be thinking about it. Besides, the press is not going to find out from me or you. Promise me."

"Ella, I'd never go to the press. But you've got to admit, this is an interesting situation. Believe me, you've got the power."

Ella placed her hand on top of the other woman's. "I'm too emotionally involved to look at all the angles now. I'm not going to try to destroy the Brewsters unless they try to take Xander away from me. Then all bets are off. As for you, you must promise me that you will not tell anyone about this. That includes my mother or any of our neighbors. You are the only one I'm trusting with this information, so I need to know that you won't tell anyone."

"I won't," she said begrudgingly, but asked, "What do you think Jack will do about this place? Would he pull the plug on the hospital wing if it means destroying his child's home?"

"No, I think it would be more likely that he might pay me more in guilt money, which would also not make me feel good," Ella said. "I didn't have Xander to make money from his millionaire father."

"I think the Brewsters might actually be billionaires," Cricket argued. "You can get *Brewster's Rose Ale* in Europe and Asia. But seriously, don't turn down any money. It could make a difference in Xander's future. Don't let your pride make bad decisions. Xander's health and welfare must come first. He needs a college fund."

"I know," Ella said begrudgingly. "I just have always felt confident that I could do it on my own. If I must rely on Jack Brewster for help, I'll feel like a failure. I don't think I'd ever be able to look in the mirror again. You know, my mother was beholden to my father for money right up until he died. They were married for years, but they weren't partners. She had to ask him for money and ask his permission to even buy a new pair of shoes. After watching that interaction while I was growing up, I vowed I'd be self-sufficient. Having Xander didn't change anything. It just changed my priorities."

"Your mother seems to be doing well on her own," Cricket said.

"She is. She buys at least one pair of new shoes a month, just because she can. When dad died, he left her with a nice life insurance policy. She's kind of gone the other way, she feels extremely empowered, except when it comes to this shop. She hopes I'll close Marcella's and get a 'real job.' And she refuses to help me in any way. I hope if we were starving, she'd feed us, but I'm not sure."

"Don't worry, I'd feed you. I'm here for you, Ella, don't forget that."

"Thank you for that. I couldn't have this shop without you."

They both fell into a comfortable silence, the affirmation that they were friends as well as co-workers, making each of them feel sentimental.

It was Cricket who spoke first. "So could you ask Xander's Daddy for some free samples of Brewster's new rum? It sounds pretty amazing."

"Not in a million years," Ella said, shaking her head.

Chapter Thirteen

Ella was a nervous wreck Saturday morning at *Marcella's*. A few minutes before noon, Cricket arrived, and Ella was glad to see her. She picked up Xander from the back room where he'd been playing with his trucks and watching a Disney movie. They headed back upstairs to her apartment so she could get him ready to meet his father.

The day before, she had gone down the street to the Gymboree and picked out a new outfit for Xander. It was ridiculously expensive and unnecessary, but something she had to do, nonetheless. And with Cindy's help, she didn't need to buy much for Xander, so when she wanted something, she could rationalize buying it. She wanted her little man to look his best, not to say that he wasn't always the most handsome child in any setting to begin with.

But Xander was not at a stage in his life where he enjoyed having his clothing changed more than once a day. Left to his own devices, he would have preferred to run around naked.

Ella held up the new outfit for Xander to see as they talked about the sweater and the animal that was prominently displayed on its front.

"Can you say moose?"

"Oose!"

"Close enough! Great job, my big boy."

Once bolstered, he was more eager to put on the new outfit.

At one-thirty, Ella and Xander set off for Jamison Park with

Xander's stroller. Xander loved riding in his stroller, and it was a beautiful sunny day for a stroll in the neighborhood. They would be early, but Ella didn't care. She wanted to have the advantage of being there first and picking out where they would sit. Xander loved the fountain, but only on warm summer days. Soon, it will be too cold for them to even visit the park. As it was on a crisp but warm October day, the park was not crowded at all.

When Xander realized where they were, he got very excited. Ella knew that any day he would start walking, and then she would have to really worry about him. Parking the stroller by one of the modern benches, she sat down, freed him from the stroller, and held him on her lap. He was all boy and immediately wanted to get down and start exploring. The ground was too cold for that, so she walked with him and pointed out different things that were around them.

"Look at the doggie, Xander," she said pointing at a familiar Labradoodle across the way. With any luck the owner, who they'd met several times, would be walking by in a few minutes and Xander would get to pet the dog, which he loved doing.

"BeauBeau," he said, pointing.

Intent as she was on Xander, Ella didn't notice Jack's arrival until he was almost on top of them. He was very early, too, at least by more than fifteen minutes. Walking toward them, she noticed he carried a tray with three cups from Starbucks in one hand and a shopping bag from an exclusive toy store downtown in the other. Sporting sunglasses, he wore a long camelhair coat over his jeans and a black t-shirt, which probably cost more than either Xander's or her outfits together.

She'd been careful to wear a casual yet trendy outfit of jeans and a silk ribbon sweater in the lightest shade of lavender. A pashmina scarf in the same shade of lavender wrapped her shoulders. She was glad she looked good because on the inside she was a mess.

* * *

Jack felt stupid being almost a half hour early for their meeting in Jamison Park, but he hadn't been able to stop himself. It was bad enough that he hadn't slept well for the last three nights, now, he was starting to battle a constant feeling of anxiety.

He'd been hiding out in a nearby Starbucks and was relieved when he saw Ella arrive with Xander. Taking his time and trying to calm down, he'd ordered Ella a cappuccino and Xander a hot chocolate. He didn't know if either one of them would like the offerings, but he wanted to bring some sort of peace offering. Their phone call the day before had been hard on both of them.

As he walked toward them in the park, Ella's words echoed in his head. Xander did not like strangers. From the research he'd started doing on young children, he knew this was a stage in Xander's development where he was especially close and clingy to his mother. So noted, Jack thought it best to proceed with caution.

When he got close enough, he said, "Hi Ella. Hi Xander."

At the sound of his name, Xander looked in the direction of the noise and looked at Jack for the first time, causing Jack's troubled heart to skip a beat.

Ella regarded him wearily but faked it well as she said, "Xander, look who's here."

Xander looked to his mother as if to say, "Who are you kidding? I don't know this guy."

"Hi, Xander," Jack said, standing a few feet away from the bench where Xander sat with his mother.

"Jack, why don't you sit down?" Ella asked, her smile warm enough to fool the baby but not Jack. She wasn't enjoying this moment one bit. She'd rather be anywhere than here.

"Xander?" She asked, pulling the little boy's big blue eyes away from his father. "Say hello."

Xander looked shyly at his mother and then looked at Jack and said, "Hi."

Jack had to swallow for fear of drowning on his own saliva. "Hi, Xander," he said, "Can I sit down?"

"Sure," Ella said, turning her body with Xander in her lap so they were facing the spot where Jack sat.

"I didn't know what either of you would like, so I brought you a cappuccino and a hot chocolate. I have a couple kinds of juice in the bag. Is he allergic to anything?" Jack asked, feeling stupid for not knowing if his child might be allergic to dairy, as he took off his sunglasses and put them away.

"I'll take the cappuccino. Hot chocolate is usually too hot, but what kind of juice do you have?" Ella asked.

"Orange or apple."

"Xander, would you like some apple juice?" she asked.

"Pple," he said enthusiastically.

"Apple juice," Ella corrected and waited, but Xander was too busy watching Jack, who was watching Xander with the same intensity.

Jack smiled at Xander and watched as Xander shyly looked down at the stuffed animal dog in his hands and then back up to Jack. His son had the sweetest face he'd ever seen. Big blue eyes that were the same shade as Ella's, with long lashes that took in every detail around him. Everything else about the boy resembled Jack, from his dark, almost black hair to his dimples.

"Jack, here you go," Ella said, handing him a sippy cup. "Just fill it about one third full, and we'll take it from there."

Jack did as she asked with shaking hands. Then he handed her the cappuccino, which she set beside her and then the sippy cup.

"Xander, look what I have here," she said, handing him the sippy cup. He took the cup in both hands, the stuffed animal dog dropping to the ground. Jack retrieved it and handed it to Ella.

"Thank you. Xander, can you say thank you?"

Xander murmured something, then shyly hid behind his cup.

"You're welcome, Xander," he said, not quite believing that this beautiful child was part his.

Ella was looking at him strangely.

"He's beautiful."

Ella nodded and added, "He's perfect."

Jack watched Xander drinking his juice, who watched Jack as he did so.

Ella looked away and then back to Jack. "I don't think there is any reason not to tell him who you are. So, if it is okay with you, I'll tell him about you being his f-a-t-h-e-r. Okay, by you?"

"Yes, very okay," Jack said and smiled down at Xander. "Thank you."

"Xander," Ella said, drawing the toddler's attention back to his mother. "Do you know who this is?"

Xander looked at Jack for a long moment, then back to his mother.

"This is your daddy," she said. The word was obviously familiar to Xander, for he regarded Jack seriously for a moment.

"Da-da," Xander said and pointed at Jack, whose heart stopped and restarted.

Jack stretched his hand out to Xander, who handed him his cup. Ella laughed, drawing his attention as she wiped away a tear.

"Do you think it would be okay if he sat on my lap?"

<h1 style="text-align:center">Chapter Fourteen</h1>

The frog in Ella's throat didn't want her to talk yet, so at Jack's question of whether he could hold his child, she had to take a moment and find her voice. Jack had asked the question as if he were a little boy himself, scared of her answer. It was another layer to the man she still didn't know. And for reasons she could not understand, it made her attraction for the man go deeper. As they sat on that bench, they looked like a family having an outing on a Saturday afternoon. It wasn't the kind of idea or fantasy she should have, but she was having it, and it made her feel very uncomfortable and even heartbroken.

"Xander," she said, drawing her son's attention. "Daddy would like you to sit on his lap, okay?" As she said it, she lifted Xander and held him out to an awkward Jack, who set down the sippy cup and took Xander in his arms.

For a moment, Xander looked up at Jack and then went back to playing with BeauBeau, who Ella had handed to him.

"He's got his BeauBeau."

"Is that the dog?" Jack asked uneasily.

"Yes, he loves BeauBeau."

"Do you like dogs, Xander?" Jack asked.

Xander nodded but looked away shyly.

"He's kinda quiet," Jack said, looking down at Xander, who'd settled on Jack's lap.

"He's shy and doesn't know a lot of men," Ella said, feeling like a failure for sheltering her son. "Besides, he's just learning to talk."

"I brought him a toy, but I don't know if it is right for him," Jack said.

"What is it?" Ella asked.

"Check out the bag."

Inside the bag, she recognized from a high-end toy store she couldn't afford. She saw a stuffed giraffe. How had he known about her fondness for giraffes? Was it a guess? She'd loved giraffes since she was a kid, but there was no way he would've known that.

"It's very cute. I'm sure he will love it. Why don't you give it to him?" Xander was already checking out the bag and had figured out it was something for him.

Ella handed Jack the bag and watched Xander's eyes grow wide as Jack pulled out the kindly-faced giraffe and wiggled it at Xander.

"Wow, look at that," she said, trying to sound as enthusiastic as possible. She would do her part to make this a successful meeting, even if it came at a high personal cost to her.

"Raff," Xander said, surprising both her and Jack. She watched Xander and Jack play with the giraffe. Giraffe was a word she and Xander had worked on from one of the bedtime stories they read every night. Still, hearing him almost get it right was very impressive.

After about an hour of watching the interaction between father and son, Ella looked at her watch and frowned. "We need to be heading back to the shop."

"Could I walk with you?" Jack asked.

"Are you sure you want to be seen with us?

Jack hesitated for a moment and said, "Yes, as long as it doesn't bother you."

"I think we should part ways within a couple of blocks of the shops. We don't need a scandal," Ella said and watched as he put on his sunglasses.

"Fine," he said and stood, Xander still in his arms.

Was he scared of being seen with them? Probably, after all, he was considering a run for mayor. How would it look if he was out in public with his baby mama and baby, who incidentally he was trying to evict for his hospital project?

Cricket was right. It sounded like a scandal. A very costly scandal for all of them.

Reluctantly, Jack put Xander in his stroller. Ella felt his eyes on her as she strapped Xander in. Xander insisted on holding both his new giraffe and BeauBeau. Jack pushed the stroller as Ella walked by his side, making her way back to Lovejoy Street.

She wondered if actors felt this way. They were acting a part but knew that part of the scene they were in was real. The leaves were rustling under the wheels of Xander's stroller, and the brightly colored trees seemed even more stunning in the afternoon sun.

"Lots of pretty leaves," she said.

"Smells like fall. It's my favorite season," Jack replied.

"My favorite is spring," she said.

"I like spring too," he said.

It might be her last fall living in the neighborhood, she realized. They wanted to demolish her shop in January and begin construction on the new hospital in March. That left her with three months.

"I don't like the early darkness. It is hard to keep the store open when it is dark. It gets scary sometimes. Different crowd of people after the sun goes down."

Now, why had she told him that? Hadn't he complained about the neighborhood? What was she doing, playing into his plans? What was wrong with her?

"Maybe your winter hours should be a little shorter, except at the holidays."

"Sometimes I close a bit early, especially if it has been a slow day."

"Do you have any protection? A bat under the counter? Pepper spray?"

"No," she said with a shake of her head.

"Have you ever been robbed?"

"Only once, four years ago."

"Ella?!" he exclaimed, stopping on the sidewalk, and turning to face her, "How did that happen?"

"Old news, and we are all fine. I have a new security system with a panic button, so it is handled. Do you ever have a slow season?" she asked to deflect the attention away from her own business.

"After the holidays. February is slow. Ironically, no one believes that beer is a good Valentine's Day beverage. But then we have St. Patrick's Day, and we are saved until January 1st with its New Year's resolutions."

"Do you drink a lot?" she asked, thinking this could be the one thing that really wasn't in his favor.

"The most I've had to drink in the last year was three beers in one night. I know that at a certain point, it stops being about the integrity of the product and more about getting a buzz. I know where that fine line is. Besides, I'm a cheap drunk."

She listened but said nothing. Where did they go from here? She didn't want to offer anything or sound like she wanted to have sex with him again, but she kind of did. Her body still tingled at the sight of him. She couldn't look at his fingers without feeling a charge between her legs, where he really liked to touch her with so many different parts of his body.

"Well, I think this is about as far as we should go," she said when they were two blocks away.

"I guess so," he said and stopped the stroller. Xander looked up at his parents as if to ask what was going on.

"Thank you for the drinks and the giraffe," she said and reached for the handle of the stroller.

"Please, when can I see you again?" he asked, a phrase that was both familiar and lovely at the same time.

"Let's give it a couple of days," she said.

"You're open tomorrow?"

"Yes," she said and shook her head. "But Sunday isn't a good night. I don't work on Monday. Maybe we could meet then."

"How about dinner?" he asked. "I could bring something over, and we could talk after Xander goes to bed."

Talk would not be what they'd be doing if Xander went to bed, and they both knew it.

"Why don't you call me on Monday, and we'll see how it goes?" she said.

Jack pulled his cell phone out of his pocket and said, "Okay, give me your cell number."

Ella realized she was giving away another part of her privacy. "I don't have yours."

"It's on the business card I gave you. It is my direct line. It works if I'm in the office or out. You can call anytime. Please. Call."

Ella recited her number for him and watched as he put it in his phone. What he did next shocked her. Before she could step away, he leaned forward and kissed her. It wasn't the kind of passionate kisses they'd shared two nights earlier, but it made Ella blush.

When he drew away, a confident smile graced his face. Before she could make a less-than-kind comment, he kissed her again, wrapped an arm around her waist, and pulled her close.

"Jack," she said, pulling away and looking down at Xander, who was engrossed in his giraffe.

"I made sure he wasn't looking," Jack said and then bent down to speak to his son. Petting the giraffe, he said, "Bye-bye, Xander. I'll see you soon."

"Bye-bye, da," he said as Jack ran a gentle hand through his son's hair.

Xander sounded so sad that his new friend was leaving that it tugged at Ella's heart.

"Monday?" Jack asked, sensing Xander's reluctance to see him go.

"Fine, make it six o'clock."

"I'll bring dinner," he said.

"Come on Xander, let's go home," she said and left Jack standing on the curb.

Chapter Fifteen

On Sunday evening, Ella sat inside *The Curry Leaf* with the other business owners who were affected by the new hospital wing. Padma and Hiram, as they always did for neighborly/friendly gatherings, had provided large platters of food to make sure that no one went hungry during the meeting. As usual, Cindy had provided the wine. As for Ella, she'd brought a cake that Cricket had made. It was their kind of potluck.

Ella bounced Xander on her knee as Cliff Potter, the attorney who'd taken their case as Ella suspected to further his own career, talked in circles about how they had no chance to win against eminent domain. Unfortunately, she agreed, but she wished he would try before throwing in the towel.

Growing tired of the diatribe, Ella said, "So, you're telling us there is no way that we can win this fight, and we should just give up?"

"Well," he said, adjusting his wire rimmed glasses one more time with his middle finger, "I think the best we can hope for is successful relocation and the money to make that happen. We are talking about two very powerful entities, the hospital and the Brewster family. It might be time to cut your losses and move on with your lives. I would propose that you accept the current offer of compensation for relocation."

"Which is far too low. I thought you said we had a chance to fight this and the offer was too low?" Hiram asked.

"Well, if you could get more public opinion behind you," the lawyer offered, then paused for effect, "that would be something else. But now you've only had a couple of small articles written about you by the neighborhood newspapers. You need the city paper, who will carry it on their website, and a few television stations. You would need to rally the community. But you shouldn't count on it because the Brewsters spend a lot of money advertising their business in this town. None of the local media would jeopardize that kind of advertising revenue. They won't say a bad word about any Brewster."

"So suddenly this ad revenue stuff is an issue? Two weeks ago, you told us that you were going to arrange some press releases and talk to a few friends of friends. You told us to gear up. We've designed some flyers and are getting ready to paper the neighborhood," Ella said and then asked, "What changed?"

"Well," he said and shrugged.

"Didn't you say you were going to help us campaign to keep big business from tromping on small businesses?" she asked. "You were going to rally some support on our behalf? Make sure the launch was timed just right?"

"Well, you know I've just been swamped with other cases lately. And, you know, it isn't like you all are paying me anything. I've been more of an advisor to you. I'm not really your attorney of record."

Ella instantly understood. This jerk, who'd stood up for them and volunteered to help them, now wanted to extort money from them. Or had someone else gotten to him? Thinking of Jack, anger washed over her. He wasn't to be trusted. Hadn't he shown what he was capable of in Saint Barts? As for good old Cliff, she knew it was all too good to be true. They needed a real attorney, someone who was vested in them and not enamored with the Brewsters or the hospital. It would take money, but between the three businesses, they should be able to come up with something better than this.

"You told us not to pay you," Hiram stated, his accent getting stronger as his temper began to rise. He had come to America forty years ago with Padma as a young married couple. He believed in the American Dream, but the idea of losing his business and his home was starting to weigh heavily on the man. Ella was concerned about his health and hoped Padma and Hiram would have the drive and support to be able to start over in another location if it came to that.

"What is this, some kind of bait and switch?" said Cindy, a woman with long gray hair that she wore up in an elaborate twist. She was in her early seventies and had the hottest temper of any of them.

"Hey," Cliff said, holding up his hands, "I'm just being honest. I've had to give preferential treatment to my paying customers."

Ella shook her head in disappointment. They'd backed the wrong guy and now it was going to potentially cost them.

"If I'm to understand you correctly," Ella started, "if we want to get your full participation, even your full attention, the fastest way to get it would be to pay you. That way, we could make our way into your busy schedule. The situation you explained earlier, where we tried to pay you, and you refused, has changed. Only, you didn't tell us."

"Well," he said with a shrug.

"You say that a lot," Ella said and glanced at her fellow shop owners. "But let me guess...maybe it is too late to even start paying you? Are your interests already getting served elsewhere?"

"I don't like what I'm hearing," Cindy added. "I think Ella just hit on the ugly truth."

Xander fussed, and Padma took him off Ella's lap. Padma, the honorary grandmother in Xander's life kissed him on the cheek and he immediately calmed down. Ella always hoped

Padma would be part of his life. She was incredibly grateful for the other woman's unconditional love for Xander.

Ella noticed that Padma preferred to remain quiet when the business issues got heated.

Cliff seemed to take great interest in the spotless yellow and white batik tablecloth, refusing to make eye contact.

"I see," Ella said, her icy tone drawing everyone's attention. "At last, we have finally gotten to the truth."

With one last glance to Hiram, who nodded encouragingly, Ella continued, "Cliff, I can't speak for everyone, but I want to take my chances with another lawyer. I find your representation to be seriously lacking. And if I must face the Brewsters, I want someone on my side that I trust. The truth is, I don't trust you. You're not coming right out and saying it, but I think your loyalty has switched sides, which is completely unacceptable. You need to leave now."

"I'm with her," Cindy chimed in.

Padma and Hiram looked to each other, and then Hiram said, "You heard Ella. Go."

The lawyer stood, grabbed a piece of butter Naan with the hand not holding his briefcase and said, "You're all going to lose. The Brewsters get what they want. And right now, they want a hospital wing in their family's name. Get real. Take the money and move on with your lives."

"Just out of curiosity, how much did it cost them to get to you?" Ella asked, her mind spinning with the thought of Jack bribing her lawyer.

"I'm not going to validate any of your accusations," he said.

"Fine," she said, "you don't need to, but I know they got to you."

Hiram was more direct. He ordered, "Get out." Then he pointed at the door.

Once Cliff vacated the premises and Hiram had locked the

door behind him, they all sat back down and tried to digest what had just happened.

"Do you really think they bribed him?" Cindy asked as she helped herself to some butter chicken.

"Yes. Or maybe they just hired him away. It really doesn't matter, they got to him, and he is no longer an asset to us," Ella said, thinking of Xander and how much he looked like Jack. She only hoped he didn't have his father's questionable integrity. He looked like a Brewster. She only wondered how long it would take for Hiram, Padma, and Cindy to figure it out.

"What bullshit!" Hiram said, surprising them all. In the seven years she'd owned her shop, Ella had never heard the man swear. It was such a surprise; it made her laugh. Soon, all of them were laughing as Cindy poured more wine.

"I'll toast to that," Cindy said.

When Xander looked wide-eyed and tried his hand at the phrase, Ella quickly distracted him with a toy. The last thing she needed was a swearing baby.

"We've been pretty quiet about this," Ella said after a few minutes of composure. "We've played nice and not made a big stink, but I think it is time we took the gloves off and started speaking out. I think it is time they got to know us as people."

"Gloves?" Padma asked as she smiled at Xander.

"As in boxing," Cindy offered, her multi-colored billowing silk dress and matching bright makeup taking on a more shocking intensity if that were possible.

Padma looked frightened at the idea of a physical battle.

"Not actual fist fighting," Ella clarified, although she did think of how good it would feel to punch Jack as she took Xander back onto her lap. "I meant we need to fight smarter and really get the word out. We know we might lose. We always knew that. But here is the thing. We've been polite. We haven't made a big ruckus or been angry. But they got to our lawyer, which is, believe me, no great loss. Maybe it is time to show them what we are made of. The hearing is in three weeks from Wednesday. We need help, and I think it's time for us to ask for it."

Over the next hour, they came up with a strategy that made all of them feel something they hadn't felt in a long time: hope.

As Ella carried Xander back upstairs, she felt sad. They would lose, and she would lose this family. This moment in time would never be the same. It made her sentimental. They had all been so kind to her when she'd opened *Marcella's*, when she'd moved into her apartment, and when she found out she was having Xander. She couldn't have done it without them, and now she was harboring a secret. If she was the strong woman she wanted to be, she'd summon them all to her apartment and come clean about who Xander's father was, and then she would also tell the press. There was one thing stopping her. She looked at her sweet, innocent child, who deserved everything she could give him. She couldn't do anything but protect him, and that meant keeping his parentage a secret.

* * *

Jack hated Sunday dinner with his parents, but when Charles had his accident, the tradition had started, and short of being bedridden with a broken leg, his attendance was mandatory. Charles, the lucky bastard, had gotten off lucky by simply leaving town. And there hadn't been any judgment because, even when Charles had turned his back on the family, he was still perfect.

"Guess who called today?" Jack's mother said with enthusiasm she rarely showed for anything but the *Nordstrom* Anniversary Sale.

Jack didn't want to play, but she wanted him to.

"How is Charles?" he asked.

"He is building a well somewhere in Africa. He called on the satellite phone to let us know he was all right," she said.

"That boy has always been such a go-getter. If the governments would let him control all the social issues in the third-world countries, he could solve them, by god!" Charles III, Jack's father, said.

"Something about schools, wasn't it, darling?" his mother asked.

"And girls," his father said.

"Oh, yes. Period poverty. If you'd have ever told me that Charles would be interested in such things, I wouldn't have believed it," Dolores said. "Girls, yes. Periods, no!"

"Maybe this is a good education for him," Jack said as he cringed at his mother's words.

"I appreciate that he is always trying to better himself," Charles III offered.

Jack wanted to say, "Stop being so impressed with him. He's always been a jackass." But instead, he kept quiet.

"Oh, and I have other news!" Jack's mother said excitedly as the butler, an older man named Davis who'd been with the Brewster family for about three hundred years, served butternut squash soup with garlic butter croutons.

Jack, still trying to digest the fact he had a son, thanked Davis for serving him and asked, "Which news would this be?"

"Well, I called that sleazy lawyer those pathetic shop owners were using for their little fight against us, and I hired him to do some work for us."

Jack's thoughts immediately went to Ella. This was playing dirty pool, not that it surprised him coming from his mother. The moment Ella discovered what his mother had done, she would blame him. And he couldn't blame her for it. But when it came to Ella, he didn't need any more bad press. What would his mother's reaction be if he shared his news about Xander? It wasn't a secret he could keep indefinitely.

"Hired him for what?" he asked. "Wasn't he on a retainer for the shop owners? That would be a serious conflict of interest."

"That's the best part," his father said with a wicked smile. Never one to get in his wife's way, he had strangely joined forces with her on this task and seemed to be enjoying himself. "It is quite simple. They'd chatted, but he hadn't even asked for a single dollar in retainer. Officially, he wasn't their attorney. He lived in the neighborhood and just visited them. Can you imagine? Anyone knows you should hand the shark at least a buck before speaking to him."

"Did you ever think how it will look when he gets disbarred for this kind of behavior?" Jack asked. "You can't give legal advice and then go work for the other side. It just doesn't work like that. That turd will name names, and when he does, this relationship will not look good on you."

"Now, Jackson, listen to your father. The man said he only chatted with them as a neighbor would. He wasn't representing them," Dolores said. "There is nothing to tell. We didn't hire him. We asked him to help us."

Jack hated this kind of thing.

"Sounds like he's a real unscrupulous bastard. Just what job did you give him? And it better not be anywhere near me," Jack said, knowing how much his mother hated it when he was, in her opinion, crude.

"He's looking into the land that we have out in Hillsboro that we were thinking of developing. You know, Brewster Estates? Little mini McMansions for homeowners with only three to five million to spend…he is a land use attorney, after all."

They'd been trying to dump the Hillsboro land for years. Twenty-five miles from the heart of downtown Portland and with many severe traffic issues in between, the land was too far away for anyone to commute for work downtown. Only with high-tech expansion in Hillsboro in the last year did the land look to have potential.

"And I'm sure that land will be much more profitable for him than defending a bunch of store owners," Charles III said.

"Really, Jackson, I sometimes wonder where your loyalties lie," his mother began. "You sound like a bleeding-heart liberal. If you start setting up homeless shelters, we will know you've taken a wrong turn."

"How is that different from building a well or trying to stop period poverty?" Jack asked. "At least I look at improving the community we live in."

"I was hoping we could have a nice family dinner," Charles III said, stopping all further conversation as Davis reappeared to clear the soup dishes. A moment later, he returned with roast goose with a rich red wine cherry reduction on a bed of sautéed chanterelles and steamed asparagus spears. Dolores had decided they would be eating low-carb, so potatoes and rice were no longer on the menu.

"Now, Charles, I promise we will talk of other things in just a moment, but there was one other item that has come to my attention," Dolores began. "I need to discuss it with Jackson before we move to more pleasant subjects. Is that okay with you, darling?"

Jack set down his fork. Could she have already found out about Ella and Xander? He wouldn't put anything past his mother. She was the toughest, most unscrupulous business-woman he'd ever dealt with.

"Of course, my love," his father replied.

"What is it, Mother?" Jack asked coolly, his mind on Xander and Ella.

"Well, this is an area where you could really make a difference. Did you go to visit the shop owners and make your position clear?"

"Don't you mean your position?" he asked.

He thought it was best to be evasive. She knew something, he just wasn't sure what, and he wasn't about to show his hand.

"I don't know what has gotten into you this evening," Dolores said.

"I'm just asking a question. Haven't you successfully torpedoed them with your new lawyer?" Jack asked as he finished off his glass of *Brewster's Mount Hood Ale*.

"Jackson, don't speak to your mother in that tone," his father said, his eyes narrowing in warning.

"It's all right Charles, I just don't think that Jackson fully understands what this hospital wing means to our family. It just isn't a priority. His mind is all rummy with his new sugar alcohol."

"You could be right, dear," Charles replied, and they both laughed at their son, who was in the room, as much as they had done when he was a child.

Jack swore under his breath. There was no way he was going to get out of this mess without hurting someone that he loved.

Breaking up their joke, he said, "I spoke to Marcella Martin earlier this week."

"Oh, that bohemian tart with the sex shop," his mother said.

"She is lovely," he said feeling incredibly uncomfortable and disloyal to Ella. Part of him wanted to lash out at his mother for her unkind words, but it wouldn't do him any good, so he would defend her. "It isn't a sex shop. Please don't call it that. It is filled with very eclectic things that I would call upscale gifts. She lives in an apartment above the shop with her-year-old son. So, for her, it won't be just losing her business. It will also be losing her home. I think she is very worried about how much it will cost to relocate her shop, and I can't blame her for being worried. Her location is fantastic. She gets a lot of business from the hospital, and there isn't any place nearby that can accommodate her. I know because I looked."

His mother was looking at him strangely, and he realized he might have said too much about Ella.

"Why doesn't she live with her husband? Or is the child a bastard?" his father asked.

"That is a horrible thing to say," Jack said, feeling the heat on his cheeks, enraged with anger. "I didn't ask as it is none of my business."

"I think that says a lot about her," his mother began. "I've looked in the shop windows. From what I saw from the window displays, we would be doing the community a favor by removing her business from society."

"Have you actually been inside?" Jack asked and then realized his mistake too late. Not only was his tone challenging, but his mother also loved any sort of challenge. He'd just dangled a steak in front of a hungry lioness.

"Perhaps you're right," she said, smiling at her husband as if it were all some sort of joke. "I shall make a point to stop in next week to see exactly what kind of business this woman owns."

Jack had only consumed one beer, so he couldn't blame the alcohol. How he could be so stupid, he did not know. He supposed it came from a desire to protect and defend Ella and the life she had created for herself. Not to mention the protectiveness he felt for Xander.

"Let me know when you are going, and I'll go with you," he said.

"That would be lovely, Jackson."

"I think we should change the subject. Enough about the hospital," his father said. "Tell me about our new business venture. How long do you think it will take for us to see profits from your little rum experiment?"

When Jack had to assume Charles's position, the only way he could see to keep moving forward with *Red's Rum* was to offer his parents a vested interest in it. But he'd been careful to make sure he could cut them out anytime he wanted. Lucky for him, they didn't know that he had given himself an escape hatch. They would have never suspected that he was capable of such strategic game play.

Chapter Sixteen

E lla and Xander spent most of Monday morning on her new mission to get public support behind their efforts to save their businesses. It wasn't easy getting in to see reporters at two of the newspapers in town, but once she'd told them her side, including the story about their sleazy attorney, she'd seen the lights come on inside their brains and knew her mission was accomplished. They were papers that did little or no advertising with Brewster International Brewing.

What helped her case, too, were the special takeout packages from the *Curry Leaf* that she brought for her visit to each reporter — a personalized lunch, along with one of Cricket's cookies, and Ella's plea for help. And, happily, when she came bearing food that smelled delicious, no one turned her down.

Back in her apartment, she played with Xander, and they spent most of their free time trying to say the alphabet and learning the names of different animals.

Ella held up Xander's new stuffed giraffe, and Xander smiled.

"Giraffe," she said.

"Dada," Xander replied.

"Yes, your Dada gave you the giraffe." Ella then shook her head. Xander was a smart child.

Each time they played this game, Xander impressed her more and more. Despite her confused feelings toward his father, she had to admit Xander came from good genes.

When he went down for his nap, she designed a flyer on her computer that was less than flattering for the hospital or the Brewsters. Through a bit of creative enhancement, it showed the hospital wing depicted as a big bully with a large fist crushing three sweet little shops that appeared to be trembling. When it was finished, she called Cindy and Padma over to have a look, and after, they gave their mutual 'thumbs up.'

"I just wish I could see the look on Dolores Brewster's face when she sees the flyer," Padma said.

"It won't be good. She'll fall off her Ferragamo heels," Cindy said with a laugh. "Good job, Ella."

Ella placed an order with a local printer for five thousand copies. That task accomplished, she thought ahead to her evening with Jack.

He had played dirty pool with the attorney. The attorney was an idiot, but he was their idiot, and the way Jack had stolen the man made her very angry. Feeling as she did, she pushed her coffee maker in front of her butcher block, which contained all the knives. It was ridiculous, but she wasn't going to take any chances with a moment of uncontained rage.

She was not going to make love with him again. Not when she felt this way. No matter how much her body wanted him, craved him, she wasn't going to give in. As a safeguard, when she dressed for the evening, she wore the ugliest, least sexy underwear she owned.

* * *

"Jack, sorry it took me so long to get back to you."

Jack wasn't sure what he'd expected when Flint called him back, but his sudden case of nerves wasn't it. And he was nervous for interesting reasons. He was nervous at the idea that somehow Xander wasn't his. He believed Ella, and he certainly was an active participant in the kind of activity that gets someone pregnant, but he certainly didn't want to hear any bad news.

"I thought about calling you to satisfy my curiosity, but I wasn't sure I wanted to hear what you had to say," Jack said.

"I don't have anything definitive, just a few more questions. What we really need is a DNA test. Would the mother be open to that?"

"Flint, Xander is my son," Jack said, feeling a strange pride that came with the knowledge.

"Buddy, you'll need to take a DNA test to be sure. Don't take it on the chick's word alone."

"Xander looks exactly like me, and I trust Ella. She doesn't want my money. She'd like me to walk away. Actually, I think she'd like me to drop dead."

"That explains a few things, but trust me, kids look like a lot of people at a young age. Besides, it isn't like she named a father on the birth certificate."

"What?" Jack said as his heart took a direct hit.

"She left the father's name blank on the birth certificate."

"Why would she do that? Well, she didn't know my last name."

"Don't sleep with people who you don't know," Flint said, sounding a bit disgusted. "Actually, you are a lucky son of a bitch. Can you imagine what would happen if the press, hell, if Dolores knew about Xander? You wouldn't need to fear Xander's mother. You'd need to fear *your* mother."

Jack made an excuse to get off the phone. Flint promised to send a full report by the end of the week. Jack wasn't sure how much more he could take. The news Flint had given him stung like a bee sting to the heart. Would Ella be open to changing the birth certificate to add his name as Xander's father?

"Wait, wait, wait, Jack, how much deeper do you want me to go? You want me to do the full background? If she's the mother of the child, I think you'd want to know a few things. Like, is she involved with someone? Has she been married before? What's her financial background. Does she have any ex-husbands?"

Jack sat behind his desk, trying to take in every one of Flint's deeply disturbing questions. *Ex-husbands?* Shit. It was too much to absorb. His heart and head beat in perfect rhythm with each other. His flushed skin began to sweat as Jack contemplated putting his head between his knees to keep from passing out.

He sat there, feeling awful, and he was to blame. It must've been incredibly embarrassing for Ella when they asked her to name the father of her child, and she didn't have a name to give. The more he thought about it, the worse he felt. And it was in that realization that he knew how much more there was to the story and how awful it must have been for her to explain her pregnancy without even being able to name a father.

He thought of the letter that he'd quickly written explaining everything and apologizing for not only his quick departure but also his fake French accent. He remembered everything in detail, placing the letter and the business card in the envelope and then handing it over to the concierge with the €300 to ensure it was delivered. At that moment, he wanted to fly down to Saint Barts, find that concierge, and beat the crap out of him.

"Jack? You still there?" Flint asked.

"Yeah, I'm here. Listen, stop with everything. I'll get back to you if I want more information. I'd rather have her fill in the details as we talk."

"Oh, man…"

"What?" Jack asked, scared of what Flint would say next.

"Bro, I'm worried. Do you have feelings for her? Crap. You don't love her, do you? You sorry sack of sentimental shit."

"Thanks," Jack said and hung up on his best friend.

A few minutes before six o'clock that evening, Jack tried to relax. He wouldn't bring up anything to do with lawyers unless she did. Unfortunately, there were a lot of ways she could go with that particular subject. He'd parked the Audi in the hospital garage using his special VIP pass and spent the last three minutes trying to think of how he could bring up the subject of Xander's birth certificate with Ella. Possibly, it was a subject that could wait for a more opportune time, but he wasn't the most patient person. Besides, wouldn't she want to get it fixed? Xander deserved a birth certificate with a mother and a father.

Taking his packages with him, he made the block walk to Ella's apartment and hoped he'd made the right choices. He didn't know what babies ate. He didn't know what Ella liked. Well, he knew she liked Indian food. He should have called her and asked if he was getting the right things.

He knocked lightly on her door, not wanting to wake the baby if Xander was by chance asleep.

A long moment later, Ella opened the door and stepped back for him to enter. He didn't know what he was expecting, but it wasn't what he got. She looked at him as if he were bothering her. The smile she offered was one of tolerance, not happiness. And in her arms, she held a shy Xander, who was trying his best not to look at Jack as he buried his face in Ella's neck.

"Come on in," she said and pointed to the small kitchen. "Just put everything on the counter."

"Hi," he said, adding, "Hi, Xander."

At the sound of his name, Xander turned his head away from his mother and looked at Jack. For a moment, neither of them moved and then they both smiled at each other.

"I think he remembers you," Ella said as she bounced Xander on her hip.

"Good," Jack said, unsure of what to say next. "I didn't know what you liked, so I brought a few things."

"Thank you. You could have called and asked. What did you bring?" she asked politely, but with no warmth.

"I'm sorry, I should have called. I brought a lot, hopefully something that will work. I've got vegetarian lasagna, chicken fettuccini alfredo, macaroni and cheese, spaghetti with meatballs and salad. There is also some tiramisu, which should probably go in the fridge. Do you think he will like any of that? Do you like any of that?" Jack asked nervously. He desperately wanted to kiss Ella and hold Xander. The urge to do both in short order was killing him. But he knew both such ideas would be rebuffed before he got a chance to execute his moves. She was angry with him. He could see it in her face, and rightfully so. He had to tread carefully. Yet again, Jack beat himself up for everything that had made Ella's life hard since he'd met her that day in Saint Barts.

Chapter Seventeen

"We will make it work," Ella said flatly, glancing from the takeout bags to Jack and back again.

Ella thought that, on some level, she must hate Jack. And possibly, he could see it in her eyes. She had strong feelings that she could only, unfortunately, categorize as hate for too many reasons to count. And now, he was trying to manage her. She felt it. How dare he? She had a baby and figured out life alone without any help, aside from the kindness of her neighbors. She ran a business and kept the doors open despite being pregnant and then recovering from birth. She'd figured out childcare and found a way to make her life work. Now he thought he could buy her dinner, a dinner she hadn't been consulted on, and make it all better. What a bunch of bullshit.

She couldn't get over it or let it go. Jack had bought out some poor Italian restaurant when he could have simply called her and asked her what Xander could eat. And hey, he could have even asked what she might want. But it was better to assume. Like he assumed the concierge would deliver a note to her instead of stopping back by her hotel to tell her in person. This man was a mess. Well, he could be a mess on his own time.

He was a selfish jerk.

He was also spoiled. Spoiled, rich, and stupid.

He thought he could worm his way into their lives by

showing up with dinner and flowers. Seriously? How did that make up for the last twenty months? Yes, he'd brought her flowers. She could see them on the counter and wasn't about to acknowledge them. She hadn't been given flowers in years. And so he'd guessed correctly and brought something that was velvety red and smelled like roses, her damn favorite. She wasn't going to give him the satisfaction of knowing he'd guessed correctly. They didn't even come close to making up for what she'd been through. Besides, she didn't have a vase. Were a bunch of roses going to look good in an old peanut butter jar? Probably not. Served him right.

"Let's have a look at the mac and cheese. It is one of Xander's favorites. But if the cheese is too strong or sharp, he won't like it," she said, stepping forward as Jack started placing container after container on her counter. "I make it for him just the way he likes."

"Can I put the tiramisu in the fridge?" he asked.

"Sure," she nodded. "Put it next to the Curry Leaf takeout boxes."

Yes, it was a dig. She wondered if he'd take the bait.

"How was your day?" he asked, surprising her after he'd put away the tiramisu without comment. Apparently, he missed the jab or ignored it entirely. So, what? He wanted to play happy family? She could play this game.

"Busy coming up with ways to save my business and my apartment, which I'm sure you will hear about soon," she said and watched Jack tense. *That's right*, she thought. *Did you think a little Italian food would make me forget what you and your family are trying to do to me? Think again, jerk! I'm coming for you. Hard.*

"Good for you," Jack said without condescension as he opened the container with the mac and cheese. "Smells like normal mac and cheese. I think he'll like it. What do you think?"

What the hell game was he playing with her? Damn it!

Ella bit her lip from offering an unpleasant comment as she glanced at the container and nodded. What Jack didn't know was that Xander had sophisticated tastes, despite the occasional smooshed Vienna sausage. She set Xander in his highchair and said, "Here you go, sir. Your dinner will be here in a moment." Then, she took her time tying a ducky bib around Xander.

Jack stood back, but she felt his eyes on her as she moved around the kitchen and got the things Xander would need for dinner. "Don't wait for me. As soon as we get him situated, I'll sit down," she said as she passed him, got out baby silverware, and filled a sippy cup with milk from the fridge.

But Jack didn't move. He just watched her, which was completely unnerving. Well, he was in for a surprise. Eleven-month-old babies didn't know the first thing about manners, but she'd worked with Xander, and he could use his fork pretty well.

Placing little pieces of salad at one end of his tray, she added a tiny amount of dressing and then blew on a spoonful of the mac and cheese before placing it on the other end and smashing it to a pulp.

"Let's try a meatball, too," she said and held her hand out for another container. If Jack wasn't going to serve himself and sit down, then he could help her. Before she had to ask a second time, the container with meatballs was placed in her hand.

Jack appeared mesmerized by the entire process of getting Xander his dinner. Welcome to Baby 101, she thought. She was pleased she wouldn't need to worry about the temptation to sleep with Jack. There was no way her actions now would bring about any lustful thoughts for the man watching her.

As she cut up a small meatball into tiny pieces, she heard a cork extracting from a bottle. Was he seriously opening a wine bottle? Like this was some romantic evening? Turning, she watched Jack smile as he poured wine into two lowball glasses, as if he was adding civility to this evening meal.

At last, Xander was exploring his food, and they were looking at each other.

"Chianti?" he asked.

"What, no rum?" she asked sarcastically.

"Thought you might have lost your taste for it. Besides, it doesn't go well with Italian. What would you like to have? Or should we just do this buffet style?" he asked.

"Really, help yourself, and then I'll do the same," she said, hearing the edge in her voice. She'd had a long day, and he wasn't making it any easier. His politeness was pissing her off.

"Ladies first," he said and made himself busy with the bouquet of red roses that neither of them had mentioned.

Would he just schlep some food and sit his butt down in the chair? This polite hero crap was gnawing at her.

As she watched out of the corner of her eye, he opened a box that contained a beautiful cut-glass crystal Waterford vase. Then he added water and a packet of flower preservatives. He placed the roses, of which there were at least two dozen, in the water. The man knew he was being watched and didn't know what he was doing.

Ella set down the empty plate she was holding and took over the flower arrangement.

"They are very pretty," she offered flatly and wished she could have kept her mouth shut.

"I should have brought them last time," he said, his body close to hers, too close.

"I wouldn't have liked that."

"Why not?" he asked standing beside her so that his lips were close enough to her ear that she thought he might try to kiss her.

"I don't know," she whispered. "But it would have been wrong. This is kind of wrong, too, but since they are here, I'll try to enjoy them."

"I hope you do," he said.

His arm gently wrapped around her from behind. Initially, she stiffened, but her body would not allow her to fight as she knew she should. Leaning back, she brushed against the more solid form behind her. She didn't want to fight. Heck, she wanted to go back to one of the best times in her life. She just didn't know if it was all real.

"This isn't wrong," he said, kissing her neck. "Nothing that feels this good is wrong. It might be a little strange, but I'm finally where I need to be."

Steeling herself, she placed her hands on the counter for support as the scent of roses wafted up and around her. "Would it be possible for us to sit down and share a meal without sex getting in the way? Maybe we could even talk, like real people, and get to know something about each other."

"This isn't sex. This is just attraction. This is me needing to touch you and be close to you. Two people and their child, hanging out like other families do," Jack said as he kissed her one final time, just in the hollow of her throat where her neck met her shoulder. A spot that he knew was not only sensitive but one of her very favorite places to be touched.

"Now, let's eat, and we can chat about mundane things like your first pet and my first car. Would you like that?"

"Yes," she whispered in surrender as he let go of her and grabbed an empty plate. Damn him for knowing what buttons to push when it came to her.

Ella's hands were shaking as she dished up a small portion of spaghetti and meatballs to go with a large portion of salad. Apparently, Jack shared her taste in food, as his plate looked almost identical to hers.

They sat across from each other at the café table in her kitchen, Xander joining them with his tray touching the edge of the table. She tried not to think of the fact that this was their first family dinner. He'd used the word 'families.' It was okay for her to say it, but when he said it, that was different altogether. It just meant more to him to join the family she'd already created with Xander. And she wasn't ready to give him that access.

How long had she dreamed of this? And now that Jack was in their lives, she was a mess and throwing up boundary walls. To what? Stop him? Make him go away? What was wrong with her? He was what she had wished for, what she had dreamt about, and now he was here. And there wasn't anger or denial on his part. Heck, he had acknowledged that Xander was his son. He wanted to help. He wanted to be a part of Xander's life. It was the best-case scenario for their situation, so why was she being such a bitch to him?

Fear. She was terrified. What if he went away? What if he left her again? What she went through in Saint Barts had been so awful. To think he didn't care...She hadn't felt pain like that ever in her life. She still wasn't over it. And this time, the stakes were much higher.

She hadn't slept well since the moment he'd stepped into her shop. Looking down at her dinner, she no longer had an appetite. And it wouldn't matter. He'd want Xander, but he wouldn't want her. If she kept acting like a bitch, he'd sue her for custody of Xander, marry some other woman, and create a family without her. And what about her hospital expenses and student loans? She could lose everything.

"How is it?" he asked expectantly.

"Fine...good," she said and took a sip of her wine. "Thank you for all of this. I just don't have much of an appetite. I'm sorry."

"Is it the hospital expansion or me?" he asked, placing his fork on his plate and taking a sip of his wine as he waited for an answer.

"I don't know how to answer that. It is just a lot to take in. My emotions are all over the place. I don't mean to sound like such a bitch. You've been nothing but nice, and I guess it isn't what I was expecting," she said. She would have continued, but

Xander dropped his fork to the floor. Ella bent down, but Jack was quicker. He got up, went to the sink, washed the fork, and dried it.

"I understand. This is a lot for both of us to take in," he said as he returned the fork to Xander's outstretched hand.

"Thank you," she said and then turned to Xander. "What do you say?"

"Tankyu," he said and smiled at Jack. The effect was devastating. Jack couldn't speak for a moment, and she didn't press him, but she did mutter, "I need some time."

When he regained his composure, his words startled her.

"I understand. I want, no, I think I need...I need to know everything. From the moment you suspected you were pregnant to how it felt to hold him for the first time. I need to know. I missed it, and had I known, I'd have been there for every moment. I'm so sorry." His hand slid across the table and grabbed hold of hers. She couldn't meet his eyes. She didn't want to let him know how much he'd gotten to her. What his words meant.

Blinking away tears, she nodded and glanced at Xander, who'd lost interest in his food, but was staring at his mother wide-eyed. For the next few moments, no one said anything, but Ella allowed Jack's hand to remain where it was. Finally, she broke the silence.

"And I want to know about the father of my child. I need to know what kind of person you are if you intend to be a part of our lives. There are traits that Xander has that aren't mine, and I wonder if they are yours."

Jack's fingers rubbed gentle circles over the top of her hand as he smiled at her. "That would be wonderful. If he did anything like I do, wow, that would be so...I don't have words. And for the record, I intend to be in your lives. You can ask me anything."

Pulling her hand away, Ella folded her arms over her chest

and asked, "Okay then, subject change. Did you bribe my sleazebag lawyer to find out everything we were planning to use against you and the hospital?"

Jack set down his wine and swallowed with great difficulty. Then, to Ella's irritation, he started laughing. She hadn't seen that laugh in almost two years. She wanted to sink into the sound of a laugh she had only heard for one night of her life, but she could not forget who he was, her enemy.

"Okay, onto the easy subject. Nice transition, by the way. But seriously, to answer your question. No, I've never met your lawyer," he said once he contained himself, "but he's got to be a jerk if he could be hired away by my family. My mother, to be exact. She bragged that she did it at dinner last night. Trust me, he's an idiot. You can do better, and I think you should."

"Your *mother* hired him?" Ella asked, having momentarily forgotten that Jack came with a family which included Dolores Brewster, Xander's grandmother and one of the largest, most influential socialites in the city. Ella hadn't considered how personally Dolores Brewster might be involved in the hospital expansion.

"She is ruthless. And she scares me a bit."

"She raised you, really?" Ella asked.

"Look, I don't think we should talk about the hospital expansion. I have a special interest in you and Xander. I think my parents feel my lack of loyalty, but they don't know why. But I wouldn't trust them. I *don't* trust them. I'm no longer so much on the Brewster side of things. I want to be there for you, to support you, but the project is way beyond my personal understanding of the matter. It is business and way beyond my influence at this point. Here is my best advice. Get a better lawyer. Stress how much you and the other two shops are part of the community. Try to gain community support. Start talking to anyone who will listen."

"You care about my shop and this apartment?" Ella asked as she wiped off Xander's hands and face with a damp paper towel.

"I care about you and Xander. I care about anything that upsets you. You will have to be satisfied with that answer. Once the hearing is over, we'll sort the rest out," Jack said as he released Xander from the highchair and pulled him into his arms.

To Ella's surprise, Xander went willingly. Seeing the two of them together was almost more than she could take. They were carbon copies of each other. She knew almost exactly what Xander would look like as an adult. He'd look exactly like his father except with her blue eyes. He was going to slay the world. Women would fall at his feet.

"Can you say Dada?" Jack asked Xander, who smiled as Jack bounced him and then walked him around the kitchen. "How about Daddy?"

Ella just watched as Xander shyly buried his head in Jack's shoulder, which made Jack smile so tenderly that she thought she might break. Xander knew there was something special about Jack. She could see it in the way her son looked at his father. She thought about telling him about the giraffe incident that afternoon but held back.

It took Ella a few moments to find her voice. "I think it's time for his bath."

Knowing that there was no way she could get rid of Jack, nor did she want to, she led them into the bathroom and started drawing a bath, to Xander's delight.

The next half hour knocked the wind out of Ella's sails. She sat next to the bathtub and watched as Xander and Jack played with Xander's toys. Xander was delighted to have such an enthusiastic playmate. At one point, she wondered if Jack was going to get in the tub with Xander. Silently, she wondered if Jack was the missing piece they needed in their lives. He added something, but she wasn't sure it was the right thing. As a single parent, she'd tried her best, but it was so obvious that Xander basked in the attention of a father figure.

At last, the water was growing cold, and Xander's energy finally started to ebb. When she took him out of the tub and wrapped him in a towel, he cried and cried.

"I know," she said, rubbing his back as she dried him.

"What can I do?" Jack asked, his shirt drenched with bathwater.

"Nothing, he's just tired. He ran out of steam. We'll get him into his pajamas and then read him a story. He should fall right to sleep," she said as she walked with Jack into Xander's bedroom and laid him down on his changing table.

After she got him into his diaper and pajamas, she handed him to Jack so she could get his crib ready. Unfortunately for Jack, Xander only wanted his mother at that moment and began crying in earnest.

Jack looked stricken as he bounced with Xander in his arms and tried to soothe him. Ella took him back in her arms and handed him his BeauBeau. Then, she sat with him in the rocker and started to rock him to sleep.

* * *

Jack sat on the floor beside the rocker, where Ella rocked their child. He thought of all the nights she'd done this same routine. He couldn't figure out how she did it all. He wasn't just impressed. He felt ashamed for not being there for her. She was the most remarkable woman he'd ever met.

She didn't know it yet, but he was going to do everything in his power to give both her and Xander a great life. He just hoped she'd want him to be a part of it.

After a few minutes, Xander drifted to sleep in his mother's arms. Ella stood gently and put Xander in his crib. Then she covered him with a blanket and put his BeauBeau beside him.

Grabbing his arm as she passed, Ella led Jack out of the bedroom and gently pulled the door closed.

Glancing at her watch, she shook her head, "Amazing, it's only 8:30. How did we manage that?"

"Is that early?"

"Yes, about twenty minutes. I can't believe it."

Jack pulled her into his arms and held her close. He was surprised she didn't try to resist him, but then she was probably too tired.

"That was amazing," he said. "You're amazing. I'm in awe of you."

Sighing, she relaxed against him, her body relaxing. "It was nothing I haven't done a few hundred times. Now, I'm tired, and you're damp."

"How long has it been since you've had any time to yourself?" he asked.

Lifting her head, she said, "I usually get between nine and ten each day. That is my catch-up time."

"I have an idea," he said, looking down into her tired face. She was exhausted, he could see it. Maybe he could help.

"I don't think it is a good idea for us to have sex—"

"Hear me out, please," he said, kissing her forehead.

"Okay," she said and leaned against him. Maybe she shouldn't have ruled sex out so completely.

"How about you draw yourself a bath in that tub while I clean up the kitchen? I'll bring you another glass of wine or dessert, or both, you pick."

That sounded better than sex. Well, basic sex—not sex with him.

"Why are you being so nice to me?" she asked, suspicious.

"Because I haven't been there for you, and it is something I can do today to make you feel better." He placed his finger to her lips. "Don't argue, don't speak. Get undressed and go soak in your tub. Oh, you can tell me if you'd like another glass of wine or dessert or both, but don't say anything else."

"Wine," she said, a sparkle coming into her eyes.

"Good, now go. I'll deliver."

Ten minutes later, just as he'd finished picking up the last of the mac and cheese from the floor, he heard the water stop running in the tub. He poured a glass of wine for Ella and another for himself and made his way to the bathroom.

The lights were out, and she'd lit candles, which reminded him of another night when she'd done the same thing. Stepping inside the bathroom, he found her lying back in the tub, her eyes shut, the water bobbing around the swells of her breasts.

Sitting on the damp bathmat next to her, he watched as she slowly opened her eyes and looked at him, showing tenderness for him for the first time that night.

"You do constantly surprise me," she said. "I don't know how I feel about that."

"I try to use my prowess for good and not evil. Want me to rub your back?"

"I think it would be best for all parties concerned if you didn't touch me."

"Really? That's no fun. Besides, I thought your body needed me," he said, watching the small smile form on her lips as her eyes closed.

"Yes, my body wants the satisfaction of you," she said. "I wouldn't want you to feel used, and that would be what I was doing. Using you for sex. I'm sure that's wrong."

"I'm not complaining. What do you say you scoot over in that tub and let me join you? Then you can use me all you want. Use me up for all I care."

Ella opened her eyes and looked at him, letting all the niceties she displayed for Xander's benefit drop away. "Fine, get in the tub and make me feel good. But don't for a moment get the idea that you've wormed your way into our lives. Trust is earned, and you are on probation. So you've made points tonight. Don't blow it. This is about me making sure you feel guilty for what you're doing to my business and my home, even if your mother is to blame for the lawyer. I want you to care, so it hurts you as much as it hurts me. Still want to get in the tub?"

Jack looked at Ella, saw through the tough façade, and knew they were both equally affected.

"Absofuckinglutely," he said and began to shed his clothing.

Chapter Eighteen

What had Ella told herself all day when she thought of her evening with Jack? No sex.

What was Ella about to do? Have sex.

She drank down the glass of wine, moved the empty glass out of harm's way, and moved over as Jack joined her in the large, clawfoot tub. She loved the sight of him, his body. She couldn't wait to touch him. She had it bad. By the time he'd settled himself, she was leaning back against him, the hair of his chest gently tickling the skin on her back. She turned and sought his mouth as his hand found her breast.

It was a large tub, but not large enough. Too much wet skin was exposed to the air, and the need to get close caused a certain amount of contained frustration.

Before long, they'd left the bathtub behind for her bed. Before she could catch her breath from the veracity of Jack's kisses, she was on her narrow queen-sized bed. Was she drunk? No. Tipsy? Oh yes.

When they were finally one, she forgot all about hospitals, gift shops, and family empires. She wanted only this, she thought, as a moan escaped her lips.

"Right there," he whispered, feeling her pleasure as his eyes locked with hers. Angling his body, he hit the sensitive spot again and again, causing her breath to hitch.

"I like to touch you right there," he whispered as she took

hold of his face and pulled him close, kissing him only to break away as her body spun out of control…she looked at the ceiling, feeling his eyes on her. Meeting his gaze, she felt the wave of emotion rapturing in her body and looked away.

She couldn't help it; she stole a glance at him again and saw passion in his eyes.

His climax followed soon after, their arms reaching for each other, doing everything they could to get closer. Ella clung to Jack, savoring the moments as their connection was its strongest. Eventually, her brain stepped in and made her separate from that which she craved.

Ella reached for a pillow and pulled it close. Jack wasn't finished with her. He pushed through her resolve and encircled her with his arms. She let go of the pillow and burrowed against him. She was so tired, and he felt so good. She drifted to sleep in the soft, warm bed with the father of her child holding her in his embrace.

Awaking with a start, she sat up, the morning sun bright in the windows. Last night had been so sensual, so wonderful, that it reminded her of only one other night in her life. Happily, both nights involved the same man. For a moment, she was confused. Had it really happened? Or was it a wonderful dream?

Grabbing the clock next to her, she yelped in alarm. It was eight thirty, and she was alone in bed. She was already two hours late for her schedule. Jumping out from under the covers, she landed on the ancient hardwood floors with a thud. A moment later, she found her robe and threw open her bedroom door. Xander must be crazy with worry. Poor guy never slept past six-thirty. What was she thinking?

She ran to his room and found his crib empty. Filled with panic, she ran to the living room and stopped.

Xander and Jack sat together on the couch watching something that from the noise of it was very child friendly.

Jack turned his head, looked at her, and smiled.

"Look, Xander. Mama's awake."

Xander smiled broadly and said, "Mama!"

Ella put her hand on her chest to quiet her thudding heart as she looked at Jack and said, "I overslept."

"I turned off your alarm. I thought you needed your sleep," he said as his eyes ran over her. "Especially considering how little sleep we got."

He winked and smiled. She remembered more of the night before. They'd made love three times. She remembered waking him twice with kisses to initiate intimacy. He didn't turn her down. He just stepped up to the plate and delivered. She felt feral, wanton. She hadn't been able to get enough of him. From the look he gave her, he didn't seem to mind.

"Don't look at me. I don't look good in the morning," she said, adding accusingly, "You stayed over." State the obvious, why don't you?

"You look beautiful, and I slept better last night than I have for almost a week. I didn't realize how tired I was. Would you like some coffee?"

Ella sighed and said, "Sure. Hey, could you stay until I get out of the shower? I won't be long."

"Take as long as you want, Xander's already had breakfast, and if the office needs me, they can call me," he said, looking very much like the pirate with his five o'clock shadow, rumpled hair, and wrinkled clothes. If Xander was still having morning naps, Jack wouldn't be safe from her. She needed to get a grip.

"Thank you," she managed and turned toward the bathroom.

As she took her shower, she thought of the night before and felt shivers as the water cascaded over her skin. They'd fallen asleep in each other's arms, and it had felt wonderful to snuggle against Jack and feel his body spooning hers. Then she awakened and made the most of having him in her bed.

A moment later, there was a knock on the door.

"Yes?" she asked, peeking out from behind the shower curtain.

Jack arrived with a coffee mug in one hand and Xander in the other.

"I didn't know how you take your coffee, but I can get some sugar or cream," he said as he placed the mug in her outstretched hand.

* * *

"Black is fine. Thank you," she said and smiled. It was the first genuine smile he'd seen on her face since Saint Barts and its loveliness had a serious effect on him. Leaning forward, he kissed her quickly on the lips. When she didn't retreat, he kissed her again.

"You are so beautiful," he said, and she shook her head in response. "No, I mean it, you are incredibly beautiful."

"Thank you," she said shyly and kissed Xander on the cheek, avoiding Jack's gaze.

"Last night was wonderful," he said.

"I'm sorry if I was a bit…um…relentless."

"Don't be," he said, turning and taking Xander with him back to the living room, where they sat and happily watched cartoons.

By the time Ella was dressed and had dried her hair, Jack was trying to think of ways to stay longer but knew he was fighting a losing battle. He wanted to make plans and tell her he would be there that night, every night, if she'd let him, but he knew it was too soon and that she would rebuff him. Heck, she was already regretting what they had shared the night before, he could see it in her eyes. He wished she could just see it for what it was: a relationship, an attraction they could not and should not deny. This kind of connection was rare. He'd never had anything like it before.

"You don't need to stay while I put on my makeup," she said, appearing in a black leather skirt, red silk blouse, black stockings, and stiletto heels.

"Do you only wear red and black?" he asked, taking in the outfit and silently wondering why she didn't have a horde of men at her door that she had to beat off with a stick. The very idea had his jealousy sparking to life.

"Only in the store," she replied, "I dress a little edgy, but red is my favorite color."

"I guessed that," he said. "You look gorgeous. Take your time with the makeup. I don't have any pressing engagements this morning."

"Thank you, but don't you need to go home and change? You can't go to the offices looking all rumpled and in need of a shave," she said.

"I live very close to here," he said.

"Where?" she asked, coming out of the bathroom with a mascara wand in her hand.

Jack got off the couch, taking Xander, who was in his lap, with him. He walked over to the window facing the west hills and pointed to his house, which was becoming more visible as the leaves fell off the large maple trees lining the street below.

"I'm just up there," he said and turned toward her. The desire to reach out and touch her was overwhelming.

"You live on Vista Hill? Which street?"

"Vista Drive."

"You live on Vista?" she asked, the tone of her voice going from warm to guarded in an instant.

"See the red brick house with the white windows and black shutters?"

"That's *your* house?"

"It was my grandmother's. It's cold and big and not at all cozy. Not like your place. I kind of hate it, actually."

"Wow," she said and went back to the bathroom. Some of

the magical happiness that had surrounded them disappeared. Jack once again felt the rift of their different worlds. He thought of all the things he wanted to say, including that he felt more at home in her apartment than he'd ever felt in that drafty old mausoleum, but it wasn't the right time. The mood had shifted, and she would not take his intent in the right way.

Looking down at Xander, he kissed his son, hugging him close. Xander smiled up at him and managed, "Dada."

Jack looked down at him and whispered, "I love you, little man."

Xander smiled and sucked on his giraffe.

Five minutes later, Ella walked into the living room and announced, "Okay, I think we're ready. Thanks for staying while I was in the shower. Come on, Xander, time to go."

Xander looked questioningly up at Jack. "I'm sorry buddy. Time to go to work." Turning to Ella, he said, "You didn't have any breakfast."

"I don't usually, but if I get hungry, I grab a bagel on the way back from Xander's daycare. Okay, Xander, we need to go. We'll be late if we don't hurry." She took Xander from Jack and helped him into his coat. Turning to Jack as almost an afterthought, she said, "Before you leave, I'll look outside and make sure that the alley is clear."

"I think we need to talk about this," Jack said, not liking the idea of sneaking around. Sitting on the couch, he crossed his legs, indicating that he wasn't going anywhere. "I don't know if keeping this secret is a good idea anymore. I don't think I want to keep Xander a secret anymore."

"Oh really?" she said with a certain measured censure, looking at him as if he'd grown a dunce cap out of his forehead.

"Please sit down. Let's talk for a moment," he said and reached out for Xander, who dove willingly from his mother to his father.

Ella sighed and sat down. "You aren't worried about your personal reputation or your family's reputation?"

"No, not really. It will be a shock, but they'll deal with it," he said.

"The timing is lousy. Think about it. What would the hospital board think? Did you uphold their standard of morality? A child you didn't know about? Especially when the mother owns a store that is rumored to be an upscale sex shop?"

"Ella, please...it won't be that bad."

"Yes, it will. Your family's name wouldn't just be taken through the mud. It'd look like I blackmailed you or seduced you, or something I haven't even thought of yet. I'll come out of this looking like an old-fashioned harlot. If the hospital paid me money, which they will, it would look like you tried to score one for the mother of your child. Then they will suspect you of something fraudulent. You really haven't thought this through, have you? How about that mother of yours who keeps setting you up with nice girls from the right families? Do you think she'd welcome a surprise grandchild with open arms? How about the sex shop owner who claims you are her baby daddy?"

Jack knew she was right. It would be a huge mess. He had his own selfish, determined reasons for wanting what he wanted, and he was going to find a way to make it happen.

"I just think that his birth certificate should list me as his father," he said. "And I want to be in his life. I want to be in your life."

Ella shook her head. "His birth certificate stays blank for the time being. I'm doing this for you. Now, promise me you won't tell anyone about your relationship with Xander. I mean it, Jack. Not anyone. Oh, excuse me, except your lawyer. But I really want you to think hard about this. Maybe you should just walk away. I'm sure it would make your family happy in the long run."

Jack saw red but tried to keep a handle on it.

"What the hell are you talking about?" Jack asked, keeping his voice even, his eyes moving down to Xander, who was playing with BeauBeau.

"I've been thinking a lot about this. It would be easier for you," Ella said, her voice cracking a bit as she said it.

"You actually think I could just walk away?" Jack asked, pulling Xander closer as he spoke. "From him? From you?"

"It would allow you to continue on with your life. Someday, your mother will find you a nice girl with whom you can have the perfect wedding, everything. You'll have more children. We won't bother you," Ella said, the words not matching the emotion he could see in her eyes.

Jack smiled, but inside, he was seething.

"I'm going to try to remain calm because of who I'm holding. Don't you ever say this kind of thing to me again," he said. "If I went away, it wouldn't be easier for him. He needs a father, and I need him. I want to be that for him. I'm here. I'm in your lives, and I'm not going away. And by the look on your face and how it feels when we make love, I don't think you want me to go. And that's good because I'm not going anywhere."

"What if your family convinces you to take him away from me?" she asked, the tears forming in her eyes.

"Ella, I would never, ever let that happen," he said. "Is that why you won't put my name on the birth certificate? You don't want me to have any paternal rights?"

"No...I don't know," she said, her eyes filled with pain. "I don't know what you're capable of, but you have the one thing I don't: power, backed with money."

There was no way he was going to convince her. He needed to de-escalate the situation. "Let's get past the hearing, and then we can re-evaluate. We will have time to think about everything and how we want to move forward. Would you be open to that?"

"What about *Red's Rum?*" she asked, raising a single eyebrow, a trait he didn't know she possessed. Years in the future, he would remember that single gesture as he sat across from Xander, who was his doppelganger, while they ate family dinner and discussed Xander's future plans. He was always surprised when he would say something, and Xander would raise one eyebrow like his mother. And in that moment, Jack would smile and realize that their smart, talented boy had picked up more than a few of Ella's lovely traits. It was easier to see Ella in their other children, but Xander was special and kept things close to the vest.

Jack smiled at Ella's raised eyebrow. A part of her body he wanted very much to kiss. He didn't know how all the chips would fall, but there would be winners and losers. People he loved were going to get hurt, but his focus was now on Xander and Ella. Everyone else could jump off the Broadway Bridge for all he cared.

He smiled, knowing that she was testing him, seeing if she could scare him into leaving. "Nice try," he said. "But next to you and Xander, *Red's Rum* and the hospital expansion mean nothing to me. I'd give it all up in a heartbeat."

"You don't even know me that well," she said. "You just know very basic things about me, but you don't even know if we are compatible. We know there are a lot of things we don't agree on."

"Do you think the passion that we have for each other you can find with just anyone?"

"I'm sure it will wear out in time," she said, her sparkling eyes looking uncertain.

"Trust me, it won't," he said, glancing down at Xander, who was watching the cartoon with deep interest. "We haven't even begun to delve into the depths of the passion we have for each other. And I could mention that I know you very well. You are the mother of my child. Hopefully, my children. Because I'd like at least one more, maybe two."

"I..." She didn't know what to say to that and he just nodded. He watched as her lip trembled and he smiled, she was a very complex woman. He liked each and every layer she chose to reveal to him. Today, it was vulnerability and fear. He wanted to pull her close and make everything okay, but she still didn't trust him, not yet.

Pointing to his heart and then to Xander, he said, "That child is mine, my son. I'd give my life for him. Believe it or not, I care very deeply for you, too. I've never felt this way. When I think of my time in the Caribbean, I don't think about learning to make rum. I think about you. I don't know what it means, but I'll be damned if I walk away to make things easier for me. That isn't happening. So I'm not going anywhere. You're not going anywhere. There has to be a solution. We just need to give it some time."

Ella looked away from him, took a deep breath, and said, "I don't know what I'll do if I lose the shop and my apartment. I'm scared."

"I know, but you don't need to be. I'll help you," he said. "You have me."

"I don't want your help," she said, as she stubbornly crossed her arms in defiance. "I built my shop by myself. I don't want a partner."

"Then maybe I should say that I will make sure that Xander's welfare will always come first," he said. "And by default, that means I'm watching out for the mother of my child as well."

"Maybe we shouldn't see each other until after the hearing," she said, her voice barely a whisper.

"I can't do that," he said, "I have to see you and Xander. I just have to. But if you're worried about your neighbors, we can start meeting at my house."

"I need to think about it," she said, pulling back. "I never thought I'd see you again. And here you are."

"I'm very happy that fate gave me a second chance. And I don't think I can ever tell you how thankful I am for this sweet little boy," he said, looking down at Xander, who looked up at him and smiled.

"I need a couple of days to think about this."

"Please don't take him away," he said, looking at Ella to see if he could detect any sort of motive in that direction.

"I wouldn't do that," she said, her eyes twinkling with anger. "I just want a few days without you here to think about all that has happened. I'm starting my war with the hospital and you today. I'm sorry it must be this way. I don't want it to be this way."

Turning to Xander, he said, "Hey, Xander, we need to go, buddy. Your mom will be late and wants to wage war on Daddy."

"Dada," Xander said and smiled, happy that whatever talk had been happening was now over, and they were all friends again.

Jack kissed Xander and then Ella. She kissed him back, and for the first time, he felt hope.

Chapter Nineteen

"Ouch," Ella said as she used a staple gun to tack up another poster on a telephone pole on busy 23rd Avenue. Her wrist was really starting to give out. She felt the power of the staple gun all the way to her elbow. She thought it might have given her tennis elbow. Damn it!

She could have paid one of the neighborhood kids to staple up the posters on the poles, which was the normal neighborhood practice, but this way, she could visit each shop between telephone poles and ask them to display her poster on their doors or windows. Her success rate for neighborhood support for her campaign of the "Small Business Coalition of NW Portland" was a whopping 90%. They'd even started to get donations for their legal fund. And, best of all, it saved her wrist.

She had even perfected what she said to her fellow store owners. Once she'd pleaded her case and gotten them to feel the vulnerability she was now experiencing at the hands of big business, her case was all but won.

Each afternoon for the last week, Ella had left Cricket in the shop, thanks to Cricket's new class schedule. Ella had taken her message about the impact of the new hospital wing to the streets. Sometimes Padma went with her, adding her heavy accent to their rehearsed speech about business owners taking on big corporations. Ella really liked it when the store owners talked about the hospital wing as just another way for the Brewsters to try and get their name on something that had to do with

Portland. It was a hospital. So what? They seemed to really like to name parks. Why didn't they stick to parks?

Thanks to their daily walks, Ella had been interviewed by three of the local television stations. She even had volunteers offer up lovely documented research that seriously put into question Good Faith Hospital's actual need for a huge orthopedic wing. What was becoming known as "The Anti-Expansion Protest" was moving the needle. The Small Business Coalition of NW Portland was becoming a familiar name to the public.

They had hired a new lawyer who could smell the blood in the water with the changing tides. He'd rejected the last two offers from the hospital and was preparing for a fight. Steve Stevenson was a tall blond man who sported a tan and liked getting his photo taken with Ella as she went door to door with her message of underdog unfairness. He looked good on camera, and the feeling was mutual. Ella wasn't sure he was a vast improvement over Cliff, but at least he'd taken a retainer, wouldn't be purchased by the Brewsters, and was known around town for helping the underdog. He made a good set of hands to help hand out fliers. He had probably already picked out the actor that would portray him in the movie version of these events. Ella's money was on Ryan Gosling.

Some of Ella's television interviews had been so successful they'd forced the hospital to make ill-worded, harried rebuttals. Sometimes, the news stations got crafty and followed hospital board members going about their business in their natural habitat. One such rebuttal had come from a member of the board with a personal interest in the hospital wing and Ella.

* * *

Jack was caught by one such aggressive reporter as he left his plush office in the Brewster Building on his way to his new distillery to check on the bottling of *Brewster's Red's Rum*. Moonshine had alerted him that they were being followed. The three-block walk was meant to be a nice distraction from his thoughts of Ella and Xander. Over the last week, Ella hadn't allowed Jack to see them. She was citing fatigue and the need to put some distance between them so that she could think about what she wanted to do regarding Xander.

He'd about reached his breaking point. Sleeping was a fantasy. Fatigue was becoming a familiar friend. As stressed and needy as he was, he totally missed the KPDX news anchor when she bombarded him five feet outside the new distillery building. Despite Moonshine's early warning system of a growl, Jack nearly jumped out of his skin when she shrieked at him.

"Mr. Brewster! Mr. Brewster! Could I get you to comment on The Small Business Coalition of NW Portland's campaign to stop the hospital expansion project?"

"I really cannot comment about the plans for The Brewster Orthopedic Wing at Good Faith Hospital," he said with a tight smile. "Please don't get too close to my dog. He might bite."

Moonshine only bit his specially formulated kibble, table scraps, and treats. He'd tried for some squirrels in the backyard, but they didn't discuss it because his lack of finesse was still embarrassing to both dog and owner.

"But Mr. Brewster, as a business owner, don't you have sympathy for the store owners? You'll be putting good people out of business for this monument to the Brewster Family. Do you think about that?" the smiling, toothy reporter asked.

Jack paused and then offered a surprising, "Yes, I do. It's not fair to them at all. I don't want to put them out of business. I respect what they have done. It might not be on the scale of a global company, but having your own business is a big deal. It shows a great determination and should be celebrated. These people are brave entrepreneurs, and what they have done is no small achievement. I want to help them relocate at no expense to them and little or no impact on them. I don't want to cost them business. I want to help improve their business with a better location, better traffic, etc. That is my goal. Now, if we could get everyone on the same page, I think it would be a good deal. Unfortunately, few agree with me. I need to see more flexibility and creativity from all parties. Then, we can have a win-win. Without it, we have a really sad situation."

The reporter, now surprised, recovering with the skill of a recoiling snake asked, "Well, then why would you endorse moving forward if the parties are unwilling to work together?"

"Who said I do? The expansion was voted on and approved by a majority vote of the twelve members of the Good Faith Hospital Board. The voting is sealed, but I can tell you it was not unanimous. I didn't vote for it."

"Are you saying, Mr. Brewster, that you personally didn't want The Brewster Wing? A hospital wing meant to celebrate your philanthropic family?" she asked excitedly.

"I didn't say that. But there are a lot of things to consider. The way everything is currently set up, someone is going to lose. It might not be today. It might be a year from now. But this isn't a win-win situation. If the business owners lose, we will relocate them and place them anywhere they want to go. And for their trouble, we're going to pay them a lot of money. But I don't know if the money is enough. I don't know if their customers will find them. I don't know if they will have the same success in a new location.

"If the hospital loses, people with severe orthopedic injuries might not be able to get the treatment they need at Good Faith Hospital. Good Faith is in the business of healing. They need a state-of-the-art facility to improve upon what they currently have. They have growing pains and have reached full capacity. But the way I see it, this isn't the best solution for any party involved. We have to come to the table with more compassion for all the parties. Someone will have to be willing to negotiate and give up a little to get potentially a lot. It is hard to say at this point."

"Spoken like a man with mayoral ambitions. Anything you want to tell us, Mr. Brewster?" the reporter said, flirting a little with a coquettish smile.

"I have no further comments. Have a nice day," Jack said and stepped inside the distillery with Moonshine at his side.

By the time Jack got back to his office, his parents were already aware of his impromptu press conference. He knew he was in trouble when his mother let his father speak first.

"May I assume, Jackson, that you had sampled a bit of *Red's Rum* before speaking to the reporters today?" asked Charles III as Jack stood in front of his father's desk and watched as the old man snapped an illegal Cuban cigar in half, as someone might snap the neck of a chicken to kill it.

"No, I was on my way to the auxiliary plant," Jack answered, wondering if Ella had heard his press conference yet. He'd said it for her. He hoped she'd see it.

"Do you recall what you said?" his father asked.

"Something about not everyone winning but wanting everyone to win," Jack replied as he sat in an empty chair and glanced at the chair across from him where his mother sat, seething.

"What is wrong with you?" Charles III asked.

"I don't like the idea of the hospital wing as it is currently planned. My eyes are open to why it is a bad idea. You chose to ignore public opinion. I embrace it, face it, and bring it to the light. Let's fix it and move forward."

"Do you want to run this company one day?" his father asked. Underlying his words was a threat. Jack saw it for what it was and gave it no power.

"I hadn't planned on it. I wanted to make rum. My ambitions didn't assimilate for anything much higher than that because I'm the second born. I know my place. I mean, come on, you've been telling me since I could understand words that this would never be mine. I heard you," he said and waited for the words to hit their target. From the time he could understand his place in the family, he was aware that there was someone else ahead of him in line. It had always been that way in the Brewster Family. None of his uncles or aunts worked in the business. Each Brewster child was paid off at the time of their twenty-first birthday. The eldest son got something different. He got the family business, whether he wanted it or not. He thought of Xander and promised never to make him or any of the other children he hoped to have with Ella one day feel like they were less-than.

Jack was an anomaly for several reasons. First, he'd been allowed into the business when he took a liking to the idea of manufacturing hard alcohol after getting master's degrees in both business and chemistry. Second, they'd needed him when Charles IV, for lack of a better phrase, "had a break with reality" and thumbed his nose at the company, thereby flipping off his family.

"You are going to put your father in an early grave," his mother said.

Jack raised his hands in mock surrender as if to say, "So be it."

"I don't know what is going on with you for the last couple of weeks, but I want you to think seriously about the ramifications of your actions. There are two different pathways you could travel on, Jackson. There is a path that involves being a leader in this community and giving back to the hometown that has given us so much as you lead them as their mayor. That's right: if you run, you will win. How many other citizens can say that?" his mother asked.

Jack did not answer. He didn't want to be mayor. He wanted to kiss Ella and see Xander. He was going to call Ella as soon as this conversation was over and force the issue.

"You're thirty-five. Your mother and I have high hopes that

soon you'll find a nice girl with the same community ambitions, settle down, and have a family. Once your civic duty is completed, then you will take your position here as the future leader of this company."

Ella was right about one thing. His family would not approve of her. She was about as far from a "nice girl" that they had in mind for him as she could get. They wanted someone they could influence and dominate. And no one dominated Marcella Martin. Maybe that is why he couldn't get her out of his mind.

"What about Charles? You know, my brother?" he asked, feeling sorry for the distancing that his parents so easily showed for their firstborn when he didn't follow their rules.

"As far as I'm concerned, your brother has had some sort of break with reality that came shortly after he hit his head on a chunk of ice on Mount Hood," his father said, looking away from Jack and at the window that looked down on busy northwest Portland. "Your comment brings up another unpleasant discussion that I feel the need to have with you. There is, of course, another alternative that is on the table for reasons that I can only describe as being born out of erratic behavior on both your part and the part of your older brother.

"I don't have to leave Brewster International Brewing to either of you. I could simply sell it to one of the interested parties that have approached us in the past. I have to tell you, in light of the behaviors I've witnessed, especially in the last couple of weeks, it might be the best alternative for all parties involved.

"And instead of having our legacy be a family business and a hospital wing that you seem so uninterested in, we could simply give the proceeds of the sale to a charitable foundation. You and your brother could see what it is like to live without the benefit of a lucrative family business and reputation to back you."

His father seemed to have forgotten the wealth that had been bestowed to Jack on his twenty-first birthday. Jack was the majority stockholder in Brewster's Red's Rum LLC. There was a caveat in their original partnership agreement that allowed him to buy out his partners. If he lived to be five hundred, he wouldn't be doing it in poverty.

Jack hated to admit it, but he'd been proud of what Ella had been able to accomplish with her battle. She was really starting to get some traction. He wondered what his parents would do if he mentioned her and how she was the mother of their grand-child. Simple, they'd throw him out, change the locks, and all his Sunday nights would suddenly be free. By chance, he needed to start preparing for this eventuality. And he didn't need to think about how wonderful that would be.

"Thank you, Father, for explaining your position," he said and stood.

"Jackson," his mother began, but he cut her off.

"I need some quiet time to reflect on Father's words of wisdom. I'll get back to you both in a few days."

Jack retreated to his office, grabbed Moonshine's leash, which signaled to the dog they were about to leave. The Vizsla got up from his dog bed and stretched as if he was annoyed at having to do it.

"Seriously, Moonshine. You act like a human sometimes."

He attached the leash to Moonshine's collar, grabbed his car keys and his coat, and was about to leave when his office phone rang. Glancing at the number, he thought of not answering, but he knew Flint wouldn't call unless he had more information about Xander and Ella.

Moonshine whined at the interruption.

"Hey Flint," he said by way of answering.

"Jack," Flint replied, but just with the way he said Jack's name, Jack was concerned.

"What's the matter?"

"I know you asked me to stop, but I wanted to check out one last thing. I did a credit check and found a very large hospital bill. I did some digging. Did you know that when Marcella Martin had Xander there was a complication?"

"No," Jack said, flashing on an image of Xander, who looked absolutely perfect. The child was smart for his age and seemed completely normal, if not advanced. Ella had mentioned nothing about Xander's birth. He now realized another layer of loss. What if the complication was with Ella?

"What's your blood type?" Flint asked.

"A positive," Jack replied, not liking the direction this was going.

"Have you ever heard of Rh disease?"

"I've heard of it. Does it have something to do with a mother and a baby not having compatible blood types?"

"Exactly. I'm speculating here from looking at the bills and the procedures, but my guess is that Marcella's blood type is something like A negative or O negative, which led to an Rh issue with the baby when he was born, as he must be Rh positive like you. She might have had treatment for it when she was pregnant, injections to lessen the risk, but needless to say, when Xander was born, he was severely anemic. They would have known there was an issue for sure if you'd been there because they would have tested your blood as the father. As it turns out, Marcella and Xander had to stay longer than expected in the hospital."

"But they are okay now," Jack said, a cold sweat breaking out on his forehead.

"Well, I'm not sure. I'm good, but medical records are sealed. I had to pull a lot of strings with some unsavory friends to look at the hospital bills. I think you would know. Has she mentioned it?"

"No," he said. "How long were they in the hospital?"

"Marcella was in for three days, Xander for four. She's got shitty health insurance, to put it mildly. It paid about sixty percent with a $10,000 deductible. As of last month, she owes

Good Faith Hospital about $47,000. And she has $24,000 in student loans. If you take away her shop with your new hospital wing, there is no way she can relocate. She's got no other assets but the merchandise in her store and an old car. She is paying the hospital about $800 to $1,000 per month and about $300 to student loans. The hospital would like her to pay more and tell her so frequently."

"How did you find all this out?" Jack asked as he leaned against his desk for support.

"Don't ask, but I thought you might want to help her out, so I've got the account numbers for the hospital and the student loan company as well as contact numbers."

"Good. You thought right. Give them to me."

Once Jack had the account numbers and contact information, he thanked Flint and called the billing department at Good Faith Hospital, then the student loan company.

Jack knew that Ella wouldn't want him to be doing this, but as he looked at the balance, it was the least he could do. Ten minutes later, both outstanding bills had been settled. No wonder she lived in an apartment above the store. How could she afford a house? Or even a better apartment?

Weathering that storm, he grabbed his coat and keys and an irritated Moonshine and left the building. Once in the privacy of his parking garage, he dialed the number he knew by heart.

Chapter Twenty

Ella was walking with Padma when her cell phone barked from her pocket. She had her ringtone set to bark when Jack called, because he was a bad dog.

"Hey Mom," she said, aware that her mother was in Seattle finding herself at a glass workshop put on by artists who'd were former students of the famous glass sculptor, Chihuly. They spoke only about once a month. And when they did, her mother liked to remind her that she was living her best life and would never be the doting grandmother that Ella had hoped for and Xander deserved.

"I need to see you. I don't care where, how, when… I just need to see you and Xander today. I'm not going to take no for an answer. It's been a week, and I need to see you, please," Jack said.

"I'm a little busy right now. I'm gathering support to save my shop against the hospital and the Brewster family. It's going very well. In case you hadn't heard."

"I know it is, congratulations. If you don't want to meet me at your place, come to my house. I've got everything you need for Xander. Plan on spending the night. I want to take out my personal work frustrations by allowing you to use me for sex. Any way you want."

"Wow, Mom, tonight? I don't know. Overnights can be difficult with Xander," she said, but her body was already turning molten from the inside out. She'd turned Jack down every night this week, wanting to put some distance between them. She was falling too hard for him and needed perspective, but at just the sound of his voice, she was weakening. She couldn't take another night without him. She wasn't sleeping. Worse, she kept rolling over and reaching for him in the night, but he didn't need to know that.

"My housekeeper got the exact same crib that you have. She bought everything that would make Xander comfortable at my house, including a baby monitor. When can you come over?"

Padma was looking at her strangely. She'd never met Ella's mother because Ella's relationship with her mother had been very strained. Her mother hadn't seen Xander until he was two months old, even though they lived in the same city. The only reason she knew her mother was in Seattle was because her mother had asked if Ella would be interested in selling any of her mother's glass creations "in your little store."

"Well, if it is important, Xander and I can be there around seven. Give me the address again."

"2137 NW Vista. The gate will be open for you."

"The gate?"

"By the way, have you seen my press conference yet? I think you'll like it. I've gotten a lot of frustration from my stupidity and loose lips. My parents are barely speaking to me, so guess what? I don't care. Just come."

"What did you say?" she asked.

"I didn't mention you or Xander, but I did talk about the hospital being a mixed bag of winners and losers."

Ella hung up and smiled, a smile not lost on Padma.

"Good news?" she asked.

"An old friend is staying at my mother's."

"A man," Padma said and smiled knowingly.

"Well, yes, an old friend. It should be fun," Ella admitted.

They made their way back to their shops in time for Padma

to start with dinner prep and Ella to relieve Cricket, who was only set to work until four that afternoon. Pausing in front of one of the neighborhood newspaper boxes for the largest alternative newspaper in town, *The Columbia Weekly*, they read the headline, and then Padma let out a rare yell of delight.

"Yippie, about time we get after these bastards," Padma said, shocking Ella as she tried not to think of how this particular headline might impact Jack personally.

The headline was brutal: **Brewster's Leg-Breaking Tactics Force Hospital to Spread Its Wings**.

Part one of a three-part article suggested the hospital was kowtowing to pressure from the Brewster family to build something, anything that could further promote the family name and reputation in the community. An anonymous source went on to be quoted that the new wing of the hospital was a "needless monstrosity" that would create "chaos for the neighborhood." The second installment, scheduled for the following week, promised an exposé on the Brewster family, their company, and a new product with an ominous foreboding name: *REDRUM*.

Jack had told her they had changed the name to *Red's Rum* to avoid litigation, but it looked better in the newspaper when printed as *Redrum*.

"To just what extremes will the Brewster family go to see their dreams realized?" the article went on to ask. It also suggested that not all the Brewsters (Jack) were onboard with the messy situation. It praised Jack for trying to be a peacemaker. Ella wondered what he had said to bring on that perception.

Ella and Padma grabbed half a dozen copies and took them back to their shops. After reading the article, which wasn't kind to Jack's mother, Dolores, Ella almost felt sorry for Jack. She wondered what kind of mother Dolores had been to Jack. If what she was reading was true, the woman hadn't been a good one.

It surprised her to think of what a loving person he was to Xander…and to her.

At six forty-five that evening, Ella bundled Xander and two overnight bags into her old red Volvo.

"Guess who we are going to go see?" she asked Xander, who smiled and chewed on his giraffe.

"Daddy," she said, feeling strangely nostalgic.

"Dada!" Xander said, pulling away from his giraffe.

"Yes," Ella said, wondering if she was doing the right thing for Xander. Every time she saw Jack, it was harder to be apart from him. The last week had been almost more than she could take. What would Xander go through if Jack suddenly disappeared from their lives?

Even Cricket could tell how much the absence of Jack was affecting Ella. At one point earlier that week, she'd said, "Look, it's messy. I get that. But for fuck's sake, call him! Use your lady-part power. Sleep your way into getting him to drop this whole hospital thing. And guess what? Side benefit, you'll enjoy it!"

"Even if I took him to another dimension sexually, it wouldn't change anything," Ella said, trying not to laugh at her friend's suggestion as they polished silver jewelry in the case. "Besides, if I thought it would, I'd feel weird about it."

"Prude."

"It's more a pride thing," Ella admitted.

"Then, at the very least, get laid for those of us who aren't getting any action."

Cricket had recently ended things with a loser boyfriend, but the woman never stayed single for longer than a week or two.

"It's complicated. We live in two different worlds. He wants to be a politician. I hate politicians. If Hiram, Padma, or Cindy knew about him, they'd disown me. I'd lose my family."

"You're making it more complicated than it is. And just for the record, you wouldn't lose me."

Ella hugged the other woman and said, "Thank you for that. I just can't see that there is any way we could live in each other's worlds. I think he will keep seeing Xander until his family finds him the right girl whom they approve of. Once that happens, he'll be gone. I just have to hope Xander isn't totally crushed." She hoped she wouldn't be totally devastated as well.

"Did you ever think he might care more about you and Xander than his family? That he'd be willing to stand up for you and Xander?" Cricket asked, throwing down her polishing cloth in frustration.

"No. He has too much to lose," Ella said, throwing her cloth on top of Cricket's.

"Why? Because he left you before?"

"Yes. To be very honest, nothing in my life has ever been easy. So why should I get a break when it comes to Jack? To design and stock this shop cost me my small inheritance from my dad's insurance. A few years later, we were making a profit, but then I got pregnant. I always thought I'd have a baby, but with a father to whom I was married. I don't regret Xander for a minute, but he had his issues at birth, and my low-cost health insurance put us right back in the red. And now, we're going to lose the shop to the very hospital I owe money to."

"The Brewsters are loaded. Why not ask Jack for help?"

"I can't do that," Ella said. "I want to solve my own problems. I can't be a burden. I want him to choose Xander. If he chooses me too, well, that would be a miracle."

"Did you ever think the two of you might be falling in love?" Cricket asked.

"No. I might have deep feelings for him, but he's only in the picture for Xander. I'm under no illusions. So stop sniffing the silver polish. I think it's affecting your brain!"

Ella's logic that Jack couldn't ever fall for her was exactly why she hadn't allowed herself to call Jack. She was done using him. She felt guilty for using him for sex. It wasn't her. It wasn't the person she wanted to be. Besides, she wasn't as good at separating her body from her emotions. Despite all the things she didn't know about Jack, she liked what she saw so much that she had to concede, yes, she was a little bit in love with him. Jack didn't need to know that detail. After tonight, she'd distance herself a bit farther. But she'd give herself this evening as one last fling before starting to think with her brain once again.

Once she was sure Xander was secure in his car seat, she got in the car and made the short trip to Vista Drive. As promised, the big, imposing black wrought iron gate had been left open for her. Pulling into the circular driveway, she stopped in front of the entryway and turned off the engine. Xander liked riding in the car and seemed to say, "What? We're here already?" as she untangled him from his car seat.

Jack appeared just as she was pulling Xander into her arms. Jack took Xander from her and lifted him high over his head before pulling him close for a quick snuggle. Xander smiled and laughed with delight and said, "Dada!"

A moment later, Jack turned his attention to Ella, wrapping an arm around her and kissing her quickly, almost chastely, on the lips. He grabbed the larger of her two bags with his free hand and led her up the stairs to his house. The red brick mansion loomed before her. He must think she lived in a tenement.

The first thing Ella noticed when she stepped inside Jack's mansion was her belief that she had somehow stepped into a museum, in, say, Eastern Europe, where not a lot of sunlight ever penetrated the fortress. It was cold, dark, and foreboding. It smelled like mothballs. It felt like a place where dead people had once lived and maybe still made an appearance. It gave her a creepy vibe that made her feel cold when she was dressed warmly.

"Before you make any conclusions, allow me to say that this house has been in my family for a hundred years," he said before she could comment. "It is cold and dark. I don't like it."

"I noticed it is kind of dark, but maybe that is the eastern exposure," she said and set her small bag down in the entryway. "Does it ever see the light of day?"

"Not really. Sometimes, in summer, the backyard actually dries out and isn't a swamp. And the darkness gets worse in the fall and winter months. I love fall, but not in this house. I just finished remodeling the living room, trying my best to make it homey, but I fear I've failed miserably," he said and led her into a much homier space that looked down at Northwest Portland. It was done in soft colors of beige and sand, surprising Ella as she pictured him with lots of black leather and chrome furnishings. It was a pleasant surprise. An oasis in the frigid desert. Immediately, she went over to the window and looked down at her neighborhood.

"Wow, what a view," she said. "You can see my shop."

"About ten blocks as the crow flies."

Xander made motions to get down to explore. Ella's protective mother side immediately kicked in as she looked around for dangerous objects.

"I childproofed the place a couple of days ago," he said, reading her mind as Xander crawled furiously toward a window. "Heck, I decorated the living room with Xander in mind."

"I can see that," she said, taking in all the overstuffed furniture with no hard edges. He was trying too hard, and she liked the effort. This room was the exact opposite of every other room she'd seen in the house.

They had a dinner of meatloaf and mashed potatoes made by Jack's housekeeper, who lived over the garage. It was excellent and something Xander really liked. They ate in the old-fashioned kitchen that Ella thought had to be in worse shape than the kitchen in her apartment. It still had milky green tile counters and matching cabinets with crystal doorknobs. The modern dishwasher looked like a spaceship in the middle of a parking lot of cars. Curious and out of place.

"Aren't you scared your housekeeper will tell someone about all the baby stuff you had her buy?" Ella asked.

"No," he said. "Greta signed a confidentiality agreement when I hired her, and quite frankly, she doesn't care because I'm a fairly laid-back boss. I think she enjoyed herself buying all this baby stuff. It might have been the first smile I've ever seen on her face. She is rather dour."

"She sounds scary," Ella said.

"She is," Jack said, "But she loves my dog, so that is a plus."

"You have a dog?"

"Moonshine. He is having a sleepover with Greta. They both get excited when that happens. I sometimes think I bore my dog."

"Doggie," Xander said and clamped his hands together.

"That's right, Xander. I have a red dog named Moonshine," Jack said. "He loves people, but I didn't want him to be too overwhelming today. We will meet him soon."

"Xander and I like dogs," Ella said.

"Good," Jack replied.

After dinner, they sat across from each other on the floor in the living room and watched as Xander tried to walk.

"I know he's going to figure it out eventually," she said.

"I think he already has," Jack said as he stood and bent at the waist, walking slowly with Xander in front of him, guiding him to take a few steps while he hung onto Jack's hands.

Ella grabbed her purse and pulled out her cell phone. Thinking of their delicate situation, she asked, "Do you mind if I take a few pictures or maybe a movie of Xander?"

"I don't mind at all, but would you share them with me?" he

asked, and she thought of how she would feel if she didn't have any photos of Xander.

"Sure, I can put together a few from birth to now if you'd like."

"I would treasure that. I feel like I've missed so much. I'll never forget what he looks like, but a photo of him would be something I'd cherish," he said, his smile beaming at her, melting some of her hard-fought resolve. A minute later, she was making a video of Xander walking with his father.

Jack pulled out his own cell phone and asked, "Could I take a picture of you with Xander? I want a picture of you just as badly as I want one of him."

"I hardly look photo-worthy," she said with a self-deprecating tone as he led Xander back to her.

"I think you're beautiful. Now smile," he said and then took dozens and dozens of photos. She couldn't blame him, but she was struck once again by how attached he seemed to already be to her child.

Once Xander was asleep in a bedroom the size of her apartment and Jack had turned on the baby monitor, he walked her to the bedroom next door. He opened the door to a dark space, and flipped a switch that illuminated amber-shaded lights on either side of his bed. The lamps were meant to bring warmth to the room but fell short.

"Welcome to my room," he said and pulled her close for a kiss. She sunk into his arms and felt the warmth she so desperately needed. When they broke free of their embrace, Ella scrutinized the room.

It was masculine, all ebony wood and big furniture, including a huge King-sized bed that looked oddly small in the large space. And again, Ella described it with one word: *Museum*. She might have decorated her apartment frugally, but it was home. This space wasn't anything remotely warm. In fact, she wouldn't be surprised if Jack told her it was haunted.

* * *

Jack loved every moment he could spend with Xander, but once his little boy was asleep and cuddled up with BeauBeau, all his attention focused on the woman he could not stop thinking about. His need for Ella, from the first moment he'd seen her in that skimpy red bikini, was almost otherworldly. It was certainly like nothing he'd ever felt for another woman. Maybe this is how it felt when you've met your soul mate. He'd dated a lot of women before he'd met her, but never felt close to the way he was feeling now. Ironically, the idea didn't scare him. However, the thought of losing her or Xander to something stupid like the hospital expansion scared the hell out of him.

It was as if he knew she was to be the mother of his children before she'd uttered a single word. His need to make love to her kept him up at night. He fantasized about different ways to bring her pleasure. He had always wanted to be his best self with any woman he was with. But when it came to Ella, he felt insecure, wanting to constantly improve himself. He still hadn't figured out how he would convince her that he was the man for her, that whatever else happened, they were destined to be together. And it was that need which turned his strategic business mind into self-doubting mush.

"Would you mind if I took a shower?" Ella asked as he pulled her toward the bed. She didn't need to be clean for him. Hell, he liked it when she was a little sweaty, but if he knew anything about women, he knew when to shut up.

"Sure, may I join you?" The bathroom was the first thing he had remodeled after he'd moved in. He couldn't wait to see her reaction.

She appeared to think about this. Then, smiling, she nodded, and their dance of seduction began. Inside a large, white marble walk-in shower with gray veins running through the stone, Jack turned on four perfectly mounted shower heads, which hit them

194

both from every angle. He watched as surprise turned to delight when the rain head turned on, and water rained softly on them. Ella smiled gleefully and Jack decided he would forever think of the shower as the "fun shower" from that moment on.

Ella smiled and tilted her head up at the soft rain.

"Do you like my shower?" he asked.

"I love it," she said. "I wish I had something this large."

He wanted to tell her that she could move in and use his any time she wanted.

"It was the first thing I installed when I moved in. I wanted something indulgent. I call it the 'fun shower.' Yet you're the first one to tell me if I got it right."

Ella opened her eyes, which he noticed were heavily lidded as she smiled. "You are a man of your word."

He laughed, bent down and kissed her almost chastely, then picked up the waiting washcloth. Grabbing the imported French soap that smelled like the most exotic location anyone had ever visited and had the fat content of butter, he got the washcloth foamy, heavy with suds.

He gently ran the soft washcloth over Ella's skin, paying particular attention to her breasts. He loved her breasts and couldn't get enough of them. They were large and firm, possibly bigger than they had been that first night they were together. He noticed when they made love that he always started with her breasts, paying particular attention to her rosy nipples. The very thought of how they had strained the red bikini fabric as she walked along the sand had his heart rate accelerating.

When he had run the washcloth over every inch of her skin, and she had moaned more than once at the intimate attention, she grabbed the cloth out of his hand. She rubbed the plush cotton against the French-milled soap that now scented the air around them with green tea and jasmine. Then she turned the tables on him and began to rub him with the same exotic technique he'd used on her. He loved that she seemed to like to touch him as much as he liked to touch her.

"Does that feel good?" she asked as the cloth ran over his back, her breasts brushing lightly against him as she rubbed.

"You have no idea," he said as he turned to face her and kissed her like a starving man.

Chapter Twenty-One

Sex in a shower was a logistical nightmare. Usually, showers were small, but not this fun monument to bathing.

Ella dropped the cloth she'd been using on Jack when he kissed her and then nuzzled her neck. Damn this power he had over her. He pulled her against him, and she leaned her weight into him, her knees going weak. Wet skin and chest hair brushing against sensitive nipples and an erection slipping between her legs and trying to gain access to her wet warmth was more than she could take.

She moaned, not sure which of the teasing, taunting ministrations had pushed her to vocalize her need. Hands on her hips, Jack lifted her to his body, then buried his erection deep as he balanced her with his hands under her butt; all the while, she was tickled by the warm water sluicing against her skin as the rain continued to fall on them. Automatically, she wrapped her arms around his neck to hang on and met his gaze. She'd never done anything like this before. It was wild and kind of animalistic, feral. She loved it. She had a moment of panic that was soon replaced by pleasure.

"Oh…oh," she said. He wasn't wearing a condom, but he felt so good, like heated silk, as he moved within her that she couldn't find her voice to stop him. She wanted to feel him inside her, and oh, could she feel him. The gravity of her body against his as he held her in this position had him as deep as he could get. She felt impaled by his erection, and that was before he started to move.

His strength was more than impressive.

"How does that feel?" he whispered. "Are you okay?"

"You're so deep. I love it," she managed as their eyes met, and they kissed.

She'd never made love standing up. There was no point of reference, just his body to rest upon. But they weren't resting. Her body bounced a little as he slid in and out of her like a finely oiled piston, her feet never touching the floor.

"You feel so good," he said, his labored breathing next to her ear, letting her know instinctively that he couldn't keep up the pace for much longer.

"You feel like silk," she murmured. He slipped a little and almost dropped her, caught her in the nick of time and kissed her.

"Am I too heavy for this?" she asked.

"You're perfect," he said, kissing her again.

And then her back was leaning against the marble wall, and he was moving even faster, using the cool marble for leverage. The different textures added to the sensuality of the experience. There was no lead up, just release as her body uncoiled, and she bit her lip as she screamed. Jack joined her, succumbing to his own climax and pumping her body until her breath came out in tiny spurts of air, mingling with the sound of water from the fun shower.

Later, she stood naked in the bathroom and used a hairdryer on her hair. She'd never liked going to bed with a wet head. Over her shoulder, Jack leaned against the door jamb, wearing a fluffy white terrycloth robe. He watched her with a lascivious look on his face as he sipped a glass of brandy. He'd placed her glass on the counter next to her.

"Did you check on Xander?" she asked over the whine of the dryer.

"He's sleeping peacefully with his giraffe in his arms."

"Good," she said and wondered what he was thinking. Normally, she would have been self-conscious about her body, but after what they'd just done in the shower, she simply didn't care. This was personal growth. Enjoying the body she had. Yes, there were stretch marks on her hips, and her boobs felt bigger, stretched, and not as perky as they once were. But as she reached up to fluff her hair, her breasts bounced and looked good in the mirror. At least, Jack's smile seemed to indicate he liked what he saw.

She paused, then looked over her shoulder at him.

"What?" she asked as his eyes seemed to appraise her.

"You're absolutely gorgeous." She hadn't expected that.

"Sure," she said doubtfully. "I don't have the same body I had before Xander. I can feel the difference and it bothers me."

"Don't be bothered. I want you to really hear me when I say your body is my ultimate fantasy. I love every inch," he said admiringly.

After a long pause, she said, "But I'm different since the baby."

"Our baby, my baby. And you are better," he said. "Lusher. Sexier. I just wished I could have seen you pregnant. I bet you were ethereal."

"Keep thinking that," she said with a small laugh.

When her hair was dry, she turned off the dryer and grabbed a brush. Before she could start taming all her blond tangles, Jack was there, placing his glass of brandy next to hers.

"Allow me," he said and took the brush from her hand. With gentle tenderness, he untangled her hair, smoothing it into long, glossy ribbons. They had just made love, but this was sensuous on a whole different level.

As he moved the brush and then his fingers through her hair, Ella shivered. When he finished with her hair, Jack opened his robe and wrapped it around her.

Looking up at him, she said, "Thank you. I was getting a little chilled."

They kissed, and she indulged in her own fantasies, touching every part of him that she wanted. The bathrobe was the perfect foil to her exploration.

"Let's get into bed and get you warmed up," he said. But he made no move toward the bedroom. He simply pulled her close and began to kiss her deeply as his hands roamed over her body.

How long they stayed like that, *naked necking* as she would later come to think of it, she couldn't say. But the need that had been so quickly quenched in the shower began again. By the time they made it to the bed, sleeping was the last thing on her mind.

Jack's bed was an impressive four poster that reminded her of the bed in her room in Saint Barts, only instead of white-washed wood, his room was dark and more than a little cold. Once she slipped between the crisp white sheets, Jack pulled her into his arms, kissed her, and then smiled. She was glad he had the same thing in mind that she did.

* * *

Jack hadn't meant to make love to Ella in the shower, but he just couldn't help himself. All that tactile infusion of slick skin, warm water, silky soap, and cold, hard marble had taken control out of his wheelhouse. He just hoped Ella wouldn't be too mad about the condom. Being inside all her warmth with nothing between them had taken normal sensations to a complex and profound level. It was intimate and meant they were only with each other. He didn't want to ruin the mood by defining it and saying it aloud, but she was his and he had found home with her and Xander.

Tonight would be special for several reasons. Not only had they made love without the condom, but she was also now in his bed, and it was a place he intended for her to spend a lot of time. He just didn't want to scare her by telling her that he didn't see his life without her and Xander in it.

Pulling her into his arms, he asked, "Are you warm enough?"

"I am, and I'm sure it's about to get a lot hotter in here," she whispered and kissed his cheek.

Jack took that as a challenge. "I like the way you think. We will take it slow this time. I'm not in a rush."

"Sometimes I like it fast, but please, take your time. Let's savor it," she said and smiled.

"You let me know when it gets too much for you," he said and lowered his mouth to her erect nipple.

By the time they were both on the edge of begging the other to fully join their bodies, the blankets and top sheet had been pushed to the end of the bed. Jack had kept the lights on, wanting to see each expression on Ella's face as he did his damnedest to show her how much he felt for her. And when had these feelings turned to love? Maybe it started in Saint Barts. He didn't question it, he just knew. He loved her. He loved Xander.

"Jack ..." she murmured, her eyes twinkling as she looked up at him.

Stopping his assault on her body, he reached for the bedside drawer where he'd placed a box of condoms earlier.

"What are you doing?" she asked, sitting up on her elbows.

"Getting a condom?" he asked.

"I think we are way beyond that after the shower," she said. He glanced at the box in his hand and then tossed it across the room and smiled.

"Well, good, because I don't want anything between us. You feel too good..."

She nodded and reached for him. Feeling her arms encircle him, he bent and kissed her, letting his tongue mingle with hers as they came to a new agreement, a new level of intimacy. Touching her knees, he spread her wide and settled between her legs. She sighed and looked at him, her eyes heavily lidded and sexy. She smiled and softly demanded, "Please, Jack."

He loved how sexy she was, how she wanted him. It had never been this way with anyone else. In that moment, he'd never been happier in his life as he slipped into her waiting warmth.

Chapter Twenty-Two

Something wet and damp touched Ella's hand. A moment later, something large and muscular jumped on her, causing her to scream even before she opened her eyes.

When she finally looked, she was nose-to-nose with a sleek, short-haired, rust-colored dog, who immediately ran his tongue over her cheek good-naturedly.

"Yuck, stop it!" Ella yelled as the dog seemed to wind up, with more tongue and a wagging tail.

Jack immediately appeared in the doorway, holding Xander in his arms. "I see you met Moonshine. Moonshine, off!"

The dog looked as if he had no idea who Jack was and, therefore, could ignore him easily.

The dog now settled next to Ella, taking Jack's position in the bed, his tail thumping wildly against the mattress as he lowered his head and wagged his tail adoringly at the woman he'd just met and fallen hopelessly in love with.

"So, this is your dog?" Ella asked as she wiped at the remnant of the dog's kiss on her face.

Xander pointed at the dog and laughed as Jack walked over to the bed and sat on the edge next to Ella. Moonshine immediately scooted toward Xander, wagging his tail and sniffing.

"How is that dog with children?" Ella asked warily.

"He's very gentle," Jack said as Xander stretched out a hand toward Moonshine and laughed with delight.

"He loves children and is very protective," Jack said, trying to reassure her.

Xander touched the dog and laughed louder. He loved dogs and had learned to be gentle when petting them. Moonshine basked in the attention of Xander, even lowering his head and moving closer to Xander's little hand which he nuzzled with his eraser pink nose.

Xander squealed with delight when Moonshine licked his ear.

"I don't want that dog licking him on the face," Ella warned. Jack immediately pulled Xander out of range of Moonshine's tongue, causing Xander to cry out in protest and Moonshine to do a full-body scoot toward him.

Xander reached out for his mother, and Ella pulled him into her arms for a morning snuggle. She could not help noticing the longing look in Jack's eyes. Their situation felt like the Titanic headed for an iceberg in the shape of a steel and glass hospital wing. But for the moment, she would do her best to enjoy the sweet times like these.

As if knowing there might be an expiration date for their time together, Jack leaned forward and kissed Ella softly on the lips and then bent down and kissed Xander's cheek.

"How does Xander like blueberry pancakes?"

"Just ask your housekeeper not to drown them in syrup."

"She doesn't start until noon, as per her employment contract. She isn't a morning person. Around here, I handle breakfast all by myself."

"You can cook?" Ella asked, a smile playing on her lips.

"I make a mean breakfast, so there is no need to rush," Jack said, kissing her again.

"I have to get to the shop by ten," she said.

"It isn't even eight yet. Lay back and relax while the man in your life spoils you."

* * *

Two hours later, Ella walked dreamily around Marcella's and tidied up different displays after the night at Jack's. The store had been open for ten minutes, and she figured she had about five more minutes of this foolish, dreamlike state until a customer or fellow business owner would remind her of the war she was waging against the hospital and the Brewsters. This lack of concentration was obviously Jack's influence. Every time he gave her an orgasm, her IQ appeared to lose a few points. At this rate, she'd be brainless by the time of the hearing in two weeks. Thirteen days, to be exact. Well, at least she was still capable of simple math.

Thinking about Jack at all made her smile, the big jerk. He was trying too hard, and it was working. *Let's see how it will be after the hearing. Then he'll show his real colors,* she thought as she dusted a display of crystals that did not need dusting. They'd made love three times without a condom. It felt amazing, and she was smiling like an idiot on this chilly fall morning. She felt like she was wearing a neon sign that announced, "Hi, I'm sexually satisfied!"

Taking a deep breath, she tried to think straight. She was going to have to start paying a little better attention to her birth control pills, or Xander was going to get a sibling, which would certainly push her life from the "complicated" column to the "insane" column. She wasn't sloppy, but she knew that everything that might happen could happen.

The bell over the front door jingled, announcing the first customer of the day. Ella turned to greet the person with a bright smile, but upon seeing who arrived, the smile fell from her face. To her surprise, Dolores Brewster marched in as if she owned the place. In a couple of weeks, that might be the truth. Wondering what had brought the woman to her shop, Ella tried to force the reluctant smile on her face and crossed the distance to where Dolores pretended to scrutinize the jewelry case.

"Good morning," Ella began. "Welcome to *Marcella's*."

"Good morning," Dolores said with a pert tone that indicated it was anything but a good morning.

She scrutinized the woman. Did Xander look like her in any way? She couldn't see it. Jack favored his father, and so did his son.

"Welcome. Is this your first time to *Marcella's*?" Ella knew it was, but she needed to appear very cordial.

"Yes, it is," the tone continued.

"I'm Ella, and this is my shop. If you have any questions, I'd be more than happy to answer them for you. To start, the jewelry in the case is made by local artisans. We like to support the community. Would you like some coffee while you browse?"

"This really isn't a social call," Dolores Brewster said, then announced, "I'm Dolores Brewster."

Dolores Brewster paused after saying this as if Ella needed a moment to grasp the greatness standing before her, maybe curtsy. Ella was very proud of herself, and she did not react in any way except to widen the fake smile on her face. After all, this woman was Xander's grandmother. It was hard to believe that she was Jack's mother. Poor Jack. She bet his childhood had been pure hell.

Ella stuck her hand out to the other woman and said, "It's a pleasure to meet you Mrs. Brewster. I've heard a lot about you. Thank you for all you do for the community."

"Thank you. And I've heard a lot about you, my dear," Mrs. Brewster replied and frowned unpleasantly. "It's unfortunate that we have to meet under these circumstances."

"I would have to agree," Ella said. Since the offer of coffee had fallen on deaf ears, she tried another approach. "Would you like a warm cup of tea? Maybe we could sit and have a chat?"

"No, thank you," Dolores said.

Ella suddenly felt dirty, as if she and her store did not measure up.

"May I ask why did you come here today, Mrs. Brewster?"

"I've seen quite a bit of you in the news in the last week, so I won't try to persuade you that we will treat you fairly and help you to establish your business in another area of the city, as I fear I would be wasting my breath. But I wanted to see you in person."

"I can respect that you seem to understand my passion," Ella said. "As a fellow business owner, I'm sure you can understand how protective I am of something I created."

"Oh, I must disagree with you there. I don't think it would be fair to compare us as fellow business owners. My husband's family business has been in this community for over a hundred and fifty years. I've been an officer of the company for over thirty years. I've helped my husband to grow it into the international company it is today. I believe your business has only occupied this location for the last seven years, if I'm not mistaken."

"You've done your research. I don't have an entourage or proven track record that dates to previous generations. It's just me," Ella said, wondering when the woman would get to the point. The moment she left, Ella was going to call Jack and rip him apart for not warning her that his mother was going to stop in for a visit.

Dolores Brewster's light green eyes, which were several shades lighter than her son's and lacking all warmth, scanned Ella's shop as if she was searching for a dead mouse.

"How exactly would you describe the items you sell?" she asked.

"You mean aside from the books, tea, cookies, and jewelry? Well, since we are in such close proximity to the hospital, I heard doctors refer to this shop as a place to fulfill a prescription for love," Ella said with a straight face. It was the first time she had had the desire to personally endorse the vanilla oil in her

Lover's Kit. Fantasizing about the reaction she would get from Dolores Brewster when she explained exactly how Dolores's son had used it on Ella's body…well, it brought out the first genuine smile from Ella since Dolores had stepped over the threshold.

"I've seen titles in the bookcase that include eroticism, and there is something in the corner that is an edible lover's kit. And I'm not sure, but I think I saw voodoo dolls for love. Those items hardly seem child-friendly. I'm surprised the neighborhood has rallied behind a shop of this kind and that it is next to a Catholic institution of healing," Dolores Brewster said, pulling back her lip into a grimace as she did so.

The older woman, who wore a black camel hair coat over a herringbone patterned designer suit, hadn't stopped by to make friends. Dolores Brewster might be a well-dressed, well-bred society woman, but Ella knew a bully when she saw one.

"I'm confused. Mrs. Brewster, with all due respect, this isn't a seedy sex shop. This is a high-end boutique with a bend toward romance. We don't sell dildos, edible underwear, or pornography," she said watching the other woman's eyes narrow in surprise only to be replaced with anger a moment later. "This boutique is the place all those cold-blooded surgeons from next door come when they want to make sure their spouse knows they thought of them, remembered a birthday, an anniversary. We don't judge somebody for buying a *Lover's Kit* for a romantic weekend or a book on beach houses in the south of France. I'm here for the person who wants to escape their own life for a few moments. This place makes people feel better. That's why we need to be next to a hospital. If they can't make someone feel good and need a brief reprieve, this shop probably can help them."

"If a book on the eroticism in Rome isn't pornography, I don't know what is," Dolores Brewster said with a hiss. "Your little shop should be closed to minors. I won't just take away this shop to enhance medical progress; I'll shut you down because you shouldn't be open to begin with."

"I'm glad that all my customers don't feel the same way you do, but I respect your opinion, Mrs. Brewster. You aren't my clientele, and I'm sorry I couldn't help you."

Before Dolores could retort, Jack burst into the store, looking from Ella to his mother and then back to Ella, as he slid to a stop between them.

"You're late," Mrs. Brewster said coolly as she regarded her son, who wore an expression of a storm cloud. All the sweet seduction that had been there only two hours ago was gone.

"I only got your message ten minutes ago. It's almost like you hoped I wouldn't come," Jack said to his mother and then looked back to Ella. "Good morning, Ella."

Ella liked it better when he said it to her the first time this morning, much earlier, when their warm bodies were spooning in his big bed.

"Good morning, Jack. Thank you again for that quote yesterday to KPDX. I appreciate that you understand what this hospital expansion will mean for the *Curry Leaf, Cindy's,* and my business," Ella said, smiling and watching as Mrs. Brewster flinched. "Your mother seems a bit confused about the impact."

"I know this can't be easy on any of you. We'll do our best to make sure that if you must relocate that you all are well taken care of."

"Thank you, Jack. Your mother was just telling me that if she had her way, she'd close my shop permanently, which seems a bit more serious than just moving me in need of community progress."

Jack turned to his mother, who glared back at him.

"I merely made the point that a shop of this nature wasn't for the discerning consumer. It should possibly be in a less trafficked area for families and not next to a hospital. I am very sorry if Ms. Martin took it the wrong way. She seems overly sensitive."

"I didn't take it the wrong way. I heard you clearly the first time," Ella said. "But if you like to change your story for your son's benefit, I'll let you do that."

Jack held up his hand before his mother could retort. "Mother, I would suggest you not say another word. I really don't want to add a slander suit to this mess."

"Jackson!" his mother all but shrieked.

"I'm serious, do not threaten her," he said and then turned to Ella. "Sorry for bothering you this morning, Ella. I didn't mean for this to happen."

"No problem. Thanks for stopping by," Ella said and plastered her fake smile on once again. "It is always nice to see you, Jack. Would you like a coffee to go?"

"Thank you for the kind offer, but I've already had a couple of cups. I'm not sure if we will see you before the hearing," Jack said, his eyes boring into Ella with silent apology. "But I wish you a lot of luck in your campaign and look forward to seeing you there."

"I'll be there with bells on," Ella said and winked. "Let me know if I should bring a bodyguard. I don't feel like being publicly stoned by your mother's friends for the lurid nature of my shop."

"I guarantee that we will be on our best behavior," Jack said, glaring at his mother.

"Thank you," Ella said condescendingly.

"Jackson, just whose side are you on?" his mother said.

"You're not winning any friends today," he said. "Let me escort you back to your lair."

Jack took his mother's arm and led her out of the store. As he reached back to shut the door, he flashed Ella with a quick smile and a wink of his own.

Later that afternoon, when the store was empty and Cricket

had not yet arrived, Ella picked up the phone and dialed Jack's private number, which she hated to admit she now had memorized. He answered on the first ring.

"It's me," she said, trying not to be excited at the prospect of talking to him.

"I'm sorry about my mother," he said. "She didn't tell me she was going to visit you. But now you see what I deal with daily. I'm sorry."

"Your mother's a bitch, and I don't say that often," Ella said. "Any chance you're adopted?"

"It's a question I've asked myself often. Unfortunately, our eyes are the same. If it is any consolation, I think she feels the same way about you, but I don't care what she thinks."

"Good, because all I could think about was how horrified she would be if she knew what you'd done to me last night. And your eyes are much more spectacular than hers."

There was a pause as he took in this information.

"Thank you. And think of what my mother would say if she knew what I'm going to do to you tonight," he said and then added, "Can you bring one of those brown boxes? I want to pour that vanilla oil all over you again and lick it off."

The bell chimed, and Ella waved to a customer. "I could arrange that, or there are other flavors as you might enjoy. Pear, chocolate, peppermint, cherry..."

"Bring them. Bring them all. We will get to them eventually. I can't wait to see you and Xander."

"Okay," she said, feeling a quickening in the bottom of her tummy. "By the way, you don't have to put the dog away. Xander loves dogs. Just try to make sure he doesn't lick Xander in the mouth."

"I'll work on it," he said and then added, "Thank you."

"For what?" she asked, immediately suspicious.

"For liking my dog and not liking my mother."

"You don't like your own mother?" she asked.

"Not especially. And I think it will get worse when she finds out about Xander."

"That's not going to happen for a long time, if ever," Ella said, her heart beating fast in her chest. She wouldn't let that horrible woman near Xander. "I don't want her to hurt him."

"I'm going to tell my family about you and Xander. I just haven't decided how I want to approach it yet, but they won't get near you. They will have to go through me," Jack said, his voice taking on an edge she didn't like.

"Why do they have to know anything?" she asked.

"Because Xander is a Brewster, and I want him to be a part of my family," Jack said with certainty. "I'm his father, and I don't care who knows it."

Ella hadn't missed that she had been cut out of the equation. Whether it was a slip or intentional, she didn't like it. All of the warm feelings she'd had toward Jack frosted over in an instant. "According to his birth certificate, he's a Martin. Until I decide otherwise, that is how it is going to stay."

She heard him sigh, then, "Ella, please. You can't be serious. Eventually, you've got to change the birth certificate."

"How would it look if the man running for mayor has an illegitimate child conceived after a one-night stand? Especially with a mother of questionable reputation?" she asked, matching his tone.

"I'm not going to run for mayor, and you were not a one-night stand. You do not have a questionable reputation. You're my Ella. The mother of my child."

"Actually, I was a one-night affair, and according to your mother, I'm of questionable reputation—"

"Ella, please don't listen to my mother—" Jack tried to interrupt, but she wouldn't listen.

"If you run for mayor, Xander won't be part of your life."

"Ella," he said, sounding exasperated, "we don't have to settle all of this today."

"I don't think we should see each other until after the hearing. I don't want to make this any more complicated than it already is. And it is complicated."

"You can't mean that. I don't want to be away from you two for thirteen days. I want to see you and Xander tonight. I want to make love to you. I want you in my bed."

"You'll be fine," Ella said, digging in for the fight, ignoring that he seemed to want to see her as well as Xander. And that she couldn't figure out how she would be without him for the next two weeks. "Maybe your mother can fix you up with some nice, appropriate girl with the right background."

"Ella, I want you. This is becoming a ridiculous conversation —" he began.

"Oops…sorry, I have to go. A customer just walked in," she said, cutting him off as the bell chimed over the door, and she waved at Cricket.

"Please. Aren't you and Xander coming over tonight?" he asked, the disappointment in his voice clearly coming over the phone.

"No, I don't think so," she said, but she was mad at herself. "See you at the hearing."

"Wait, what about your need to use my body for your own personal satisfaction?"

"I think I'm satisfied. See you on the seventh." Then she hung up and wanted to kick herself. Why had she been such a nasty bitch? Had his mother rubbed off on her? Or had she purposefully driven a wedge between them? It was alright to prove a point, but at what cost?

Or was she just testing him?

This separation was going to hurt her. If Xander registered that Jack was gone from his life, it was going to hurt him.

She had acted recklessly, and now she would let the chips fall where they may.

Chapter Twenty-Three

J ack knotted the green silk tie that his mother told him set off his eyes against his favorite navy suit, and looked in the mirror. The tie, just like Jack, looked disheveled. Pulling at the knot, he wrenched the tie free and threw it at the mirror. He hadn't slept well for thirteen nights since Ella had refused to see him. Calling Ella every day, he tried to get her to relent on her decision to punish him by refusing him access to both her and their son, but she hadn't wavered. At least she'd spoken to him in monotone syllables. She'd steeled herself against him. When he watched the local television news coverage and was given a full account of exactly what she'd been up to, he could feel the distance that now existed between them.

It didn't have to be this way. If he could go back in time, he'd have told anyone who listened that he had a sweet child with the beautiful Ella Martin, the woman of his dreams, who was currently making his life a nightmare. Maybe it wasn't too late for a big, grand gesture.

He'd been a coward, afraid of his family's reaction. Brushing it off as shock hadn't done him any favors. He didn't care what his family, the media, or even the hospital thought. Not anymore. He only cared about Ella and Xander. At least he was clear on that.

This thing with the hospital wing should never have gone this far. At two o'clock this afternoon, the matter would be settled, for better or worse. And by God, he wasn't losing Ella. No way.

He thought again of what he should have done. He should have publicly proclaimed Xander, but he'd also have pulled all the parties together and…

What? Had some sort of bullshit kumbaya moment?

His personal life shouldn't interfere with business, but on this matter, it had not only interfered, but it had also trampled all over him.

His parents were already chilling champagne, confident as they were as to the outcome of today's hearing. Well, after he told them what he planned to say after the hearing today on the steps of the courthouse, that champagne would stay corked. He might be unemployed. He didn't care.

Ella and her neighbors' campaign had led to picketers outside of Good Faith Hospital. The Small Business Coalition of NW Portland had promised to boycott all Brewster products, including *Red's Rum* if the hearing found in favor of the hospital and the Brewster Family by default. That hurt, but he understood their perspective.

He figured there were at least thirty restaurants, brewpubs, and cafes that sold Brewster products whose names he'd seen on the membership list for The Small Business Coalition of NW Portland.

Jack took pride in being able to judge people's character. When it came to Ella, he'd seriously underestimated her skillfulness, her ruthlessness, her durability, and, unfortunately, her passion outside of the bedroom. She was a brilliant marketer, and fighting with her was both exhilarating and maddening. She was the perfect match for him.

He didn't like being her opponent. He should have changed sides the moment he'd found her again and learned about Xander. Instead, in the beginning, he'd put business before her. She would punish him for that decision. And at the moment, he didn't know what he could do to change her opinion of him.

Moonshine trotted into his room, jumped on the bed, and looked at Jack. Today, the dog was the only friend he had in the world.

"I know. I'll try to get them back," he said, looking at his dog's soulful eyes.

* * *

Ella thought carefully about what to wear to the hearing. In the last couple of months, her reputation had taken some hits from the more conservative of reporters who'd covered the "Brewster Hospital Scandal." They'd called her an unwed mother who'd refused to name the father of her child. They'd quoted Dolores Brewster, making the woman sound virtuous in trying to rid the neighborhood of something akin to a local brothel.

Ella didn't have the money for a new suit, but then something changed, and there was an extra eleven hundred dollars in her account to spare. Damn Jack had paid off her hospital bill and her student loans. She didn't know how he found out about them. If she hadn't had so much to do, she might have called the hospital and the credit union and complained. They would probably laugh at her. Not that she could blame them.

But what Jack didn't understand was that the way to make her happy wasn't with money. Just like this hearing, all parties involved thought they could throw money at her and make her go away. Money to them was power. They'd assumed she'd take it, but they hadn't asked nicely, nor had they treated her or her neighbors with respect. She hoped she'd made them think twice with the development of The Small Business Coalition of Portland, many of whom would be in the courtroom supporting her today.

She would confront Jack about how her two largest bills got

paid off on another day, but today, she had other things on her mind. And it wasn't like they didn't have a few things to discuss. She hoped the outfit she'd picked out would give her an extra boost of confidence that would help her side to win. It was a crazy notion, but when you were dressed well, you felt more confident. As she looked in the mirror after placing her grandmother's pearls around her neck, Ella felt powerful.

The Kate Unger suit had a simple cut, but the fabric, a black-on-black cheetah print, dripped of money. She wore her long blond hair up in an elegant twist. Walking around her apartment, she warned herself to step carefully. She wasn't used to the black silk Stuart Weitzman pumps she'd borrowed from Cindy's shop. They were not opposed to dumping her on her behind if she proved unworthy of them. Adding to their danger was the fact they were half a size too big, but they looked good, and that was all that mattered today. She added another shoe pad to the interior of her left pump and hoped for the best.

Regardless of today's outcome, she'd have to talk to Jack. She'd made several contingency plans. If she lost and had to move the store, she was seriously considering moving away from Portland. She didn't know exactly where she and Xander would go, but one thing was for sure: She wasn't sure she could stay so close to Jack if he and his mother won today.

Besides, there was another thing that had happened. She'd seen a photo of Jack with a curvy redhead alongside his parents in the local newspaper's City section in yesterday's edition. She knew that before she'd come into his life there had been a string of girlfriends, but to see it after all they had been to each other, well, it hurt.

They were at some charitable event for the hospital. The woman, wearing a black sequined gown, was draped all over a tuxedoed Jack, who looked incredibly handsome as he smiled for the camera. Despite his daily phone calls, he hadn't let any grass grow under his feet. Obviously, he hadn't been completely honest with her. It hurt her to the core. He was making contingency plans. She could feel it.

If she and the other shop owners won today—which, according to her lawyer, was a long shot more akin to a snowball's chance in hell—there would still be fallout to deal with. She could not continue to live in a location where she could see his house. Next, she'd be spying on him with binoculars. The fact she'd already thought of it was deeply concerning.

At 1:15, just as she was getting into her car to go to the hearing, her cell phone started buzzing. Hiram, Padma, and Cindy had left earlier to get good seats. They'd elected her as their spokesman, so she would be sitting with their attorney, Steve Stevenson.

Recognizing the number as her daycare, Ella immediately turned off the Volvo's engine and took the call.

"Ms. Martin?" the woman Ella recognized as the director of the daycare asked.

"Yes, what's wrong?" she asked. She didn't have time for pleasantries.

"Xander has a fever. I need you to come get him."

"Today is the hearing. I'm just leaving now. Can you keep him isolated for an hour, hour, and a half?"

"I'm afraid I can't do that," the woman said in a tone that was familiar with begging parents.

Ella knew there was no way she could miss the hearing. Cricket was in class for another half hour and wouldn't open the store until three o'clock. Quickly, she put together a plan. She'd pick up Xander and have Padma hold him during the hearing. He was a good baby. He wouldn't make a big fuss. At least, she hoped he wouldn't.

At three, she'd see if she could get Cricket to meet her, or maybe there would be a recess, and she could run Xander home for Cricket to watch him. She'd work it out, somehow. She had no other choice.

Chapter Twenty-Four

J ack looked around for Ella. Where was she? It was almost two o'clock, and she was nowhere to be seen. Had something happened to her? Was Xander all right? His heart skipped a beat with the thought that either one of them could be in trouble.

He sat by the aisle next to his parents in the second row, right behind the hospital's attorneys. He'd been asked to testify on behalf of the hospital and all the money they'd raised.

"Who are you looking for?" his mother asked.

"Why do you think I'm looking for someone?" he asked in the same accusing tone.

"You're restless. I recognize the signs," she said, smiling.

"Marcella Martin isn't here. She is the spokesperson for the store owners."

"Good, maybe she won't show. Maybe we scared her off."

Jack ignored the comment and scanned the crowd of reporters and interested parties.

At 1:58, just as the judge was taking his seat, Ella burst into the filled courtroom with Xander in her arms. After a quick moment with the woman who owned the *Curry Leaf*, she handed over Xander and made her way to the front of the courtroom, where her lawyer stood waiting. Jack looked over his shoulder at Xander, who was dressed in a red and white striped sweater with a teddy bear on the front. It took all of Jack's resolve not to get up and cross the distance to Xander. He hadn't realized how much he missed his son.

Instead, he looked at Ella, who was breathtaking in a black suit. It was like seeing her for the first time. He wanted nothing more than to pull her into his arms and kiss her.

"Look what the cat dragged in," his mother whispered.

"She looks beautiful," Jack observed, drawing a sneer from his mother, who didn't dare a snarky comeback as the judge had begun talking.

Judge Caldwell, an older man with prominent jowls, looked directly at Ella and said, "Young lady, did you bring a child into my courtroom?"

"Yes, your honor," she replied. "I apologize. I had a daycare emergency about fifteen minutes ago. If he makes a sound, he'll be removed."

"First peep, do you understand?"

"Yes, your honor," Ella said with a nod.

"Can you believe that woman brought her child? Is she looking for a sympathy vote?" Jack's mother whispered, but Jack didn't hear her. He wondered why she'd brought Xander and didn't like any of the conclusions he came to. Glancing back at Xander, he didn't think the child was his usual smiley self. He wondered how long it would take for his mother to notice the resemblance between him and Xander. Maybe she wouldn't, but Dolores Brewster never missed a thing.

He tried to focus as each side presented their opening statements, and then witnesses were called. Jack watched Ella from behind and stole the occasional glance at Xander, who sat quietly on Padma's lap.

Over the next half hour, the hospital spokespeople outlined their reasons for wanting the new hospital wing. Jack, as planned, was the last witness called. When his name was called, Ella looked over her shoulder, and their eyes met. He offered her a small nod, which she ignored with a narrowing of her eyes.

* * *

Ella's cheeks still burned from the judge's reprimand. She hadn't wanted to bring Xander, but what choice did she have? She was a single mother with daycare issues. Why didn't stuff like this ever happen to fathers? Why did she think if Jack had shown up in court with a baby he'd have been praised for being a good dad?

The proceedings went on as her lawyer had predicted. The hospital only wanted to heal the hurt. If only these cold-hearted businesses could understand that the new wing was for the greater good, they would certainly move out of the way...

When they called Jack to testify, Ella looked at him, their eyes meeting, and then she looked past him at Xander, who was looking very attentively at his father. Too attentively, she thought. *Ut-oh.*

They swore Jack in, and he was seated beside the judge. At the sound of Jack's voice, Xander grew restless. Ella could sense it before she heard what the papers and television news would later refer to as "The Moment."

"Mr. Brewster, can you tell us what this hospital wing meant to your family and why you took it upon yourselves to raise the funds necessary to make this vision a reality?"

Jack looked away from his attorney and wearily at Ella. "Every generation of the Brewster Family has tried to give something back to the community—"

"Dada!"

The judge pointed directly at Ella, who turned to see Padma standing with a struggling Xander in her arms.

"Dada! Dada! Dada!" Xander screamed at the top of his lungs and strained, fighting with a panicked Padma to break free.

Jumping out of her seat, Ella started toward Xander, but her heels impeded her progress as she had to walk slowly to keep from tripping in the ill-fitting shoes. Out of the corner of her eye, she watched in surprise as Jack left the witness stand and raced down the center aisle to get to Xander.

The judge was banging his gavel and shouting for order and demanding that Jack return to the witness stand, but Jack ignored him.

"Jack, I've got him," Ella pleaded, already reaching her arms out to Xander, who continued to call out to Jack.

"Dada! Dada!"

Jack was closer to Xander and stepped in front of Ella. He held out his arms to the twisting child.

"I've got you, buddy," Jack said and took Xander in his arms.

The baby smiled and snuggled against his father's neck and quieted immediately.

Ella, too shocked to speak, watched as Jack made his way back to the witness stand with Xander in his arms.

"I'm sorry, your honor," Jack said, a broad smile breaking out on his face. "He just needed his daddy."

"Jackson! What are you talking about?" his mother asked, her voice cutting through the courtroom like an ambulance siren on a quiet country road. Somewhere in the melee, she had stood and looked like she was about to hurt someone.

By the shocked look on the judge's face, it appeared that even he didn't know what to say.

Ella had to hand it to Jack. He'd found a way to tell the world about his son.

"Is that child yours?" Jack's father asked above the roar of the crowd.

"Yes, he is. His name is Xander Martin Brewster," Jack said with a proud note in his voice as Ella sat and watched the courtroom proceedings slide off their access.

Placing her head in her hands, Ella felt the immediate onset of a pounding headache as the courtroom erupted into confused chatter.

Her lawyer pulled her wrist. "Is he serious? Is he the father of your child? Why didn't you tell me?"

Looking at him, she said, "Yes, he is my baby's daddy. I didn't want it to interfere with the case."

"Interfere? Are you serious?" he asked incredulously.

"It's a private matter between Mr. Brewster and myself," Ella said, thinking of how stupid it sounded.

"You are one piece of work, you know that? So is he, for that matter. I knew I should have never taken this case," he said, angrily shoving papers into his briefcase.

There were other sounds in the courtroom as the judge tried to gain control of the room.

When at last Ella fully raised her head back to consciousness, she looked at the witness stand and knew that Jack had been watching her. A court deputy had to stop Dolores Brewster from charging Jack on the witness stand, and the judge was threatening everyone with contempt of court. Several smartphones were raised in the air, snapping photos of Jack and Xander at the front of the room.

The judge banged his gavel in rapid succession, making Xander cry.

"Forty-five-minute recess," the judge barked and then turned to Jack. "Get that kid out of here."

Ella stood, placing her hands on the table in front of her to steady herself. She didn't want to turn around and see all the shocked and disappointed faces. Jack could deal with his messed-up family. She didn't care about them. She cared about Padma, Hiram, and Cindy. They must hate her for lying to them. The Small Business Coalition of NW Portland would be out for her blood.

Before she could decide what she should do, Jack was beside her with Xander in his arms. If he hadn't been holding the baby, she might have punched him. Might. She was kind of touched that he'd stood up and acknowledged their son in front of everyone. A place in her heart simmered with warmth at the gesture, which was also rather romantic.

Looking up at him, she waited. He didn't speak. Instead, he bent and kissed her. Leaning into the kiss, she felt relieved as Jack's free arm wrapped around her and made his intentions clear to anyone who was watching. She could feel the flashes of the cameras capture the moment. Xander beamed a smile and said, "Dada," to make sure she understood that he'd recognized his father and wasn't about to be ignored.

Charles and Dolores Brewster approached. The anger and disappointment etched into their faces like Halloween fright masks. Xander glanced at them and immediately buried his face in Jack's chest.

"Jackson, I don't believe I've met this woman," his father said, the anger barely contained.

"Pardon me, Father," Jack said, his arm tightening around Ella's waist as he met her gaze. "Ella, I'd like you to meet my father, Charles Brewster the third. Mother, I believe you already know Ella. Father, this is Marcella Martin. Ella and I met in Saint Barts. When Charles had his accident, I left unexpectedly. I left Ella a note, but she didn't get it and thought I'd walked away from her. We only met up again a little over three weeks ago. This is our son, Xander."

"You should have told us earlier," his father barked.

"The moment you found out, so we could have handled this privately," his mother added in a hiss.

"It was none of your business," Jack said, tightening his hold on Ella's waist.

Seeing the reaction on their faces, she could tell they didn't agree with their son. She didn't have time for this, nor did she want to be in the middle of what was shaping up to be a whopper of a family fight.

"I need to get Xander home. He has a fever," she interrupted and reached for Xander.

"You need to testify," Jack said, pulling his gaze away from his shocked parents.

"I'll take him home to Cricket. Then I'll be back," she said, bouncing Xander on her hip.

Then she added, "Xander, say bye-bye to Daddy."

As Xander and Jack said their goodbyes, his mother whispered angrily, "Did you get a paternity test?"

Ignoring his mother, Jack said, "I'll ride along with you. Make sure the press leaves you alone." Not waiting for an answer, he took Xander back in his arms and blazed a trail through the assembled crowd.

As they passed by Hiram, Padma, and Cindy, they all gave her long, uncomfortable looks. Cindy raised her arms as if to ask, "Why didn't you tell us?"

Ella merely shook her head, mouthed, "I'm sorry," and kept following Jack through the crowd.

By the time they'd put Xander into his car seat, the reporters had found them again.

"No comment," Jack said, waving away the reporters.

Once they were inside the car, the silence stretched between them. Even Xander seemed to sense the seriousness of the moment and remained quiet.

"Ella," Jack began.

"No, not a word. We need to get Xander to Cricket and get back to the hearing. We'll have time to discuss this later, not now."

"I'm sorry about what happened in there," he said.

"If you keep this up, I'll start crying, and then we'll have an even larger mess on our hands."

Reaching out, he placed his hand on her thigh and patted her.

"Damn it, Jack! Stop it!" she said through gritted teeth.

"I'll make all of this up to you, I promise."

"Talk is cheap," she said as she pulled into her parking spot, shut off the engine, and opened the back door to grab Xander.

Jack started to get out of the car, but she stopped him.

"Please, just stay here. I'll be back in a moment."

"Bye-bye, Xander," he said, pulling at her heartstrings once more.

Cricket happily took Xander from Ella as she quickly explained the situation. "Look, if it gets bad, if reporters start showing up, just close the store and hide out in my apartment."

"As if," Cricket said, bouncing a tired Xander on her hip.

"If he looks worse or isn't feeling good, just close the store for the day and go upstairs," Ella said, thinking that Cricket was more laid back than she appreciated.

"Ella, you worry too much. Go win your hearing. We'll be here when you get back," she said and gave her a quick hug.

Chapter Twenty-Five

Jack waited in the Volvo and wondered just how mad Ella was at him. He figured she was ready to erupt but that too much was going on for her to totally unravel.

"I don't want to talk about it," she said as she got in the car.

"Okay," he said and waited.

As she pulled out of the parking lot and back onto Lovejoy, he could see her trying to fight back tears.

By the time they were parked in the courthouse parking garage, she was dabbing at her eyes with tissue. He knew she was at her breaking point with him, his parents, and the hearing. Before she could protest, he was at her side of the car. As she got out, he crowded her, pulled her close, and refused to be rebuffed. Eventually, she leaned into his chest and allowed him to hold her.

"Either way this goes," he whispered, "I'm here for you. And tonight, we're going to put an end to this distancing moratorium. Understand?"

He felt her nod as she swallowed hard and tried to gain her composure.

"Time to face that mean judge again. Come on, sweetheart," he said as he led her back to the courthouse, holding her hand.

* * *

Ella let Jack lead her back to her seat in the courtroom. They'd gotten back right before the judge arrived. Avoiding eye contact with his parents and with her fellow shopkeepers, Ella sat down next to her very angry attorney, who glared menacingly at her.

When the judge sat down behind the bench, he glared at her and then at Jack, who was back on the witness stand and looking at her.

"Mr. Brewster, can I count on you to keep your personal drama out of the courtroom?" he asked, staring Jack down.

"Yes, your honor," Jack said and then looked back to Ella, who knew what was coming next.

"Ms. Martin, can I count on you to stop the circus as well?"

"Yes, your honor," she said, feeling her cheeks heat with embarrassment.

"Then let's continue," he said, and the attorney for the hospital, who seemed more than a little off his game, tried to bring the focus back to the debate at hand.

Ella thought that Jack had answered all the questions as she had predicted, but then he surprised her.

"I do have something I'd like to say," he said and looked toward the judge.

"What is it in regard to?" the judge asked.

"It is a possible solution for the shop owners if this expansion moves forward."

"Your honor, may I confer with the witness?" Jack's lawyer asked.

The judge, who wasn't at all happy, glanced at the man and said, "No. Continue, Mr. Brewster."

"I have a new building that is just a few blocks from the current location of *The Curry Leaf*, *Marcella's*, and *Cindy's*. It faces 23rd Avenue, which is a more traveled road than Lovejoy, so it has some advantages. My offer would be this: if the proprietors had to move, they could consider a new location in my distillery building. I'd give them a good deal on the rent, and there is a possibility of live/workspace, so they could live there as well."

Ella tried to get a handle on what Jack was offering. His distillery building was a very nice property but completely beyond what any of them could afford. She had to admit that it was a nice offer, but in reality, it just wasn't possible. She stole a glance at Padma, Hiram, and Cindy. Hiram's disapproval was more than evident as he met her gaze with a cold glare. She felt other eyes on her as well. Jack's mother dabbed at her eyes with a tissue, looking somewhat mortified by all that had transpired that day. They no doubt blamed her for trying to entrap their son.

At last, Jack left the stand and went back to sit next to his parents. Ella watched as his mother whispered something nasty to him, which made him cringe, but he didn't reply.

The judge called a ten-minute recess, and Ella's attorney, who'd ignored her for the last hour, focused all his attention on her.

"In light of this circus today, I don't think it would be a good idea to put you on the stand. I'll put anyone on but you."

"No one else is prepared," she whispered back.

"No one was prepared for what happened here today. I question your loyalty. And I'm sure they do, too."

"Are you kidding? Nothing has changed."

"This entire courtroom has turned into a soap opera. Your baby daddy will take care of you. I can see how he feels about you. But I don't know if I want to let you screw over everyone else. If I'd known, I could have leveraged this to our advantage. As it is, we are screwed."

"Why don't we ask them?" she said and looked back at her assembled friends. She had no idea how angry they were at this moment, but she knew there would be fences to be mended.

They both got up and waved to Padma, Hiram, and Cindy. Padma and Cindy stepped forward, but Hiram stood his ground at the back of the room. When they got close enough, Ella said, "I'm sorry, I didn't know myself until a few weeks ago. Nothing has changed. We still want the same things. I didn't know about the distillery building offer until just now. He doesn't want me to testify." She glanced at the angry attorney, who nodded.

"It would be stupid in light of what happened," the attorney said.

Cindy and Padma looked at each other, and it was Padma who spoke first. "So this is the family friend you went to visit that made you smile?"

Ella nodded. "But we are on opposite sides. We didn't discuss the expansion because I refused to. I don't know if we even like each other." Even though she said the words, a voice inside of her reminded her that she not only liked Jack, but she also loved him.

"Jack Brewster is Xander's father, and you didn't figure it out until three weeks ago?" Cindy asked, shaking her head.

"He looked different in Saint Barts. Remember? I told you he looked like a pirate," she said, careful to keep her voice low. There were angry whispers coming in the general direction of Jack and his parents. Several board members were confronting him, and if she had to guess, Ella thought it was a foregone conclusion that he was about to lose his VIP hospital parking pass and his board position.

"You've worked very hard, Ella. You're still our best hope," Padma said.

"Is Hiram mad?" Ella asked.

"Yes, very much," Padma replied. "He wants to give Jack Brewster a black eye for turning his back on you."

"He didn't know where to find me," Ella said, feeling like she wanted to smile from the support she was receiving.

"I can't believe this," her attorney muttered.

"Ella's our girl," Cindy said. "You be nice to her."

Chapter Twenty-Six

Jack watched over one of the board members' shoulders at the conclave happening around Ella. He was getting chewed out in hushed tones, not only by his parents but also by several angry board members who'd accused him of lying and a host of other unseemly things. He ignored most of it. Somewhere along the way, he heard that there would be an emergency vote to possibly get him removed from the board. So be it. He couldn't care less. He shocked them by offering to resign. All he wanted was to be with Ella and Xander. Everything else was background noise.

The judge reappeared, looking angrier than usual, as Ella's lawyer began to present his witnesses. Do-gooder after do-gooder said their piece about the impact to the environment and lifestyle of the NW Portland neighborhood. It was all white noise until at last, close to an hour later, they called Ella to the stand, eliciting much chatter. The judge's gavel broke up the squawking.

After she was sworn in, she glanced in Jack's direction but then focused solely on his lawyer as he took her through the questions at hand.

Dolores appeared to be so mad—her face red, her lips tight—she looked like she might explode.

"How hard would it be for you to recreate your place of business in a new location?"

"I couldn't," Ella said. "There is a lot of custom work inside my shop by artisans that would take months to replicate. The settlement being offered by the hospital would cover roughly twenty-five percent of my moving costs. It just isn't feasible. If this expansion goes forward, I'm out of business."

She had the supporting documentation which her lawyer passed on to the judge. For the most part, Ella was a great witness, adequately displaying how short-sighted the hospital was. Twenty minutes later, the hospital's attorney asked her a question based on Jack's testimony.

"What did you think of Mr. Brewster's offer?"

"Today is the first I've heard of it. It isn't in writing, so I think nothing of it," she answered.

"If it was in writing, would you consider it?"

"There are a lot of things I'd consider if I saw them in writing," she replied. "I can't answer about this until I see each point clearly identified, including lost wages while we struggle to change locations, make improvements, and incur expenses to make us whole."

A moment later, Ella was told she could step down, and the judge listened to closing statements. As the hour was late, he said he would offer his ruling in writing within seventy-two hours. And then they were adjourned.

"We'll see you at home shortly," Jack's mother said as they stood. She was barely holding it together. He recognized the signs. It was an order, not a suggestion.

"Not tonight," Jack said.

"Jackson, considering everything that has happened here today, you will obey your mother in this matter. We have a lot to discuss," his father said, and although it was barely a whisper, the tone was laced with menace.

"No," Jack said, feeling like a belligerent twelve-year-old. "My child is sick, and Ella is going to need me. I'll be at her place. Or, if she prefers, she'd be at my house. Whatever she needs or wants, I'll provide."

"Is she living with you in your grandmother's house?" his mother whispered angrily.

"No, I'm just trying to get sleepover privileges whenever she allows me over. She is very protective of Xander. I haven't been welcomed at her place for the last two weeks as this hearing was looming. It didn't help that you showed up at her shop and threatened her. That was more than a little upsetting to her. She really doesn't want you or Dad to play any part in Xander's life. That is your grandchild, and I support her thoughts on the matter. As for the separation moratorium between the two of us and Xander, well, it ends tonight. I can't spend another night without her or Xander, so don't come near us. No unplanned visits."

"Jackson, we need to talk about this," his father implored. "There are financial implications. You need a DNA test—"

"No, it's my business, not yours. I think you've really hurt your position with her. I don't know if she will ever let you be a part of Xander's life, which would be a real tragedy. He is a smart, sweet little boy."

His mother's face was bright red as she said, "If you bring that woman to my home—"

"You'll what, Mother?" Jack asked, keeping his voice low but matching threat and tone.

Glancing at her husband and then back to Jack, she said, "We'll see that you're dis-inherited."

"You're angry because you've had a big shock," Jack said, smiling at the thought of how ridiculous she sounded. "Sleep on it. See how you feel tomorrow. I should be back in the office by ten or later if Ella needs me. Sometimes, she asks me to leave if I overstay my welcome. Xander is a beautiful child. It would be a shame if you didn't get to meet your grandson because you did something rash. Trust me, it would be your loss."

Not waiting for a reply, he turned and looked for Ella. She was just leaving with her neighbors. He decided to let her go. He'd see her later.

Chapter Twenty-Seven

Ella opened the door to her apartment and found Cricket holding Xander on the couch while they watched the local television news.

"Hey, look who's here, Xander. It's movie star Mommy!"

"Very funny," Ella said, and then, "How is he?"

"Still a bit of a fever, but it doesn't seem to be getting any worse. He just wants to be held. I heard there wouldn't be a decision for a couple of days."

"Thank you so much for helping today," Ella said, reaching out for Xander, who went quickly into her arms. "Yeah, it was all a bit of a circus, which Xander contributed to. The judge was irritated. I don't know what I would have done without you today."

"No problem. Besides, the coverage of the hearing has been entertaining. Did Jack really tell everyone he was Xander's father?"

"Yes, he did," Ella said. "I don't know if I should thank him or hit him. I guess he really does want to be a part of Xander's life."

"Oh, Ella, that's a good thing. Give him a chance."

"I suppose it is good...until he meets someone who his family finds acceptable and gets married. Then he'll have other children, and then what?"

"What about you?" Cricket asked. "Aren't you in the first position for that role?"

"You should have seen the way Jack's parents looked at me. I felt cheap. It was awful.

Um…would you mind watching Xander while I change out of my suit?"

"No problem. So, just so I'm clear, you're questioning Jack's motives?"

"Yes," she said as she placed Xander back in Cricket's arms and made her way to the bedroom. Pulling her cell phone from her pocket, Ella looked down and noticed she had five calls from her mother and two calls from Jack. She decided to ignore all of them.

Five minutes later, she was back in her jeans and a red cashmere sweater set.

"I think he did it for you. I think he chose you and Xander over his family," Cricket said as Ella sat next to her on the couch and watched as Xander half walked, half crawled over to her.

"I hope you're right," Ella said quietly as her heart gave a hitch as local news turned to national news. "Would you like to stay for dinner? I got a take and bake pizza yesterday, it's in the fridge. I just need to bake it."

"No, I think I'll be heading home. I have a mid-term to study for, and something tells me that you won't be alone for long tonight."

"Cricket, Jack didn't make any firm plans with me. Stay."

As Cricket stood, there was a knock on the door. "Told you so. Don't get up. I'll let him in."

Ella watched as Cricket opened the door to Jack, who stepped back in surprise. He was still in his suit, but he'd removed the emerald silk tie. His shirt was open at the neck, and she could see the white t-shirt underneath. The whole look was sexy, and the moment she took it all in, she felt the heat start low in her belly. She had missed this man.

"Hello," he said, glancing past Cricket to Ella and Xander.

"Well, hello there," Cricket said. "Come on in. I'm Cricket, and I was just leaving."

"Jack Brewster," Jack said, extending his hand to shake Cricket's. "Thank you for the help with Xander today. We were really in a bind."

She smiled and then turned back to Ella. "Sounds like it. No problem, I adore Xander. I'm here anytime you need me."

"Thank you, really—"

"Oh, Ella, your baby daddy is here."

"Dada!" Xander exclaimed at the sight of Jack, who dropped the bags in his arms on the nearest flat surface and made a beeline for Xander.

Ella stood and handed Xander to Jack as Cricket said, "Goodnight, you all have some fun now." Then she shut the door behind her, and they were alone.

One arm around Xander left one arm free to snare Ella, which was exactly what she hoped for and what Jack did.

"Hey," he said, pulling her to him. "It's been a long two weeks."

They kissed quickly as Xander made his displeasure known.

"He doesn't feel good," she said as they both focused on Xander.

"Poor Xanderboo," Jack said as Ella looked at the bags littering the floor.

"What's in the bags?"

"Dinner, and I brought an overnight bag because I'm spending the night."

Ella smiled, despite her doubts. Good. She wanted to go to bed with him and wake up with him tomorrow morning. She realized, finally, that she wanted him to stay, not for just a night. Forever.

"It smells familiar," she said, thinking that it couldn't be what she thought it was.

"It should, it's from Padma and Hiram's restaurant. I placed the takeout order this morning and told them it was for you to make sure they wouldn't poison me. When I picked it up a few minutes ago, we had a nice conversation. I think I can help them if the hearing goes in favor of the hospital."

"You hate Indian food," she said, wondering if she would ever figure this man out. How many surprises could she endure in one day?

"When I eat it alone. I've never shared it with you," he said, his eyes sparkling.

"Xander loves it," Ella said, her voice sounding strange even to her own ear. "Maybe you will too."

"I can't wait to try it with my son and his beautiful mother," he said as his arms encircled her again. Before she could even absorb his words, he kissed her.

"What are you doing to me?" she asked.

"I'm trying my damnedest to get you to fall in love with me. Is it working?" he asked, looking down at her, his lips gently brushing hers.

"Think about your parents," she said, pushing aside his comment, which she couldn't quite believe. "They hate me. They want you to settle down with a nice girl, like that redhead I saw you photographed with." Her breath came out faster than she'd have liked.

"The drunk woman from a party I didn't want to go to last Saturday night?" he asked.

"The one who draped herself all over you?"

"Remember how I called you, and you told me to go away?" he asked, his hand brushing her breast.

"You two looked friendly. Is that why, because I turned you down, you wanted to get even?" Ella asked. She'd told him to go away every night for the last two weeks. She hadn't really meant it and had been surprised he hadn't stopped by and forced the issue. She wanted him to prove it. She needed him to prove it. Maybe that was why she was intentionally provoking him.

"My mother introduced her to me. I don't even remember her name, but the photo from the paper obviously bothered you. Glad to see you're capable of jealousy."

"Ginger Fleming," Ella replied as she stepped back from Jack.

"Oh, Ginger Fleming. Hadn't given her a second thought," he said and swung Xander into his arms, then followed Ella into the kitchen.

"Really?" she said as she pulled packages from the paper bags.

"Really. I'll prove it to you later. I've thought about you a lot."

She would reflect on those words later. Not now. Now, she was pissed.

"Look Jack, I'm not naïve. I highly doubt a man who looks like you has been without female companionship," Ella said, dropping the silverware loudly on the counter and not caring. She needed to know.

Jack sighed. Xander was placed in his highchair. Then Jack reached out a calming hand and she stepped just out of range. "Okay, here is the truth. Before I went to the Caribbean, I had a bit of a reputation as a man who dated a lot."

"So I've heard," Ella said. She didn't know specifics; it was a bit of a bluff but had the desired effect.

"Fine, but hear me out. When I got down there, to the Caribbean, something changed. I was alone for the first time in my life. Really alone. No Mommy and Daddy Brewster to save my ass. I was taught how to make rum, but then I had to show the generous family who had agreed to show me how they made rum that I was worthy of their secrets and trust. I had to show them that I paid attention and that I could do it. I had to do a good job. It was no longer the kind of work I used to do to make my parents happy. No, I had to do well for the family, my adoptive family. If I ruined a batch of rum, it affected how they would live that month. Literally, it was the difference between them

241

having electricity at their home and their factory or just their factory. It kind of put my privileged life into perspective."

Ella nodded and looked away. Jack had some depth to him. She had underestimated him. And he wasn't finished.

"So, to address your concerns. When I met you, I was looking for something different than I had, say, a year earlier. I was looking for forever. I wanted a partner. When I saw you, you took the very air from my lungs. And then to not know what happened… Torture. Fucking. Daily. Torture," he said and pulled her to him. "So when I tell you there isn't anyone else, you need to understand, I mean what I say."

She let him hug her, and it felt more intimate than making love. She whispered, "Okay."

He kissed her quickly on the lips, squeezed her once and then let her go. Without missing a beat, he turned to Xander, who was wide eyed, and smiled, as Jack said, "Look, Xander, your favorite chow."

* * *

Jack was secretly pleased. He didn't know the redhead and didn't want to know her, or any other woman for that matter. Considering everything that happened earlier in the day, he thought it was interesting that this detail was the one Ella had latched onto. Good.

He'd meant every word he'd said to Ella. She was it for him. He loved her.

He wanted to know everything he could about Ella. She'd been very private, and it hadn't been easy to get details out of her. Each little nugget of information was like hidden treasure, and he'd just hit on a large chunk.

"What would you like?" she asked, looking at the cartons of food.

"What do you suggest?"

"You got Xander and my favorite, butter chicken with Raita and Naan," she said.

"I'll copy your plate," he said and watched as she turned to Xander in his highchair and got him ready for dinner. Placing her hand on Xander's cheek she tested for a fever.

"Does he have a fever?"

"A little," she said. "After he finishes dinner, I'll give him some liquid children's Tylenol. He seems to do okay with the cherry flavor."

"Poor kid," Jack said.

He was surprised to see Xander pick at his butter chicken. The stuff was good. And unlike their other dinners, they were all starting to relax around each other. He didn't want to ruin the mood, but he couldn't help but ask Ella a question that had been on his mind all day.

"What did you think of my idea of the distillery building on 23rd Avenue?"

Ella took a sip of the chardonnay that he'd brought and tilted her head to the side as if she were trying to figure out a complex problem. She was adorable when she looked like that.

"I don't think I can afford it. The building is new, and I've seen the space. The rent would be more than I could afford. It will probably work for Hiram and Padma because if they were in a more populated area, they would get the business to sustain it. I think I might lose the hospital business, so it would be a wash. Cindy is loaded, so she can afford to do whatever she wants. I'd love to have more of a café space for Cricket, but I don't think it is feasible."

"I'm pretty sure I'll make you an offer you can't refuse. Tell me, what do you pay now for rent of the space and the apartment?" he asked as his finger ran circles around the rim of his wine glass.

Ella looked uncomfortable, and for a moment, he worried that he'd ruined the mood, but then she stood and got a warm cloth to clean up Xander. When she named a figure, he was a bit shocked. She was getting an excellent price, but money didn't matter to him at this point.

"See? I don't think you can match that," she said.

"Of course, I can," he said. "We'd put it in the rental agreement for a certain time period. Hell, maybe I won't charge you anything."

"And you'd be showing favoritism," she said.

"I'd do it for all three of you," he said and watched her. This had come as a surprise, and she wasn't sure what to make of it. So, she ignored it. Fine, he'd planted the seed.

"I think we should get Xander a quick bath and see if we can get him down. He didn't eat much. I don't want him to get any worse."

Jack held Xander as Ella ran the bath. He watched as she got his towel and washcloth ready, even turning up the heat in the apartment so he wouldn't get cold.

Xander didn't act like himself in the bath. He didn't want to play with any of his toys. Ella made quick work of it and before long, he was bundled up in his pajamas, but he had no intention of going to sleep.

"Can I try?" Jack asked as Xander grew crankier and crankier.

"Sure," she said and handed him to Jack. Sensing a difference, Xander began to cry and asked for "Mama."

"Sorry, I tried, but you're up again," he said and handed him back to Ella.

"We'll walk," she said and began pacing around her apartment. "I do have a couple more questions for you, but you might not like them," she whispered in a soft tone.

"Go ahead," he said, glancing at his watch. It was almost ten o'clock, and Xander didn't look like he had any intention of giving up the ghost.

"Did you get removed from the hospital board?"

"They had a special vote this evening. I haven't checked the results, but I'm assuming I got fired. I offered to resign, but I think they would prefer to go through the formality of a vote."

"Did your parents know you were going to offer up the distillery building?"

"No," he said. "It was a surprise."

"What if they don't approve it?" she asked, a new look of worry on her face.

"It isn't their call," he said, "so don't worry."

Chapter Twenty-Eight

Ella did worry. The distillery building, if it was the same rent she was paying, could work, at least until she could figure out what she wanted to do. She didn't believe in the free offer. She wouldn't even consider it. What about Xander? What about Jack? What happened now? She needed more from him, but what, well, she wasn't quite sure.

By eleven o'clock, Ella had taken Xander's temperature and was pleased it had gone down.

"I have an idea," she said, thinking that this would test Jack's desire to be a father in a whole new way.

He was rocking Xander in a chair, but Xander's eyes were wide open and watching the adults around him.

"We can put him between us in bed. I've never done it before because you need two people to make sure he doesn't roll off the side. But with both of us here, we can put him between us, and he'd be safe."

"I'm game," he said.

Ten minutes later, they were in her bed with Xander between them. Ella wore white cotton pajamas with white roses appliqued on the fabric, and Jack wore his t-shirt and boxers. It felt very intimate. Possibly more intimate than when they'd participated in many different activities in that bed. How was that possible? Maybe because Xander was their ultimate, best joint creation.

They each had a hand on Xander, gently comforting him as they stole glances at each other.

"Ella," Jack said, his voice soft in the muted light.

She met his gaze but said nothing as his hand reached for and found hers.

"I need to tell you something."

She tensed. What if it was too much for him? What if despite everything he'd said there was someone else? Well, she'd do what she was good at doing. She'd deal with it. No, it couldn't be. He wouldn't do that to her.

But even with everything he had done and said, his next words floored her.

"I'm in love with you."

Each of his words hit her like sweet kisses. She didn't think or ponder her words. She just looked at him, seeing the love in his eyes for her as she whispered, "I love you too."

Gently, they moved toward each other, their lips meeting as they cradled their child between them.

As Jack ended the kiss, he placed his hand on Ella's cheek and said, "Then I have a question for you."

Did he want her to move in? That was probably it. He would want Xander close. How did she feel about that? Well, maybe it would be a good steppingstone.

"Okay," she said and waited.

"Will you marry me?"

She should have known, but she couldn't believe it.

"You want to marry me?"

"Yes, I love you. I'll never love anyone like I love you," he said. "I think I fell in love with you in Saint Barts. It was immediate, and then I lost you. I felt so thankful when I saw you again. I was so miserable without you. I didn't know how much until I couldn't see you. It really bothered me. Losing you was one thing, but these last few weeks have been a different kind of misery. I was on pins and needles, hoping you would let me be a part of your life, a part of Xander's life."

"You were always going to be a part of Xander's life. But denying myself access to you... well... I couldn't do it. I know about the misery of being away from you. I can't do it again."

He smiled, "You don't have to."

"I love you, too, so much," she said but started to struggle with her words, "I don't...I can't...but your mother and father hate me—"

"I don't care about anyone but you and Xander. Marry me."

"You'll lose the company—"

"I couldn't care less. I want you in my life. I want to go to bed with you every night and wake up every morning. I want to make love with you and grow old with you. I want us to have another baby. Money comes and goes, love...our love...well, it only happens once if you are lucky to find it. And then it lasts forever."

Ella was speechless. She wanted to believe him. Needed to believe him. He made it all sound so simple.

"You really love me," she said.

"I've been trying to tell you."

"I love you," she said and felt the tortured need to be with this man to never let him go. The idea that he wanted to marry her was more than she could have ever dreamed of. "I just don't want you to regret that you chose me. Xander will always be part of your life, but you don't have to marry me."

"I want to marry you. You don't need to worry about my family or my business. I have a little something that is my own. My new rum business doesn't belong to my family. I own the distillery building. All the patents for *Red's Rum* belong to me. My family gave me the equipment before Charles left. It was part of my trust fund. I'll relocate your business and both your neighbors'. I'll make sure you have everything you want because

I can, and I want to make you happy. It will be our rum business."

Ella said, her voice cracking. "And you really want to marry me?"

"Yes, say yes to me," he said and kissed her again.

"Yes, yes, yes," she said. "When?"

"Tomorrow? I want to be your husband as soon as possible."

Jack reached over and gently wiped a tear from her cheek. She hadn't realized she was crying until he touched her. The last two years had been a long, hard struggle. She was tired, so tired, of always having to be on top of her game, never letting her guard down or taking a break. To always take care of every one of Xander's needs. Now, she would have someone there to share the good and bad times.

"You've done such an amazing job with Xander, with your business," he said. "I'm so proud of you. But from here on out, we are a team. We are in this together."

"I'm no longer alone."

"I don't think you ever were. You've got a great support system in those neighbors of yours."

"I love them for all they've done for me. I think, like me, they'd protect Xander with their lives even though he's my son, the child I made with the love of my life," she said, feeling more tears fall.

"Thank you, thank you for letting me be a part of this family, your family."

"I'll let you in on a little secret. I think, finally, you've proven yourself," she said with a nod.

Jack smiled, and said, "I'll keep proving myself to you."

"Good. I need that," she said.

"Can we have another one, you know, another baby, maybe down the road? I want to see you pregnant with my child. I want to be there for you. I want to be in the delivery room. Would all of that be okay?"

"I think it would be wonderful," she said. "Maybe two more, if you'd be up for it."

"Oh, I'll be up for it," he said with a smile.

Xander stirred between them, reached for his BeauBeau, and pulled it tighter to him.

"Hey, little man," Jack whispered, looking down at Xander. "Your mommy and daddy are getting married."

* * *

Ella was up early the next morning. Jack found her in the shower, leaning against the tile and smiling so peacefully he almost didn't want to bother her. Xander was still snoozing after a late night, so he gently pushed back the curtain as she smiled at him. He kissed her, and then they took advantage of this rare morning time together.

"Do you still want to marry me?" he asked.

"Yes," she said and pulled him close for another kiss.

Over breakfast, where Xander showed Jack just how far he could toss Cheerios, Jack looked at Ella over his coffee and said, "I think he is better this morning."

"I hate to say it, but I like the destruction of his breakfast. It is a definite sign that everything is good in his world."

Jack rubbed Xander's head, who looked at him and said, "Dada."

"I love you, Xander," he said.

Xander smiled at his father and said, "Wuv you."

"Oh, my heart," Ella said, touching her chest.

"I think that might be the best thing I've ever heard in my life," Jack said.

"Me too."

Xander continued to bombard the floor with Cheerios.

Jack looked at Ella and smiled before asking tentatively, "Do you mind if I move a few things in here, maybe a pair of jeans and a few pairs of underwear?"

"I'm surprised. Don't you want us to move into your big house?"

"I hate it. I like this place. And if there is a pet policy that allows dogs, Moonshine would be very helpful in Cheerio removal from the floor. He's a great vacuum."

"Considering that the hospital will be paying my landlord handsomely for this property, I think we can talk to him so that Moonshine is welcome, as are you, Mr. Jack Brewster, for the next few months."

"We can remodel the house on the hill, any way that you want. Make it a place you want to live and raise a family. Tear it down and rebuild it for all I care."

"You might regret those words."

"I like what you've done with your space. I think I'll like what you do," he said.

"And you made a generous offer in court yesterday. I'd like to take you up on it," she said.

"You might have won, so don't assume you get the plush accommodations of the brewery building," he said. "Did you consider that?"

"I'd bet you something that involved our naked bodies on that, but even if I lost, I'd still be winning."

He laughed, and Xander followed suit, not knowing why everyone at the table was happy but going with it.

"We are most definitely going to lose the case against the hospital, so eventually, the shop will be moving. If Xander and I move in with you, what will we do with the apartment over the shop?" she asked, accepting what she knew to be true.

"Keep it. Use it for staff or as a clubhouse. Ella, my personal wealth—regardless of whether my parents cut me or us out of the will—is over fifty million. Money doesn't mean to me what it does to lots of other people. I want you to marry me without a prenup. I want to share what I have. You are sharing Xander with me, so I think it is only fair that I share the love of my life. But all I will ask you is to put my name on Xander's birth certificate."

The coffee cup was halfway to her lips, but she paused. "You…you are worth fifty million dollars?"

"Yep," he said, smiling. "So stop shopping at secondhand shops. You can afford anything you want. Although, you do look lovely in anything, or nothing at all. Your choice."

"Xander doesn't have to have secondhand clothing…"

"No," he said, watching as she gently set the cup on the table. He took her hand and said, "And I want you to wear my ring, and I'll wear yours. Of course, yours will probably have a bit more sparkle than mine."

"Okay. I'll add your name to his birth certificate. I just need to find out how."

"I know how. I've already signed the paternity affidavit. My lawyer has it."

She smiled, wiped away a tear, and he said, "I'm kind of excited."

"Me too," she said. "I'm waiting to wake up from this amazing dream."

He squeezed her hand, "It's not a dream."

Chapter Twenty-Nine

Jack was happy the security guard didn't stop him when he entered the Brewster Building at 9:30 that morning. He had done a quick detour to his house on Vista to change clothes and to ask his housekeeper to keep Moonshine company as he did not want to take the dog into the office today in case there was an issue. And by issue, he meant his parents. They tolerated his dog, but Moonshine didn't like them. He didn't blame the smart animal. He wished he could hide out with Ella instead of being where he was.

He got to his office and sat behind his desk without issue. His voicemail was full. He had seventy-two new emails, mostly from news organizations. The only call he made was to his attorney and best friend, Flint.

"Hey Flint," he said and didn't need to identify himself in greeting.

"It is the man, the myth, the baby daddy, wow. I heard about it. Everyone with a heartbeat in Portland heard about it," Flint said. "Actually, I heard old Lester Holt even talked about it on Nightly News, but only the West Coast edition. Are you okay?"

"I'm great. I'm getting married to Ella today. I need a best man. What are you doing at 2 p.m.? Could you swing by the courthouse?"

"Hmmm, it is my day to visit the burrito lady and get a burrito, but that can wait. I'm free. Besides, I'm looking forward to meeting your new bride. She's kind of gorgeous and settling by marrying you, which I intend to tell her," he teased.

"Great. Thank you, and bring the paternity affidavit. We are adding my name to Xander's birth certificate."

"Congratulations, Dad," Flint said.

"Actually, Xander calls me Dada."

"Well, isn't that too cute for words? Is Dolores going to be there with Charles, fifteen or twenty, or whatever the hell your dad is?"

"He's Charles the third, and no, I didn't invite them."

His office door opened, and his parents marched in on cue.

"You had to mention them, didn't you?" Jack said.

"They conjured like an evil spell," Flint said.

"Something like that. I've got to go. See you later today. Let's meet on the steps at two."

His parents didn't sit. They just loomed before him. He recognized the attempt at intimidation. Heck, they'd been doing it to him since he was a kid.

"Mother. Father," he said in turn.

"I don't know where to start," his mother said, clearly upset and off her game.

His father did not have the same problem. "I do. Now, listen here, Jackson—"

"I quit," Jack said.

"What?" his father said.

"You can't—" his mother started.

"Now, you both look here" Jack interrupted. "I have a son. He is gorgeous. Maybe I'm biased, but he is wonderful. And Ella, well, she is the love of my life. I knew it the moment I saw her in Saint Barts on the beach. She was wearing a red bikini and walking along the water, right where the amazing aqua water was rolling over her toes. I spied on her to find out where she was staying. Then I sat next to her at the bar and fed her high-end Mojitos. Heck, we both ended up getting sloshed, but we had the best night of my life."

"Jaaacccckkkksssooonnn—"

"Shut up, Mother. Then, after that fabulous night, I made the biggest mistake of my life. I chose this family over her. I flew home to wait vigil over Charles's bedside, which I did to please you and was totally unnecessary. I put that asshole before the love of my life. I should have chosen her. It is the biggest regret I will ever have in this life. I will spend the rest of my life trying to make it up to her."

"I guess I don't understand," his mother said.

"Here, I'll show you a photo of Xander in case you didn't get a good look yesterday. He looks exactly like me at the same age."

His parents were silent—surprised, he guessed.

He grabbed his cell and pulled up a photo of Xander.

"This is Xander. He calls me Dada. Ella was so generous to let him do that from the beginning. I didn't realize it until just now. I need to thank her for that, but then she is a selfless, kind person. I'm lucky she even gives me the time of day."

Dolores's face softened as she took the phone out of Jack's hand and looked at Xander.

"He looks just like you," she said, using a soft tone he rarely heard. "Look at that, Charles. It is my baby all over again."

"He is my baby. He's a very sweet, smart little guy," Jack said with pride.

"When may I meet him?" Dolores asked. And in that moment, he saw her vulnerability.

"Well, it is complicated because we are a bit of a package deal. Ella, Xander, and me."

"I was thinking about what she said. First, I think we can all agree she is a very beautiful woman. Well-spoken, smart," his father said.

"She is the love of my life," Jack said. "Of course, she is smart."

"If you love her, then she is a member of the family," Dolores said, but Jack could tell that it didn't come easily.

"We are getting married at the courthouse today," Jack said.

If he'd slapped his mother, he'd have gotten less reaction.

"Absolutely not. We will have a family wedding and a lovely reception. No child of mine is getting married at the courthouse," Dolores said. "You deserve better. She deserves better. We can arrange it quickly, but in no way will we be denied such a lovely event."

Jack smiled to himself. It was easier than he thought it would be. Someday, he'd have to thank Xander.

Ten minutes later, Jack called Ella at *Marcella's*.

He could almost hear the trepidation in her voice when he asked her what she thought about the change of plans.

"Your mother wants us to have a wedding?"

"A big party, as soon as it can be arranged."

"She must really want to meet Xander," Ella said.

"Bingo. I knew you'd see through her. And Dad thinks you are pretty and well-spoken," Jack said.

"I guess this is good news."

"Honey, let's still get married today. I would feel good about it. I want to be married to you. We can still do the fancy dog and pony for my parents. What do you say?"

"Yes," she said, excitedly. "I've been dreaming of being married to you since Saint Barts."

* * *

Ella didn't know why she was so nervous, but she was as she got ready in her apartment before Jack arrived to take her to the courthouse.

That morning there had been an emergency visit to *Trudel's Wedding Boutique*, the most exclusive wedding shop in town, if

258

not the west coast, which had not only freaked out Ella, but also a nervous little woman in black—Trudel herself. Trudel was used to several weeks, if not months, in preparation for a bride to wear one of her dresses in their wedding.

"I just...I just don't know if we have anything to help you," Trudel said, looking as if she might drop over.

Another woman, who looked like Trudel but had a surer smile, appeared and put her hand on Trudel's shoulder. "I've got this, Mom. Hi, I'm Suzie. I can help you out."

Ella settled on a lovely double breasted ivory suit that had a long, narrow pencil skirt with a slit up the side. *Trudel's* also had exactly the right shoes, which were heels of the same color in raw silk.

Ella loved the suit, and they had even found a matching bow tie and vest for Xander. With a little help from Cindy, she was able to get Xander outfitted.

By the time Jack arrived at her apartment carrying several boxes, she was ready. Her heart still skipped a beat when she opened the door to him, and he smiled appreciatively.

"You're beautiful," he said by way of greeting.

She didn't greet him. Instead, she took the boxes out of his arms, set them to the side, and then stepped toward him. He wrapped her into a tight embrace, pulling her close.

"I love you," she whispered and heard him sigh contentedly.

"I love you, too," he replied and rubbed a hand along her back. The boxes held a bouquet of white roses and gardenias for the bride and one very special box held platinum wedding bands along with a large ruby and diamond engagement ring.

Cricket stood up for Ella and Flint stood up for Jack. Ironically, the judge who had been so hard on them the day before was available to perform the nuptials. He even seemed to get a kick out of it. He chuckled when he saw them.

"Not you two again," he said.

"Would you please marry us, your honor?" Ella said.

"It would be my honor." Smiling, as he shook his head, he said, "Just so you know, I think your little boy is a cute kid. Just not in my courtroom. You make a sweet little family."

"Thank you," Jack said as he looked to Ella who smiled back at him.

Chapter Thirty

After they had made everything legal, Jack, Ella, Xander, Cricket and Flint ended up having a late lunch at the *Curry Leaf*. Hiram, Padma, and Cindy joined the party, and it turned into a real celebration. When Jack's phone buzzed at lunch with an incoming text, he didn't want to read it. And when he did, he groaned. His new wife visibly tensed. He looked up and met her eyes.

"What?" she asked as he read the text and sighed.

"Mom and Dad want us to come to dinner with Xander tonight."

Ella set her fork down and dabbed at her mouth with a napkin. "Well, it is official. I've lost my appetite for Indian food, which was my favorite until ten seconds ago."

Flint laughed, and Cricket made a sign of the cross, which made Flint laugh harder. Jack looked at them, and Flint looked toward Cricket and winked.

* * *

Ella ripped the tag off her new black dress that had been hastily purchased after their lunch. Cricket had insisted Ella not even consider opening *Marcella's* on her wedding day. Reluctantly, she agreed. Jack took Ella to go shopping for a new dress for her to wear to her new mother and father-in-law's house for dinner.

"You don't need to do this," Jack said for the tenth time as he held Xander while sitting on the edge of the bed. Ella looked each way in the hallway mirror of her apartment. "You look great in any outfit."

"Don't you like this dress?" she asked, pulling her attention from the mirror to Jack. It was a black wrap-around with a sash to tie on the side that he'd bought her earlier that day, along with matching shoes and a handbag.

"I love it, but you are nervous, and you don't need to be. I'm nervous about what you will think of them, not what they will think of you. You understand the difference, right?"

"You say that because you are a man. Deep down, you care what they think. Xander at least looks cute." He was sporting a new outfit that he had not wanted to put on.

Jack stood and walked to her with Xander in his arms. "It is because I'm your husband, and I want to make sure you are always as happy as humanly possible. I love you, Mrs. Brewster." He kissed her as Xander smiled and said, "Mama, Dada."

Jack drove Ella in his Audi with Xander in the new baby seat in the back.

Jack pulled into the driveway of a large white house with evergreen shutters further up Vista Drive.

"This is your parents' house? I love this house. Every time I drive by it, I wonder who lives in it. I've always wanted to see inside."

Jack shook his head. "Now you know, and you are paying a high price to see the inside. I grew up here. It is as cold as that mausoleum that I live in, trust me," he said as he turned off the engine.

Ella tried not to notice as the uniformed butler opened the door for her, but she did thank him, to which he nodded. Maybe he'd been instructed not to talk to her. This was going to take some time to get used to.

Jack freed Xander from the car seat and told the butler that the keys were in the ignition and then thanked him.

He carried Xander to where Ella waited and held out a hand to her. Together, they made their way up several dozen steps.

"Have I told you lately how beautiful you look?"

Ella shook her head and whispered, "Have I told you lately how nervous I am?"

"Don't be. Whatever happens, whatever they say, I love you," he said.

"They don't know we are married, maybe you should take off your ring?" It was the last thing she wanted him to do. She loved seeing him with her ring on his left hand.

"No, no more secrets. I told them we were getting married. Now, they know I was serious."

The door opened to a smiling Dolores and Charles, who greeted Ella warmly as if they were meeting her for the first time. It was as if the day before never happened. Then, they made a beeline for Xander. Being that he didn't like strangers, especially when they were focused so intently on him, he reacted.

As Dolores reached for him, he immediately cried, clutched BeauBeau, and turned to his father for protection.

"I'm sorry, he doesn't like strangers," Ella explained, feeling all kinds of discomfort.

Jack was blunter.

"Xander doesn't know you well enough yet. Don't reach for him. Let him come to you," Jack said. "Just be cool for a bit."

"Remember, he was sick yesterday. He still might be recovering from his bug. He will warm up," Ella said kindly, and then Dolores did something that shocked them both. She hugged Ella, who didn't know what to do with the sudden contact except go with it. Well, fake it until you make it.

"Jackson was shy at the same age," Dolores said as she looked at Xander and smiled. "Welcome to our home. Why don't you come inside?"

It wasn't, "Welcome to the family." But it was something.

But Xander proved to be finicky, and they decided they would have a buffet dinner in the living room. They asked Ella about *Marcella's* in generic terms, but at least they asked. Jack told them more about how they met in Saint Barts, keeping more salacious details unsaid.

Xander either stayed on Jack's lap or wanted to be with Ella for the remainder of the evening. And the less friendly Xander was, the more it bothered Jack's parents.

They ate a dinner of salmon and vegetables, Xander trying a few bites, but he was mostly overwhelmed by the adults all aiming their attention at him.

Finally, Ella felt bad and decided to try something.

"Xander," she said as she held him, drawing his attention. "Let's show everyone how you can walk like a big boy. Maybe Dada can take you for a spin around the room?"

Jack, who had been sitting next to Ella, stood and held out his arms to Xander, who willingly went into them. Jack walked bent over with Xander, holding his hands as Xander walked clunkily around the large living room, drawing applause from Jack's parents.

After the promenade, Jack paused next to his mother and said, "Please make some room." Then, he and Xander sat between his parents. It did the trick. Xander crawled over to a delighted Dolores's lap. He didn't look at her, but he played with her pearls and leaned against her, to her delight.

Dolores looked up at Ella, who nodded and smiled. "See, it was just a matter of time."

Eventually, Jack suggested they leave so that they could get Xander to bed, reading Ella's mind.

At the door, both parents surprised her by hugging her again. It was a bit unnerving, but this time, she sensed some warmth.

"I'm happy for you," Dolores said to Jack as she hugged him, then she addressed them as a group. "Thank you all for coming tonight. It meant a lot."

Back in the car, Jack said, "They like you."

"How could you tell?" Ella asked.

"The hugging. Mom and Dad don't hug anyone they plan on trying to destroy."

"Oh, well, that is good," she said.

Jack laughed and said, "You know I was serious. I will always choose you and Xander, always."

"Thank you," she said.

"Okay, that first meeting is over. It will never be that hard again, I promise. And hey, do you know what tonight is?" Jack whispered later from the doorway as Ella held Xander in the rocking chair, his long lashes fluttering as his eyes closed.

"Wednesday?" she asked, raising one finger in the air.

"Our wedding night," he said, looking almost offended.

"I knew that," she said with a smile.

"Time to practice for another Xander," he said.

Xander had proven to be the great equalizer with all grandparents involved. He was soothing tensions and hard feelings like only a grandchild could. His biggest advocate was his grandmother Dolores, who couldn't believe how much he resembled his father at the same age. After that first meeting, the great melt began.

Dolores had traded in her business suits for jeans and sweaters when she babysat her grandson, which she asked to do as often as possible. It still unnerved Ella a bit, but a softer side of Dolores was wonderful to see. And, she liked Ella, calling her the 'daughter she had always hoped for,' but Ella was still a little nervous around the other woman.

Red's Rum was launched to rave reviews two weeks after Jack and Ella's private nuptials. The bottles featured a majestic Moonshine gazing contemplatively toward the sky as his velvety ears flapped in the breeze.

Everyone in Ella's life attended the launch party, which was held at the new distillery in the Brewster Building. Her mother, her new in-laws, and her family by choice—Padma, Hiram, Cindy, and Cricket, who had taken to spending a bit of time with Jack's best friend, Flint—all enjoyed the party. Jack met her mother, and, to Ella's surprise, they got along famously.

"Just tell me why," she complained. "I think she likes you better than she likes me."

"She reminds me of you, just in subtle ways," Jack said as he wrapped his arms around his wife and kissed her.

"Good thing you're handsome, or I'd have to punish you for that comment," she muttered.

Moonshine was an instant celebrity, his image not only gracing the label of Red's Rum but a slew of merchandise, including t-shirts and beer mugs. For a spiced blend, he was pictured wearing a pirate hat and an eye patch. Thankfully, he hadn't let the instant celebrity go to his head.

Their official wedding was held three months after Jack and Ella's private ceremony. Charles and Dolores hosted Ella and Jack in their large home, which had a ballroom on the third floor and could easily accommodate two hundred guests. It was the event of the year as it was planned completely by Dolores Brewster and catered by Padma and Hiram. Not surprisingly, it was covered by all the local media and was the talk of the town for months.

Before the wedding, Ella returned to *Trudel's* and got fitted for an actual wedding gown that was a halter style and reminded the groom of the first time he'd seen her in Saint Barts.

Moonshine and Xander added to the event, joining their parents at the front of the room. Moonshine carried their platinum bands from a little baggie on his collar, which made the best man, Flint, say, "I really only have one job, and the dog is doing it."

At the reception, as they were dining on Padma and Hiram's famous butter chicken, Dolores approached and leaned down to Jack.

"I've been talking to a few of the guests. They have been asking me about the next mayoral run and if you are going to toss your hat in the ring. Everyone is very positive."

Jack met Ella's gaze, smiled, then looked at his mother and said, "The only Brewster who should run is you."

She looked like she'd been slapped and then Jack added, "Ella and I talked, we think you'd make a fabulous mayor."

* * *

Jack wanted Ella to meet his brother, Charles. But all invitations to Charles went unanswered. The last they heard before the wedding, he was in some small village in Africa that even his satellite phone couldn't reach.

By the time Ella and Jack returned from their month-long honeymoon in Italy with Xander, the remodel on the first and second floors of the distillery building was almost complete.

As predicted, Ella and her neighbors lost their eminent domain case to the hospital, but even she had to admit that her new location in the Brewster Building had advantages, the most prominent being that she would be sharing office and living space with her new husband. Cindy, Hiram, and Padma had become somewhat local celebrities for their role in the "hospital love child scandal" and were excited about the new possibilities, which included being interviewed by *People Magazine* and *TMZ*. They all loved the Brewster Building and were settling in well.

They'd even warmed up to Jack after he proclaimed his love for Ella and Xander on the day of the hearing. The fact he offered them free rent for the first year, and reduced rent there-after, along with moving expenses, and a general relocation bonus, didn't hurt either.

"Well?" Jack asked as he set down the takeout box from the *Curry Leaf* on the highly polished counter in Ella's new shop in the Brewster Building. He was in jeans and a white t-shirt and had just finished installing a set of shelves on the back wall. She knew he was good with his hands, especially when it came to pleasuring her body, but she hadn't imagined he knew how to use real tools, let alone wear a tool belt.

"Well, what?" she asked, putting some edge in her voice as she set down her own takeout box and folded her arms.

Smiling at her, he stood and walked around to her side of the counter. His hands on her hips, he pulled her to him, leaned close, and whispered, "Do you want to take me up on my offer..." Then he kissed her, making her world spin. They had done their relationship in reverse, a baby before they'd even started dating. These moments were to be savored.

There had been much spinning in Ella Brewster's world over the last few months.

Ella looked down at the impressive pigeon blood red ruby and diamond ring on her left hand. It caught the sunlight and sparkled, momentarily distracting her from Jack's question as she wrapped her arms around his neck and considered the possibilities.

Jack could be very persuasive, another talent he'd demonstrated over the past few months.

Cindy's Emporium, which was right next door, was slated to open in two days. Padma and Hiram, who were on Cindy's other side, had been back in business for almost three weeks. *Marcella's* corner shop in the Brewster Building, in the heart of the Pearl District, would open in ten days. The artisans Jack hired to recreate her night sky took a week longer than originally planned, but the timing, along with their wedding and European honeymoon, worked out perfectly.

"I've got a lot on my mind. I had to pick out paint colors for the house today," she protested as he kissed her neck, suggestively nipping at her ear. Whenever he started this kind of thing, they usually ended up getting naked in their new, luxurious apartment, as long as Xander was napping or with his new nanny.

"My poor darling, so much stress," he said, continuing to nuzzle at her neck.

"In fact," she said, interrupting his tender assault, "the time estimate on the haunted house went to eighteen months just yesterday. I'm more than a little frustrated. We'll be living in our apartment for at least a year and a half."

"That space isn't just an apartment," he said, and she knew he was right. Their living space, along with Hiram and Padma's, was more like a suite in a five-star hotel. They all loved their new apartments. Jack, Ella, and Xander had moved in as soon as they'd returned from their honeymoon. Moonshine had taken to being an urban dog like a duck to water.

"But I wanted to be in by our first anniversary," Ella said between kisses.

"You sound kind of frustrated, angry," he said.

"I think that is wishful thinking on your part."

Jack narrowed his eyes, considered his answer, and said, "The new couch was delivered to the stock room this morning. What do you say we go christen it? You can take out all your aggression on me. I like it when you do that."

"Now?" she asked, her body already starting to tingle. "I thought you wanted to finish the shelves tonight."

"Xander is with his nanny for another hour, and that gives me just enough time to take care of my wife's needs. Happy wife, happy life," he said, kissing her as she tried not to laugh.

Moonshine, who'd been comfortably resting on a large dog bed behind the counter, stood and started to growl, drawing their attention.

Ella tried to calm the dog, who seemed more interested in a homeless man passing by the picture window.

"He's protecting you from that man, which reminds me. They will be here tomorrow to install your security system with a panic button," Jack said, glancing over his shoulder at the tall, slightly hunched figure who looked in at them.

A moment later, the man was at the door and trying the handle.

"That isn't good," Jack said, then, after a pause, added, "Holy shit—"

The dog ran from behind the counter and crossed the distance to the man, barking and growling.

Ella couldn't decide if she should call the police or grab a weapon, but to her surprise Jack let go of her, hurried to the front door, and unlocked it. A moment later, he opened his arms to the homeless-looking man and pulled him close in a bear hug.

The intruder, Ella realized, was no stranger at all. He wore expensive gear, but it was beat up, shredded in some places. He had a thick, dark beard, his skin weathered and sunburned.

"Charles," she said dryly, shaking her head as Moonshine returned to her side and continued to growl.

Jack smiled at his brother and said, "Welcome home, you big jerk."

Not offended by the derogatory greeting, Charles took a long look at Ella, turned to his brother, and said, "Sorry I missed the wedding. I was digging a new well in Burundi. Did you know it is the poorest country in Africa?"

Without waiting for an answer, Charles's eyes roamed over Ella. "Damn, your baby mama is hot. I bet I could steal her away in one month or less. Wanna bet?"

Ella stepped from behind the counter, walked right up to Charles, and punched him as hard as she could in his left shoulder, the shoulder he'd broken on Mount Hood two years earlier.

As he cried out in pain and looked like he might drop to his knees, "Why did you do that? We're related."

Ella said, "Serves you right. No more messes for your brother to clean up. You understand me, brother-in-law?"

As Charles nodded, she turned to Jack, smiled, and said, "Ah, now the cosmic balance has been restored."

"For what exactly?" Jack asked, his expression a mix of shock and amusement.

"You once said that Charles was competitive with you. Well, now the big jerk knows he can't have everything he wants," she said as she slid an arm around her husband.

"Man, she is something," Charles said, shaking his head as his cockeyed smile appraised Ella. "She kind of reminds me of Mom."

"Did you get kicked by the village mule on your travels? Ella is the kindest, smartest woman I've ever met," Jack said, as he turned his back on his brother and kissed his wife.

Acknowledgments

A BIG thank you to my BETA readers. I couldn't do this without you!

You might notice this has shades of another book I've written with a hero named Jack in Saint Barts. Here is the reason why: I wrote this first and my former line editor didn't like the story, so I shelved it for a few years. I had Jack and Saint Barts on my brain when I wrote *The Poison Garden*. So, think of this as the light to that dark.

About the Author

Mary Oldham is an award winning author, and three-time Golden Heart Finalist with the Romance Writers of America in the areas of Contemporary Romance and Romantic Suspense. She is a 2023 Maggie Finalist with the Georgia Romance Writers for her book, CRUSH. Mary lives in Portland, Oregon when she is not sitting on her deck and looking at the Pacific in Yachats, Oregon, the Gem of the Oregon Coast.

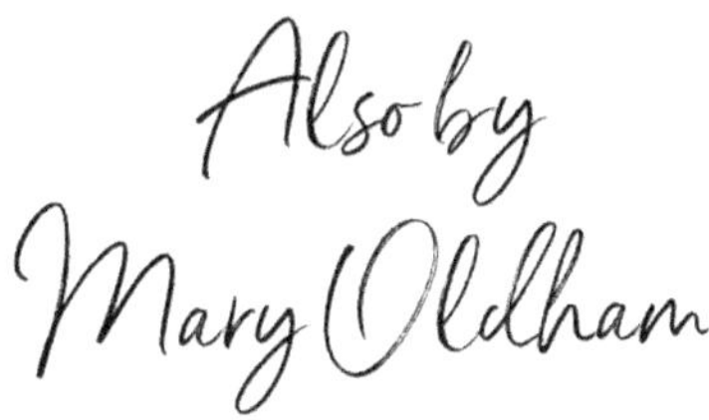

Don't miss any of Mary Oldham's other books, available in Print or Digital at Amazon or Barnes and Noble:

Stand Alone Titles

CRUSH, May 2022

Instant Daddy, Just Add Rum, February 2025

The Poison Garden Series

The Poison Garden, 2023

Madam Emma's Love Emporium, 2024

The Silver Linings Series

The Silver Linings Wedding Dress Auction, October 2021

Sisters Before Misters, August 2023

Enchanted, 2024

The Hotel Baron's Series

A Paris Affair, November 2021

A Summer Affair, December 2021

A Roman Affair, April 2022

A London Affair, 2024

The Aphrodite Sisters Series

Sage's Redemption, Book 1, October 2022

Toni's Secret, Book 2, November 2022

Roxie's Circus, Book 3, December 2022

Kimberly 's Reckoning, Book 4, March 2023

Audiobooks

The Silver Linings Wedding Dress Auction Available April 2022

Narrated by Gildart Jackson

The Poison Garden

Available December 2023

Narrated by Robin McAlpine

Mary loves to hear from her readers! You can email her to sign up for her newsletter at www.maryoldham.com.